About the Author

Daryl L. Keener was born in San Francisco, CA in Letterman Army Hospital. He is currently serving a 1,256-year sentence in the Colorado Department of Corrections for being convicted of robbing armor trucks and banks, he is appealing his conviction. He served a contract in the infamous French Foreign Legion, where his physical and mental traits were put to the test. His hobbies before coming to prison wer playing in poker tournaments, shooting guns, playing pool and sky diving. His current hobbies are writing poetry, working out, studying law and of course playing poker. Although this is a fiction book. Daryl wrote the majority of this novel based on his personal life experiences.

Acknowledgements

To my father, Maurice D. Keener who never gave up on me and never left my side when the times were tough. He believed in me when others did not. It is because of him that I had the strength to write this novel. So this book is dedicated to him from my heart. I love you Dad.

Also, to my best friend Gary Cyprian, the greatest ride is always the last ride. We walk the same paths but have on different shoes. I wouldn't change a thing brother, no regrets, Gladys and Tiffany will be missed dearly. We will meet up again soon, in this life or the next. Until then, die the way we live. And of course to Keri, you will always hold my heart.

"Freedom from jail, the sounds of clips being inserted, at the same time a man is murdered and a baby is born, it's the beginning and end."

The Deal

This morning I watched my last sunrise as a free man

This Though it was beautiful, my soul was stricken

I did not want to commit to these chains

The chains that had cost me my freedom

But when one makes a deal with the Devil

He must also pay the piper

There is nothing left but hollowness, an empty shell

A vessel that was once filled with life

Now holds nothing but death

I am bound to a new master

He will use me as he see fit

For I am obligated to do his bidding

For one never thinks about the price he must pay

To live one life without regrets

Only in the end do we realize our mistakes

But by then the hour is too late

D. Keener

Prologue

"Welcome to the Colorado Department of Corrections ladies, I am SGT Chavez. I am not your friend nor do I want to be. I don't care who you are or what you did to get sentenced to prison. I don't care how tough or smart you think you are, because I am tougher and smarter. You were brought here because society deemed you unnecessary to be in the public; you're a nuisance. Now some of you have short sentences, some of you will spend the rest of your pathetic life in here, I don't care either way. What I do care about is you following every order I myself or any of my officers gives you. I don't ask or say please, I tell you what to do. For your duration in prison I will have absolute control over your sorry asses. I will tell you when to eat, speak, sleep, shit and which direction I want you to wipe your ass. I did not ask for you to come here; you did all that on your own. I get paid to keep you away from Mr. John and Mrs. Q taxpayer until some needle dick, paper pushing prick decides you are fit, excuse me, rehabilitated to go back into the real world. And let me tell you something, CDOC has an 86% recidivism rate. For those of you who don't know what that means, it means that eight out of ten of you will be back within three years after your release. You either learn two things in prison, one: how horrible the conditions are and not want to come back or how to try to be a smarter criminal, which eventually you'll be back. For me, its job security really, I want to personally thank you for being so stupid and for putting my daughter through college. Now enough foreplay, behind you is twenty showerheads. There are eighteen of you; I want you all to get into a single file line going across and strip naked. That means everything ladies. Some of you may be homophobic, hell some of you may even be queer and like the sight of seventeen swinging dicks. Well I don't, I got some nice warm pink pussy at my house waiting for me when I leave here. Anybody else have any pink pussy waiting for them?" There were a few laughs. "Negative ladies, because right now your wife, girlfriend, or/ boyfriend is getting fucked in the ass by Jody. Who is Jody you're probably wondering? Jody is your best friend, your neighbor, the gas station clerk at 711. He's the one keeping that nice warm pussy filled with cum."

"Now arms out in front of you, open your hands, turn them over, lift your arms above your head, open your mouth, now run your finger around your gums on the inside of your mouth, lift your tongue, let me see behind your ears, lift your dick, lift your balls, turn around and let me see the bottom of your left foot, now your right foot, bend over and spread your ass cheeks and cough. Now grab a piece of the shittiest soap the state could find for you and wash your ass, you have one minute, now move!" 49 seconds later,

"Water off, get out and line up on the wall to your right and grab a towel. Dry off, when you're done, drop those towels in the blue baskets to your left and get back in line. When I call your name you will head over to that counter and will be issued five pair of boxers, five pair of socks, and five t-shirts. For you new guys that number on your shirt is your new name during your stay, remember it quickly. Ok, now that you ladies look a bit more presentable, before we proceed any further, are there any questions on what I said so far?" A hand rose, third from the back of the line. SGT Chavez walked down the line and looked the convict who raised his hand, "What!" Chavez hollered. The convict replied, "I was just wondering about the pork you serve here, is it kosher Sergeant?" Chavez eyes slowly narrowed and a slight grin appeared at the corner of his mouth. He asked the convict, "What's your name?" The convict replied, "The state of Colorado says its 97441." "Well 97441," Chavez replied, "We have a special place for people like you." Chavez looked over his shoulder and said, "Officer White, Officer Young, would you please as so kindly handcuff and escort our friend Mr. 97441to the SHU." (Segregation Housing Unit) "Yes sir," they replied in unison. "Oh and to answer your question convict, don't worry you'll have plenty of time to bless sausages when you're on your knees with your new cell mate Marvin." Chavez said. Then he turned around and yelled at his officers, "Now get him the fuck out of my face!" Chavez faced the group, "Now are there any more questions from the rest of you ladies?" Nobody raised a hand.

Chapter 1

History has taught us that all civilizations have had their sufferers. In every Country in Asia, Europe, and North and South America, live men whose life is an atonement. Some have been stricken down by tribulations or unforeseen happenings. Many have suffered by their own mistakes or they have committed some act for which their conscience chastises them. They feel that they are despised and they know that they can reinvent themselves only by escaping from their past lives. Still, some others, citizens of countries that have been or are currently going through turmoil, cannot adjust themselves to new conditions; their only resource is to exile themselves. For these human beings who society call, "Outcasts," the Foreign Legion offers sanctuary.

50 miles outside of Awbari, Libya

The explosion came without warning for those who was caught up in it. Body parts, metal dirt, and concrete was raining down within a fifty-yard radius. Two seconds after the explosion came automatic gun fire from the north and the east of the camp. Bullets were tearing down anything that was moving. Soldiers who were not blown up were screaming, running, and blindly shooting in all directions; hitting their own comrades as confusion rushed all around them. Dawn was creeping up and in about ten minutes the sun will have shown its face. Fires burned from fuel storage containers and disabled vehicles, the smoke was getting thick. From the hill above, the attackers rained death on those below.

"Dragon Fly to Ares, over." The sound in Ares' ear was crystal clear, "Ares' copies." "Yes sir, I know you're trying to have a cat-nap up there all by yourself and all, but I just wanted to inform you that the rest of us are a little busy being in the middle of a firefight and all. And we're wondering if you get a chance, could you engage in a rogue vehicle that's going south at a high rate of speed loaded with a bunch of tangos, and bless us common folk and kindly stop such said vehicle sir, over?" "Roger," was the reply.

Before Karsten was interrupted with that transmission he was already 'dialing' in on the jeep that was heading away from the camp. He had time, he thought; the vehicle was only two-hundred meters out. He took out an apple flavored jolly rancher from his back pocket, un-wrapped it and put it underneath his tongue. The jeep was now four-hundred and twenty –five meters out. The sugar instantly made Karsten wide eyed. Five-hundred meters out, Karsten was lying in a prone position looking through a high powered scope attached to the Barret BMG .50 caliber sniper rifle he was cradling. Five-hundred and sixty-five meters out, he checked his wind age one more time; it was full value blowing east to west at ten knots. Through his scope he could see the jeep with four tangos, including the driver. It was an open top jeep that had seen better days.

His primary job was to stop the vehicle, no problem there. The driver did not present much of a target, only his head was visible. Karsten thought twice, he was a damn good shot but this was not Hollywood. His first shot needed to count and then he could play. So he took careful aim and plotted a triangle profile; a course for the bullet to hit below the driver's neck, hopefully in between the shoulder blades. Six-hundred and forty meters out, it was time to take his shot. *BOOM!*

The sole shot of the .50 Caliber was distinguishable over the small caliber rifle rounds below. The chest of the driver exploded about one and a half seconds later, with it the windshield was also gone. The jeep, now at the hands of a headless driver started swerving wildly.

Before anybody could take control of the jeep, it flipped and rolled three times before it came to a stop. Bodies went flying in all directions. Amazingly, two tangos were still moving on the ground; somehow they survived the horrific crash. The first made it to his knees, and then his head went missing from his body at the impact of a high velocity round. The second, still crawling on the ground made it about four meters when he too was stopped with another round, separating his head from his shoulders as well. *Damn I'm good,* thought Karsten as he was double checking for any more survivors.

"Ares to Dragon Fly, what's your sit-rep (Situation Report), over?"

"Dragon Fly to Ares, SNAFU (Situation Normal All Fucked Up) and the vultures are heading to ground, over."

"Copy, will join the feast in about ten, over."

Karsten loved his team; they were already doing what they were supposed to, without being told. When the guys saw him approaching them, they slowly made their way to meet him.

"Hey Sarge, how was your nap?" Asked Rone, Karsten's second in command.

"A real wise ass huh? I have you know that while you and the rest of this paper plane outfit of yours were down here wasting ammo and Legion time, I was up there," he pointed to a ridge, "covering your ass from behind and stopping skinny's from escaping. Not to mention putting holes in that machine gun embankment every time somebody wanted to hop in and give you a new asshole." Karsten replied.

"Yea right boss is that why the whole left side of your face is covered with dirt?" Rone asked sarcastically.

"I was listening for buffalo asshole." Karsten said with a sheepish grin on his face.

"First thing first, Rone do you understand what the words intelligence gathering means?" Rone nodded, "I don't think you do, I said a small explosion, meaning use just a tad of RDX to blow up those barracks. Not pack in as much as you can and make a hole to the center of the Earth. Please don't speak; I don't want to hear it. You know the routine people; kill anybody that still has a pulse, repeat there are no survivors. Rone you and Tiekert check the bodies for any Intel. McLean gather any useful weapons and ammo and distribute it among the men. Nordeen, you get on that tough book and sat phone, call the priest and get us a taxi out of here. But first, I need you on that ridge doing over guard. All that noise, somebody heard it, make sure nobody sneaks up on our coattails, will you? Ok people twenty minutes, then we move out."

Wasn't much of a training camp, Karsten thought. *But then again how much training does one need to strap a bomb to his chest, scream a few choice words, and then blow yourself up?* Not much he concluded.

He was walking through debris and dead bodies with Gladys, his Glock .45 caliber in his hands at the low ready. Years of experience has taught him to never assume anything. He glanced around and saw that his team of Midnight Marauders was busy at their task, he smiled. The sun was up and blazing now. It was just past 7:20 a.m. local time and it was already 31 degrees Celsius. Karsten made his way toward the south of the camp to a small structure, that was surprisingly still standing despite the ruckus that just occurred. As he walked inside what he thought use to be a makeshift kitchen, he noticed pots, pans, and other kitchen items scattered around on the ground. A few chickens were still in cages in one corner to his right. He moved deeper inside the structure just to come out the opposite end that was blown out. Something didn't feel right, he thought.

During the raid a lot of tangos were running toward this building instead of going toward their weapons storage units. Karsten walked back inside and did a more thorough check and still came up empty handed. He gave the room one more glance and then a light bulb went off in his head. *It's the ground*, he told himself. It seemed softer in some spots. Ten minutes of searching and he found what he was suspecting, a trap door, he made a small x in the dirt and stepped out of the structure. He pressed his throat mic,

"Ares to Dragon Fly."

"I am near the south side of the camp outside the only structure that's still standing, need you here ASAP."

"Yea boss, I see you, on my way."

Two minutes later, "What's up Sarge?" Asked Rone, as he arrived.

"I marked a small x near what I think is a trapdoor. I need you to go inside and clear it for bobby traps." Karsten said.

"Well ain't I the luckiest pig on the ham sandwich. Yes, sir masta, I'll go inside and get my ass blown to kingdom come while you stand safely out of the way." Replied Rone.

"Time's wasting Toby; get your ass in there."

Five minutes later, "it's clean Sarge, want me to look inside or shall I go back to the cotton fields?"

"I didn't know they have cotton fields where you grew up in Germany Rone. Hell silly me, of course they do, that's how Hitler financed the war uh? Now shut up and give me a hand will ya." They pulled the wooden top cover off the trapdoor. It revealed a small hole in the ground, approximately ten by six in size.

"Holy shit Sarge!"

"Yea I know," Karsten keyed his throat mic again, "Ares to Bishop, sit-rep please."

"Bishop here, quieter than a moth taking a shit on a light bulb, over."

"Stay put and alert, out twenty minutes have just been extended. We may or may not have some guest showing up."

"Copy that, Bishop out."

"Well Sarge?" Rone asked.

"Well my ass, hop down there and tell me I've been in the sun too long and that I'm hallucinating."

Rone jumped down into the hole, while Karsten keyed his throat mic, "Tin man, Oxford, on the double to where Rone and I are, over."

"Damn Sarge, either you or I are hallucinating together or I say we stumbled upon something that even those Intel weenies had no idea about." Rone said.

Inside the hole were a cache of weapons, clay mores, anti-personal mines, RPG's, Semtex explosives, crates of AK-47's with about ten thousand rounds of ammo, and mortars with firing tubes. But what Karsten was looking at was the grandest of all. Four American made shoulder launched stinger heat-seeking missiles. Two in open cases, the other two in closed cases below. Karsten heard footsteps approaching from behind him, he brought up his pistol. McLean and Tiekert came through and stood over the hole.

"Now where do you suppose they got that from?" asked Tiekert.

"Maybe the missile fairy," replied McLean.

"Knock it off." Karsten said, "You two find anything on those bodies?"

"A couple of ID's, some misc. paperwork, two cell phones, and one burned up laptop, which with a little care, we might be able to get something off the hard drive." Answered Tiekert.

"And some gold rings and a couple of silver necklaces too." McLean added.

"Search the bodies, not rob the bodies McLean." Tiekert said.

"Hey who's going to know? Besides, they don't need it where they're going. They get to play with all those damn virgins anyway."

"Rone," said Karsten," Take pictures of those stingers and cases. I want serial numbers if any. Salvage any and all weapons you can, use the rest of that Semtex to wire this hole, I want nothing left when were gone. McLean, you stay put and help him. Tiekert you gather your goodies and bag them then meet up with Nordeen up on that ridge."

Tiekert was about ten feet away when Karsten called him back, "Oh and um Tiekert, could you bag two of those chickens as well, I'm hungry." Karsten un-wrapped another Jolly Rancher, this time it was cherry, and he put it under his tongue. "Rone how long before you finish rigging this joint?"

"About fifteen minutes Sarge, I want to use the remote instead of a delay."

"Fine, when you two are done, join the rest of us, we'll be on top of that ridge, take your time in a hurry." Karsten walked off talking to himself about the stinger missiles. Karsten made it to the ridge where Tiekert and Nordeen were providing over guard. "Nordeen, what's the status with the taxi?"

"Good news and bad news Sarge. Good news is we have a ride out of this hell hole. Then again the bad news is that we have to meet it here." Nordeen pointed to a place on the map he had spread out in front of him. "It's about ninety miles of desert east of here sir."

"Fucking Viva La France," Karsten mumbled under his breath, then asked," Tiekert, how are we on supplies?"

"Weapons and ammo are great, got a refill from the camp below. Water is down about one full canteen per man. The mad bomber down there blew the shit out of the water storage tanks. Food wise, just what we brought with us, not including these two rats with wings you had me bag earlier," Tiekert answered.

"Ninety miles uh, fucking Legion is going to be the death of me," Karsten said to nobody. He hit his throat mic, "Ares to Dragon Fly."

"Dragon Fly here, go."

"When you're done rigging that hole, I need you and Tin Man to head about one click south of the camp where I stopped that jeep, and see if it's still functional, Bishop will meet you there, over."

"Copy that, over."

"Bishop go down there and lend them your expertise and see if we can shorten out trek of ninety miles."

"Ok Sarge," was the reply.

"Tiekert," Karsten said, "You ever plucked a chicken before?"

"Can't rightly say that I have Sarge."

"Well, neither have I, looks like you're about to learn the hard way."

"Oh come on Sarge, I ain't no chicken plucker. And besides, why can't you do it? It was your idea to grab these damn pigeons to begin with."

"Ah grasshopper, have we forgot the chain of command? Rank has its privileges, you know that, and besides I have to go take a shit. But first, hold that chicken down; let me get a handful of feathers.

"Negative Sarge," Rone said as he, Nordeen, and McLean approached the ridge, where Karsten and Tiekert were looking through field binoculars. "Tires are flat, bent axle and the engine is halfway out of the hood. Almost looks as if the driver lost his head and wrecked the damn thing. Why did we need that jeep for anyway Sarge?" asked Rone.

"Nordeen didn't tell you the good news huh? We have about ninety miles of ground to cover before we meet up with our ride."

"Fucking awesome, it's only one hundred fucking degrees out here, yea no problem." McLean stated in a sarcastic tone.

"Could be worse," Karsten said, "Now quit crying and load up. Go tinkle, rub one off, or whatever you have to do, we clear out in five minutes. Rone what's the range on that remote?"

"Oh, about half a mile Sarge."

"Good, blow it when we're far enough. Alright wolves, time to march or die."

Chapter 2

"97441, pack your shit, you're going to G.P. (General Population) yelled a correctional officer over the intercom inside the six by eight cell. *About fucking time* he thought to himself. Thirty minutes later his escort came for him.

With his property packed, he made his way through a corridor that smelled like a combination of wax, and dirty mop water. They reached the slider to exit the building. 97441 stepped through and was hit by the blazing sun shining above. He had not seen real light in over twenty days. That's how long he was in the S.H.U. for his charge for asking a question that was advocating a facility disruption. It is a class two offence; according to the Colorado Department of Corrections C.O.P.D (Code of Penal Discipline)

As he walked forward toward the main yard, he heard the usual sounds of a prison yard, weights clanking, inmates cheering on a basketball or handball game, indistinct shouting at each other. This was not his first rodeo in prison; he had recently spent time at a U.S.P in Pennsylvania. He made his way to unit two which was a closed custody level.

"He's all yours L.T.," Said the correctional officer, as they stepped into a tiny office.

"Let's see here," the L.T said, "not here one day and already was a guest in the S.H.U. it says here in the file this is not your first time in a prison environment, and by looking at the number on your chest, I take it your familiar with the standing rules, so I'll spin this for you quick. I don't like you, I can already tell, you and I are going to have some problems. So let me explain this to you one time only, if you cause any problems for me on my shift, I will personally kick your fucking teeth down your throat. If you cause any problems when I am away, when I come back, I will personally kick your fucking teeth down your throat. If I have a dream that you are causing any problems, when I wake up, I am going to drive out here, no matter what time it is, and kick your fucking teeth down your throat. You should consider this your first and last warning, any question?"

"Uh yeah, as a matter of fact, you seem to have this fetish with my teeth, is this in any way connected to the fact that you obviously like to have things in your mouth. Because, if it is, I really do appreciate the offer, but you're not quite my type, I prefer to rock hoes not fellas."

The L.T. glared at 97441 for about two minutes, and then gave a small grin as he said, "I hope someone puts that smart ass mouth to work. You're going over to C-pod, first tier, room three, have fun. Now get the hell out of my sight!"

97441 made his way to his cell and opened the door. His new celly stood up from his rack and looked him over before asking his name, "What's up youngster they call me Ham."

"They call me Diamond," said 97441

"So you're stuck on the top bunk uh?"

"Yep."

Diamond walked in the room and put his property on the top bunk, not un-packing. Diamond looked over and sized up his new celly Ham. He was a big fucker he thought. About forty-one years old, six-two maybe two-hundred and fifty pounds, with arms the size of hams he guessed. Diamond looked around the cell; at least his celly had his own shit, a TV on the end of his rack, a coffee maker, lamp, and TV on the desk.

"So what are you here for youngster?" asked Ham.

"I don't talk about my case; it's nobody's business but mine. If inquiring minds want to know they can Google, my name and see what pops up."

"You kids today," Ham stepped closer to Diamond, "I was not asking why you were in here, I was telling you to show me your paperwork. I want to make sure you ain't no child molester of a motherfucking rapist."

"Look I ain't got no sex case if that's what you want to know, and second no one in green tells me what to do, no matter how big they think they are."

Ham stepped within two feet of Diamond's face and said," Look here cuz, you ain't hard so quit fronting. And if you say any more slick shit out of your mouth I'm going to beat the shit out of you then have my homeboys run up in you and make you the pod bitch. Now like I said before, let me see your paperwork nigga."

Diamond stood his ground un-fazed and was staring Ham in the eyes. *He we go again* thought Diamond, then without warning Diamond grabbed Ham's glass coffee carafe and slammed it into the side of Ham's face, glass and hot coffee went everywhere. Diamond following through with a left hook to Ham's right ear. Ham was nowhere as slow as he looked; he recovered quickly and smashed a meaty fist to the side of Diamond's face that sent him staggering back towards the bunks. *Goddamn that motherfucker hit hard,* I cant's take to many more of those, Diamond thought as his head was spinning. Ham charged all of his 250 pounds at Diamond, he grabbed him and lifted him off the ground and slammed him onto the desk, wall and metal bed fame all at once.

"I'm going to kill you punk ass bitch." Ham screamed as he cocked back and punched Diamond in the nose, instantly breaking it and sending him flying off the desk and onto the ground. By now Diamond was seeing so many stars he thought he was in Hollywood. As Diamond hit the floor Ham came rushing over to put a boot to his dome. Diamond saw it coming and with the strength he had left, he kicked Ham in the balls. That stopped him cold in his tracks; not wanting to waste precious time admiring his move Diamond rose up from the floor and kicked Ham in the balls again. Diamond taking advantage as Ham was semi-hunched over holding his dick, he jabbed him in the throat with the webbing of his hand. Ham who was now unable to breath finally staggered back.

Diamond then took the palm of his right hand and hit Ham with an uppercut to the chin that would have knocked most men out, but not Ham. Ham was not knocked out, just knocked down to the ground looking like a lost sheep, after a few moments he returned to a standing position and Diamond asked himself; *How in the world is this motherfucker still standing?* Diamond grabbed Ham's TV and with all his might brought it down on the back of Ham's head. That did it; Ham fell to the floor face first and was snoring. *Goddamn, almost got my ass handed to me,* Diamond told himself. With one eye closed and a broken nose Diamond grabbed Ham by the arms and drug his limp body to the cell door, kicked the door open and drug Ham into the dayroom and shouted, "Is there no one else, is there no one else, uh? Speak now faggots."

The only sound came from the group of CO's who were trying to get inside the pod through the slider. Diamond watched as they made their way toward him with their pepper spray and Tasers out. He got on his knees and put his hands behind his head. It still didn't stop the CO's from spraying the shit out of him. They were yelling, "Quit resisting, quit resisting!" Diamond was just lying on the floor taking kicks and punches to his body and face. In between the beatings the CO's managed to put handcuffs on him as well. One of the guards had a knee on the back of Diamond's neck. Bloodied, bruised, and tired as hell, Diamond just laid there. No telling how long he was lying there before he heard the voice of the L.T. who he was just talking to about minutes ago.

"Lift his head up." The L.T. told the CO who was kneeing Diamond's neck. The guard lifted Diamond's head, the L.T. bent down on one knee and whispered to Diamond, "You sure a stupid nigger aren't you boy? You know when Ham over there wakes up he's going to kill you. Never in the nine years that I've been here have I seen that boy lose a fight. You either got to be the luckiest man on this planet or the real deal." Diamond smiled a bloody, fat lip smile, "Oh that's funny uh boy," The L.T. stood up and kicked Diamond on his chin, knocking him out cold. "Get his ass to the infirmary for Decon," the L.T. told the CO's as he walked out of the pod toward his office.

When Diamond awoke he was ass naked under a shower head that was pumping freezing cold water. "What the fuck!" He screamed.

"Honey if you want warmer water you have to do it yourself, I can't come in there with you," a small blonde nurse said. Two CO's were behind her laughing. "This is not a funny matter," she said to the guards, "quit laughing."

Thirty minute later the nurse handed Diamond a towel, told him to dry off and handed him a paper gown. The guards then handcuffed him and escorted him to where the doctor was waiting, "Alright," she said with an upbeat tone as she was putting on medical gloves. "Your name please?" she asked.

"97441."

"Your height please?"

"About five-ten."

"Your weight?"

"Around two hundred and ten pounds."

"And you're 25 years old?"

"Yes." Diamond said.

"Thank you," she said, "now that wasn't so hard was it? Good, let's take a look at you.

So what happened?"

"I slipped in the shower Doc." Diamond said sarcastically.

"I see, and did this shower have fist and feet, or was it one of those automatic ones?" She smiled.

"He was in a fight Doc." One of the CO's said. "You're kidding, what gave you the idea? As a matter of fact, will you please wait outside the exam room please, after all this is Doctor/Patient conversation. He's handcuffed and if I have any problems you'll be the first to know, thank you." The two CO's left and waited outside in the hallway.

"Now that their gone, how much of this is from the boys in blue?" She asked. Diamond just stared at her. The Doctor said, "You aren't snitching if you're telling the truth, and besides you don't owe these CO's nothing."

"Snitching is snitching Doc when you're all said and done. And besides when you go home tonight I still have to be here, you do the math."

She stared at him with sad eyes for about six seconds, and then she said, "Let's see you have a broken nose, two black eyes, one of which will be closed for a couple days, a missing front tooth, and from the looks of your labored breathing, possibly a cracked rib. Amongst other various cuts and bruises on the remainder of your body. Any place on your body that was not hit?" She asked jokingly.

Diamond looked down at his dick and said, "Can't really be for sure if their swollen or just their natural size."

"Definitely swollen, I've seen bigger on the roaches in my apartment."

"Ha, ha, ha, point taken Doc." Diamond laughed sarcastically.

"You're pretty banged up; I hope it was worth it." She said.

"It's never worth it Doc."

"So why do you do it then?"

"Sometimes it's unavoidable no matter what you do, and when the time comes, you have to do what you need to do to survive."

"Well did you at least win?"

"Nobody ever wins a fight Doc."

"Who are you now, Dr. Phil?" She asked.

"Nah, just somebody who should've known better than to get locked up again."

"Well at least you're one of the few who realizes that, the question is will you be back again after you get out?"

"I don't plan on it Doc, but then again that dammed eight ball has been known to get shit wrong."

The Doctor gave a small laugh, "Anyway, the best I can do for you is give you some of D.O.C. universal pain medication, some ibuprofen, take it twice a day for a week. I'll re-set your nose before you go but other than that my hands are tied like yours."

"What about my tooth Doc?"

"What about it? It's gone, can't put it back in."

"Sure thanks Doc." Diamond said in a disappointed tone as he got up to leave.

"Oh by the way," the doctor said, "that big guy that you did not fight, he had to be transferred to the local hospital. He may lose his left eye from glass fragments, just thought you might want to know."

"Not really, Diamond said to himself as he walked into the hallway where the CO's were waiting. "Alright gentlemen," he said, "I'm ready for that nice warm single cell waiting for me in the S.H.U. And while you're at it would it be too much to ask for double blankets? I feel a slight chill coming on."

"No problem sir." One of the CO's replied.

They took him to a cell in the S.H.U. that had the A.C. on full blast, with no linens or blankets, just a bare, ripped up, stinky mattress that was thinner than a pocket bible. Diamond looked around the cell. "Assholes could've at least given me some shit paper." He mumbled. He was dead tired; he gave the thin mattress a glance, then a small shrug, laid down and passed out.

The sound of a cell phone vibrating on a glass night stand woke him up, "Mushi, Mushi."

"Hey Dee it's me."

"What's up Playa, you do realize its 3:07 a.m. don't you?"

"Yeah my bad, look I have to talk to you."

"Ok so talk."

"Not over the phone, could you meet me at the Waffle House on Fillmore in about twenty?"

"Sure, I wasn't doing anything but sleeping, I'm leaving right now." *Click,* then all he heard was the dial tone.

"Umm who was that baby?" The woman named Sabrina asked as she rolled over and put her bare breasts on Dee's chest.

"My nigga Kevin, I have to go, I'll be back in a couple hours." Dee said as he got up and started dressing.

"But it's three in the morning baby, where are you going?" She asked.

"Waffle House, to have an early breakfast, when I get back I'm going to eat you for dessert."

"You're nasty." She purred then added, "You promise?"

"Love you, got to go." Dee said as he bent over and kissed her on her mouth then walked out of the apartment.

Fifteen minutes later Dee pulled up next to a silver Yukon Denali in the Waffle House parking lot. He got out, walked inside the restaurant and noticed Kevin sitting in a corner booth in the back facing the windows. Dee glanced around while he took his time walking toward Kevin. One guy at the counter, a couple sitting at a booth opposite side of the place, one cook, and one waitress; the place was dead.

Kevin was smoking a port as Dee approached him and sat down. There were two glasses of orange juice already on the table, and Dee took a large gulp from one of the glasses. "Want to tell me why I am here at 3:30 in the morning, instead of lying next to my phat ass, blonde hair, blue eyed, cave bitch?" Dee asked.

"Joann is pregnant."

"Well I'll be damned, told you to wear a condom playa."

"Fuck you, you don't even know how to spell condom."

"That may be true but I ain't the one with a knocked up bitch either."

"She won't get an abortion."

"Ok, so be a man, step up and handle your shit."

"I don't love her."

"Well maybe you'll learn to over the next eighteen years or so."

"But she's fat and ugly Dee."

"Then why are you fucking her then? Wait don't answer that, let me take a stab at it; stop me if I'm wrong. You drive her whip, you live at her house, you eat all her food, you spend her money, and you don't do shit all day but sit around at her pad cause you don't have a job; does that sum it up or did I leave something out?"

"You a cold –hearted mothafucker Dee, here I am, I called up my best friend because I need a shoulder to lean on and all I get is shit-talk."

"Man if you don't quit fronting like your non-existence feelings are hurt, you know I got your back playa."

Kevin smiled then said, "I know, I know, look the reason I brought you down here is because I need some cream."

"Sure how much you need, a couple of thousand?" Dee asked as he pulled out a wad of cash from his front pocket.

"I'm gonna need more than you can give me pimp."

"How many men are you talking about?" Dee asked as he put his money back in his pocket.

"At least thirty-thousand."

"Damn, for what?"

"Well for starters it'll hold me over until I can find a job. Help me take care of some of Joanne's bills and prepare for this baby."

"Dude look, you know you my nigga and all but I don't have an extra thirty laying around, the most I can gather right now is maybe ten or twelve at best."

"I know that already Dee but I ain't asking for your money, I'm asking for a huge favor."

"Shit, this can't be good if you can't tell me over the phone; hold that thought." Dee said, as the waitress approached the table. "What can I get you gentlemen this morning?" She was smiling a joker smile.

"I'll have the steak and eggs and another glass of orange juice please." Dee ordered.

"How would you like your steak?" The waitress asked.

"Bloody and still moving if that's possible."

"And you sir?" She asked Kevin.

"How about a double-bacon cheese burger with curly fries, a strawberry milk shake, and your phone number please."

She smiled, "I can give you everything but my phone number, I don't think my boyfriend will like that too much."

"Ah sexy, he'll never know." Kevin said in his smooth Casanova voice.

"Oh he will, you see he's the cook."

"Oh, well tell him he's a lucky guy and that the steak is mine will ya? I don't think he's too happy at me the way he's staring over here." The waitress smiled and walked off.

"Thanks friend, now my shit is going to have extra spit in it. And damn, not two minutes ago you were crying about Joanne's fat ass now you're trying to bang our waitress."

"Shit man, I learned from you didn't I? Mr. International Diamond Dick Dee," Kevin said.

"Do as I say not what I do tadpole. Anyway, what about this huge favor you need? Spit it out because you know I'm going to do it anyway."

Kevin leaned in closer to Dee and started whispering, "I need your help to rob a bank."

Dee leaned back and away from Kevin, "Come again son."

"You heard me man, you got the guns and the know-how and I already know you gangsta about yours after all the work we put in together over the years."

"You serious ain't you?"

"Like the Aids epidemic."

"Damn, that's what I thought. You sure you don't need a kidney, any bone marrow or something?"

"Come on Dee, you supposed to be my boy, my ace, my partner in crime."

"Oh I'm all of that; I just don't want to be your celly in prison is all."

"Fuck, will you quit playing around; you pulled bigger licks in Europe."

"Absolutely, the key word being, Europe. Not in my fucking back yard."

"Look man, are you going to help ya boy or what?"

Dee took a sip of his orange juice and was remembering a quote he heard long ago, Greater love has no man than this, that he lay down his life for his friends.

3 Days Later

It was an early and chilly morning as Dee and Kevin sat in the Denali about two-hundred yards away from the bank in some apartment complex's parking lot with the S.U.V. engine turned off. It was about 7:08 a.m., the sun was still barely rising in the sky. Kevin was sipping on some PowerAde while Dee was warming up with a large cup of hot chocolate they had picked up at the 7-11 across town.

They had not spoken a word to each since then. Each man in his own thoughts. Kevin was already thinking about how he was going to get a new 'grill'. Dee on the other hand was pre-occupied with more delicate matters. He had not gone to see his parole officer since he came back from Panama, which was about forty days ago. He was quite sure there was a warrant out for his arrest. Then there was the matter of Sabrina, she was unaware of his being on parole or ever going to prison in that matter. She had no idea of his past life and not really so much of his current affairs either. For the six months that they had been dating all she knew about him was that he was a D.O.D. employee and that he worked on classified material. Which was partly true, Dee was a D.O.D. employee; he was a civilian contractor on Ft. Carson Army base in Colorado Springs. As for the classified work, yep that was a lie.

They had met at Twenty-Four Hour Fitness where he was working out. She was dressed in a pair of tight ass shorts that looked as if her ass was trying to escape. She was about five-eight, around one- hundred –twenty pounds, long blonde hair that went down to the middle of her back, blue eyes and as Dee would tell everybody, a set of D.S.L.'s (Dick Sucking Lips) that would make Angelina Jolie jealous. He had worked up the courage to finally speak to her after days of eyeball fucking her. They have been inseparable ever since; over the months they fell in love with each other. This was Dee's first love. He knew everything about her and yet she knew so little of him. She had a clue that he did illegal business when he went on his 'Business trips' outside the country, but she'd never asked nor did he volunteer any information.

Dee was head over heels in love with Sabrina. Anything she wanted he gave her, which to his surprise was not a lot. Sabrina was not a lady who was defined by material things. All she wanted was to go see movies, hiking, and go on nature walks; and would rather cook a homemade meal than go to a restaurant. To Dee she was perfect, what more could he want in a woman. He even quit fucking other women their first week dating because he felt she was the 'one'.

So now here he was sipping cocoa about to pull a lick. He looked at his Nomo's; it was about 7:26 a.m. The first bank employee normally arrives at twenty 'til eight, the other two at about ten 'til eight. They drive around the bank and make sure the first employee turns the blinds over to let them know she's safe and is not being robbed. He looked over at Kevin, "You sure you ready for the big league playa? While you over there acting all shaky-dog on me, when you go the bigger cooker on you."

"I'm cool Yo, quit bugging."

"Oh shit Kev, get down, get the fuck down."

"What's up?" Kevin asked as he slumped down in his seat.

"Just get the fuck down now, Mr. John Q law just pulled up in the parking lot heading our way."

They both were slumped down in their seats now. Kevin pulled out his .45 and Dee pulled out and cocked his .40 Cal Glock." Yo man," Kevin said," Why we down like this, we ain't do shit wrong yet?"

Dee was listening and watching the cop in the side mirrors pull up behind the Denali and stop maybe fifteen feet behind them. "Let's see," Dee said, "two black males sitting in a sixty-thousand-dollar car in the middle of the whitest part of town on a cold ass morning with the engine off. On top of that one of those if not both males probably have an active warrant. And let's not forget about the guns and masks he'll find when he decides were up to no good and searches the ride, that's why asshole, now shut the fuck up."

"Man what is he just sitting there for? Do you think he saw us and calling for back up? If so we should just ride on his ass right now Dee." Dee was thinking about it but then what he saw next took the words right out of his mouth. He saw the cop take out a glazed donut, took a couple bites, and then sipped his coffee.

"That fat piece of shit doesn't even know we're here." Kevin said.

For ten minutes they watched as that fat Bobby ate two more donuts and finished his coffee. The cop even got out of the cruiser and stretched, looked around before driving off not having a care in the world. When they decided he was far enough away they got back upright in their seats and looked at each other.

"Did that just happen?" Kevin asked.

"Yep," Was all Dee could say.

Dee looked at his Nomos again; it was five minutes till eight. "Let's get

rolling Pedro."

The plan was to park the whip behind the strip mall that the bank was located in, and then walk from behind to the strip mall to the bank. For a couple of minutes, they would be blind as to if any customers went inside or not. They were prepared either way. At 8:05 a.m. they parked as planned behind the strip mall facing a residential area. Checked to make sure their burners were locked and loaded, put on all black balaclavas and shades, and Kevin grabbed a small backpack.

"One more time Kevin, the bank don't have any security guards, so there's nothing to worry about on that end, except if a customer wants to play hero. So don't shoot anybody unless I shoot somebody first. I really don't plan on hurting nobody this morning but if I have to I will. And If I shoot one, we have to shoot them all, got it?" Kevin just nodded.

"Time to get our dicks wet playa," Dee said as they exited the vehicle.

They made their way around the shopping center and were walking in the parking lot toward the bank. Although it was a bright morning, it was cold and breezy, so nobody who was around even notices what they were wearing.

"Ladies and gentlemen I believe this is a robbery!" Kevin yelled as he burst through the front door of the bank, pointing his gun at the nearest teller closest to him, who was now frozen stiff.

Dee came in right behind Kevin and jumped over the counter and pointed his gun at the man at the drive-thru counter and the other female teller who was at the second teller station," Allo Gov," he said in an English accent, "Now be a good sport and please fill that bag my associate is carrying. And don't forget, no dye packs, bait money or G.P.S. devices please; because if I think that one of you is trying to pull a fast one I will kill you all, now hurry the fuck up! There you go everything in that top drawer, now the second drawer bitch. Yea don't look too shocked, I know what's in that one too."

Kevin jumped over the counter to assist Dee. Dee looked at his stop-watch he had around his neck. "Fifteen seconds!" He yelled to Kevin. Kevin grabbed one of the female tellers and dragged her by her hair towards the back of the bank to the vault. "Hurry up bitch or I'll put a bullet in that pretty mouth of yours." he told her. Back in the front of the bank Dee had the other two tellers lying on the ground after they finished emptying all the drawers, six total. "Thirty-five seconds!" Dee yelled. Just then Kevin came from the back of the bank with the backpack overflowing with cash. He scooped up the remaining cash Dee had laid on the counter. "Time!" Dee yelled. Almost simultaneously they both jumped back over the counter into the lobby and made their way out.

Dee let Kevin walk out first then he yelled in his best Nixon impersonation, "Remember gents, I am not a crook!" Then proceeded to walk out the bank at a fast pace but now so fast as to draw attention to himself. They made it back to the waiting ride, and as they were getting in a lady who was walking her dog on the sidewalk in front of the Denali gave them a suspicious glance and kept going.

Kevin started the S.U.V., as soon as they turned the corner to get out of the shopping center's back entrance they heard sirens. Kevin eased the Denali onto the main street toward the sound while Dee was lying on the back seat making sure there were no tracking devices or dye packs mixed in with the money.

The sirens were approaching fast and Kevin watched as two police cruisers went speeding by them in the opposite direction. "Are they turning around?" Dee asked.

"Nah, stupid mothafuckers are on a ghost chase," Kevin replied, as he made his way onto the highway Dee made his way up to the front seat and buckled –up. Kevin popped in a CD and hit track twelve; it was the song "Days of Our Lives" by Bone Thugs- N- Harmony. He turned it up to eardrum popping level, then hit the cruise control and sat back and relaxed as they made their way to Denver. Total take from the bank, $97,342.00.

****

"Wake up you piece of shit, your time is up," said the C.O. as he banged against the outer side of the cell door.

"Damn why you so hostile," Diamond asked, "Didn't get any dick last night uh? Well you can only blame yourself for that. I mean look at you, you're fat, hick, inbred pile of shit; I would've killed myself years ago if I was you. But I tell you what I am going to do, I am going to do you a huge favor; I'm not going to fuck your baby's mama when I get out of prison because I know you're gay. But ever the day I start liking big cocks in my mouth like you, I am going to come back to this small rank town of yours and I am going to fuck your old man," Diamond said then smiled a wide grin.

"Fuck you nigger, go back to Africa."

"Stupid fuck, I'm from San Francisco, and if that wasn't the case you can take your white ass back to Scandinavia," Diamond replied.

"Well you're still black," the C.O. said.

"Right, what an amazing sense of observation skills you have Billy boy."

Two minutes after the exchange of words Diamond was being walked out of the S.H.U. by two guards. As he made his way out the door the sun hit him like a brick of cement, he had to stop to shield his eyes so he could see ahead of him. Diamond was led back to Unit two, and back to the office of the L.T. where he had his first encounter. The L.T. motioned for the guards to leave after they escorted Diamond in.

"How's the jaw?" The L.T. asked.

"Great, how did it feel to touch a real man L.T.?"

"Still got that smart mouth huh?"

"And you still have those pretty eyes L.T." replied Diamond.

The L.T. gave him a *'I wish I could punch you in the face look'* then said, "You're going over to C-Pod, first tier, cell nine, bottom bunk. You don't need any speeches from me so I won't waste my time. But for you I will give you a little heads up. Word has it that Ham put out a hit on you to his boys. They want your ass bad, and if I get a chance I am going to let them have it. Then we'll see if you're the real deal or not. Now get the fuck out of my office."

Diamond got up and left without saying another word. He walked into C-Pod and when he did you could've heard a pin drop; all eyes were on him. *'Fuck it"* he thought as he made his way to his new cell. When he stepped in, a smiling light-skinned brother who had tattoos all over his face and body was standing in the middle of the cell waiting for him. Diamond dropped his bag.

The man with the tattoos said, "Damn nigga, you sure do know how to make an entrance."

Diamond smiled, "Yeah well you know, if you make a deal with the devil, you have to pay the piper." The tattooed guy smiled. "So how's the kids Tony?" asked Diamond as they both came together and gave each other props and half hugs.

Chapter 3

Her name was Keri Collins; like the famous football player to be exact. She had long shiny black hair that went almost ten inches down from her shoulders. She had creamy skin, almost almond complexion. Her figure was slim, but could tell she is athletic. Although she had large brown eyes she wore contacts, she had full lips with a smile worth a million dollars. Keri stood about 5'7" and weighed about one-hundred twenty-two pounds. And to him she was the most beautiful woman he had ever seen in his life. He knew already before he met her that he was in love.

"So this is what you do when you stay late at the office? Look out the window and watch the cleaning crew do their jobs uh?"

Daryl did not even look back to acknowledge Gary who was speaking to him. "She's beautiful Gary, absolutely beautiful."

"Come on man, get a life, she's a fucking cleaning lady. What are you trying to do, fuck your way to the bottom?"

"Nah, she's more than that, I think I am in love."

"Oh cut the shit what you need is to go out to a bar, find yourself some nice warm college pussy, fuck her in the ass or whatever it is you do, come back to work on Monday and get ready for the trip we're taking to Spain on Wednesday. Three full days in Madrid, where the pussy is all hot and spicy, what more could you ask for?"

Daryl turned around to face Gary, "Damn man, you think about pussy more than I do and you got in house. But then again maybe you're right, maybe I lost focus there a bit.

As a matter of fact, I'm done here, let's go. I'll walk you to your car."

As they both left Daryl's office he hit the lights. When they got on the elevator to head to the parking garage, Daryl asked, "What's on your agenda for tonight?"

Gary sighed and said, "Family time with the old ball and chain and kids. She's been on my ass lately talking about I don't spend enough time at home, that I am always with you. I have to keep reminding her that if I was always home we wouldn't have a house, because I don't see her paying the bills every month with the tips she gets from Applebee's."

Daryl laughed, "Tell her I said hi."

Gary laughed, "You must not want me to get any tonight uh, and you know damn well she can't stand your ass. She thinks you're a bad influence on me because you're a whore."

"Bad influence my ass, a whore well maybe. I like to be called a man who explores his options with amble interest. And if she only knew where those bad choices are really coming from, your Mexican ass will be sleeping on the couch until the kids went to college. Mr. let's go drink out of a boot until we get alcohol poisoning when we went to Germany last winter. Mr. Eat this bag of mushrooms and have a three-hour conversation with Harriet Tubman about a railroad. And let us not forget, Mr. It's legal in Amsterdam; here Daryl, take a hit of this you'll be able to hear colors, need I say more?"

"Hey if I don't show you a good time then who will? You'll probably end up waking up in a bath tub full of ice missing some vital organs. Anyway, I have to go. You want to get together on Sunday and go shoot some pool?"

"Yea why not, how about Bernie's at three o'clock?"

"Sounds good brother, later," with that Gary got into his car and drove away. Daryl walked about twenty feet to his car, got in and looked at his watch. It was 9:36 p.m.

He had been sitting in the parking lot of the building across the street for about three and a half hours before she came walking out of the building. She was saying her good-byes to a few co-workers as Daryl got out of his Lexus, hit the alarm, and started her way. He had to jog to catch up with her, as she was walking real fast to her car. Not wanting to scare her he yelled, "Excuse me miss, can I have a minute of your time please?"

Keri waited for more but none came out. "Ok, its past one in the morning in a parking lot, what do you want?"

"I uh, was wondering if you would like to have a cup of coffee or perhaps a milkshake with me sometime?"

Keri laughed, "Are you serious, you approach me in the middle of the night asking me out? I have no idea who you are, or where you came from, from all I know you might be a serial killer or rapist. Did you really think that you could come over here to my place of employment at 1 in the morning to ask me out on a date and I'd say yes?"

"Hold on, please let me explain. Daryl was fumbling for words, "My name is Daryl, I work across the street in that big black building right there, here is my card." Daryl handed her a business card, it read 'Global Security Inc. Daryl Keener – Consultant. Keri looked it over, and then looked behind Daryl to the skyscraper that had Global's name on it.

"Is there a problem miss?" The security guard asked as he was walking toward them.

Keri looked at Daryl, "No Don just giving directions," she replied.

The security guard gave Daryl a once over look then turn around and started walking back towards the building.

Keri looked at Daryl and asked, "What kind of corporation that owns the biggest building downtown lets its employees wear jeans and a t-shirt to work?"

Daryl smiled, "I am more on the field office side of the company. I travel a lot so I am allowed a few exceptions. Look I know I am skating on thin ice here. I have no idea if you're married or have a boyfriend or anything like that. What I do know is that you're a very beautiful woman and I would like to try to get to know you a little better." Keri started to speak, but Daryl cut her off, "Look before you say no, just hear me out. I am 45 years old, no kids, never married, single, I'm not a player or have time for games, and my favorite book is Ernest Hemmingway's: The Old Man and The Sea; here let me see that card. She handed him back the card. Daryl flipped it over and began writing on the back. "I am writing down my home number on the back. I will be out of town starting Wednesday and will not be back until Sunday night. Please just think about what I said. I am serious when I said how beautiful you are. Ok, well have a good night." And with that said, Daryl started to walk away back toward his car. When he was halfway there

Keri yelled, "Hey don't you want to know my name?"

Daryl yelled back, "Good night Keri," as he got into his car and drove away.

Madrid, Spain

Daryl and Gary had been on the first floor of the department store coming up four hours now. They had originally taken forty-two hostages, but now only had thirty-nine; they were shooting one every hour until their demands were met. They had half the hostages on their knees in front of the windows and entrance ways, and the other half lying face down on the ground. The negotiations were going nowhere.

"Look damn it, we got hostages and plenty of loot, we don't give a damn and we're not afraid to shoot." Daryl was speaking Spanish into a phone, "I don't care what you have to do, just get it done!" He yelled.

"Sir we are trying to accommodate your request, but it's going to take some time for something of this magnitude to get done. "

"Get out my ass and save me the bullshit and please don't feed me any of that textbook shit either. It does nothing for you ok."

"I think that if you released some hostages it would expedite matters a little quicker."

"You do don't you? Didn't I tell you not to fuck with me? There you go with that psychological bullshit again. I tell you what, you want a hostage released? No problem watch the front door." Daryl put down the phone, looked over at Gary who had his weapon pointed at the hostages on the floor and proceeded to walk to the entrance. Once he was there he yelled through the glass. "Is this what you want?" And as he said that he put his gun up to a female hostage's head and blew her brains all over the other hostages.

"Shut the fuck up or you'll be next he told a nearby male hostage who was praying to God.

Daryl walked back to the make-up counter, picked up the phone and said, "There you go Mr. Frued, one hostage released from her mortal body, do you have any more requests that will expedite matters?" Then he slammed down the phone.

Gary was pacing the floor nervously, "What the fuck you keep looking at?" Gary yelled at a hostage. The hostage had been laying on the floor staring back and forth at Gary and old RPG that was leaning on a mannequin. "Oh I get it," Gary said, "You were wishing that long shot was a big fat dick uh? Well keep eyeball fucking me and I will make sure you get that shoved so far up your ass you will be wishing for this here bullet, fucking faggot." Then he kicked the hostage in the ribs.

Gary turned to Daryl, "What's taking them so long?" He asked.

"Patience brother, you know this shit takes time, it's only been a little over four hours. We'll give them a few more hours than we blow this bitch and make our great escape.

Besides, they need more time to try to figure out how to breach the place without blowing up the hostages, we don't."

Just then the phone rang; Daryl picked it up and said, "Well?"

"We are working with the Americans to have your friends' released from Guantanamo Bay, but it will take a little more time. But we do have you bus en route and your airplane is being fueled as we speak."

"Well done Mr. Frued, I knew we could come to an understanding sooner or later. The next time you call I want to hear good news about my friends in Cuba, or dare I say, I'll start killing some more hostages; now get back to work." Daryl said as he hung up the phone.

"Gary!" He yelled, "Get the Pentolite ready, these fuckers are about to make a move on us any minute now."

Gary started arming the charges he had previously set around the department store. As he was doing that, Daryl picked up a hostage and positioned the man in front of him to use as a shield as he looked out the window. Without warning a sniper round hit him in the right shoulder causing him to lose balance and release the hostage. Immediately after that a second round hit him in his chest and down he went. Before Gary could react, the department store went into chaos.

Flash bangs began going off all around him, temporary blinding and disorientating him. Two seconds later he fell as multiple shots hit him in his chest, arms and back. As he lay there dying he heard the shouting of the police telling everyone to remain on the floor and be still. Thirty-eight seconds after the initial breach the police had the area secure with two suspects down.

Daryl got up from the floor and shouted, "Hold the exercise, hold the exercise!" Daryl walked over to the officer who was in charge of the raid, "I hate to be the one to tell you, but you and all of your people and the hostages are all dead."

How do you suppose that?" The officer asked. "We killed you and your buddy over there before you activated any charges."

Did you really officer? James please stand and reveal yourself."

As the officer watched, James stood up from among the hostages and opened his shirt to reveal a suicide vest. "As you can see you assumed that there were only two suspects, and that is exactly what I wanted you to believe; hence the reason I never tried to completely black out the windows. I wanted you to see what was happening so you can make a judgment call on how to breach the place. My objective was never for you to comply with my demands, hell I could care less. My goal was to kill as many hostages and other first responders as possible. My life was going to end here today either by you or the explosives. I came here willing to make the ultimate sacrifice. So then you have to ask yourself, what sounds better for my cause to other terrorists and those seventy-two virgins waiting for me in paradise; killing a mere forty civilians or killing forty civilians and about fifty more cops and other government officials?"

"How in the hell were we suppose to know that there was another man hiding with the hostages?" The officer asked.

"That's the question is it not? And that's why my associates and I are here. To answer that and other questions you might have." Daryl looked around the mock department store "Ok everybody, this exercise is over, thank you so much for your hard work and effort today. We will re-group tomorrow morning in the command trailer at 7:30 a.m. sharp to go over the do's and don'ts of the tactics that were used here today." With that said the police and the other exercise participants began gathering their weapons and other gear and were clearing out. Daryl began walking back to the command trailer when he was stopped by the officer in charge of the raid, "You boys really that good that you can spot unidentified accomplice huh?"

Daryl smiled, "No were better." Daryl didn't wait for a response, he continued on walking to his destination to retrieve the surveillance tapes that recorded the day activities. He had a long night ahead of him; to study and analyze everything that just went down in the past seven hours.

Daryl and Gary was in Daryl's office playing the video game Tiger Wood's Golf on the X-box 360 he had secretly hidden in a compartment in his desk, connected wirelessly to a sixty-inch flat screen TV that hanged on his wall that when not turned on doubles as mirror. They were sitting in bean bag chairs that Daryl kept in one of his closets. And by the look Daryl's face, it did not seem like he was winning.

There was a knock on the door, "Come in." Daryl said without looking to see who it was. The man who walked in was in his fifties, about 6'3, well-tanned and wearing a three-thousand-dollar suit by Tanner and Son. He coughed to get their attention. Gary and Daryl looked back to see the Vice President of the company looking down at them. They each stood up. Daryl was the first to offer his hand and said,

"Good afternoon sir, how can I help you?' Followed by Gary giving up his hand as well.

"So this is what you gentlemen do all day uh, Mr. Keener? Pretend to be busy and play games all day." He had a serious tone to his voice.

"Actually sir, Gary and I were just doing a little research on how uh, what were we researching Gary?"

"We were researching what irons to use in the upcoming company golf tournament so we could kick your old ass." Daryl looked at Gary with a have you lost your fucking mind look.

"I've been winning that tournament for the last twelve years and be damned if I lose to you two wet behind ears punks." He grinned then continued, "Anyway since you're both here, I won't have to repeat myself later. I came down here to congratulate you gentlemen on a superb well done job, you men did over in Spain last week. The Spanish was impressed, and you know those cocky bastards are never satisfied. And they have already formally asked us to come back there in about eight months; this time in Barcelona to offer a variety of training courses over an eight-day seminar. Then of course our vendors were very impressed on the cool new toys you persuaded the Spanish Government to buy. Over all gentlemen, you've hit a grand slam on this contract, as always."

"Thank you sir," Daryl said, "just doing our jobs."

"Yes I can see that quite clearly Mr. Keener," the Vice President said as he looked past him towards the TV. "Keep up the good work guys, I'll leave so you two can get back to researching." As he said that the Vice President walked out of Daryl's office and shut the door.

"Just doing our job sir, can you be even more in his ass?" Gary asked Daryl.

"Do you think he was mad at us about the game?" Daryl asked.

"Man hell no, we just made this company more than a half-million dollars in four days. Him and everybody else in corporate knows we bust our ass so they can have winter homes in the tropics. If you don't believe me, look around, your office is as big as a one-bedroom condo. Look at what you're wearing, is there anybody else in this building wearing a pair of Jordan's with their slacks, no. And let's not forget about the big fat bonus we get every quarter. We get results Daryl, we are good at what we do, and it's that simple. Good help is hard to find in our field."

"Touché, touché." Daryl replied.

"Look, I got some paper to push around on my desk before I leave and make it home at a decent time before the wife complains, you want to hit the gym later?"

"I wish could but tonight I already volunteered to pick up a couple kids from that foster home I've been telling you about for years and take them bowling, you should come."

"Man I barely have time for my three kids. And besides you know Casey ain't having that shit."

"Yeah, she wouldn't, the selfish bitch."

"Gary laughed, "See you tomorrow brother." Gary said as he walked out the door.

Daryl was just turning off the video game and getting ready to leave when his phone rang. He picked it up, "This is Daryl."

"Hey Daryl, this is Keri."

Daryl sat down, his heart stopped. He could not believe that she actually called.

Chapter 4

Fort de Nogant, Paris

"Why do you want to become a Legionnaire?"

"Because I don't have any family and nowhere else to go."

"So does three quarters of the other applicants, what makes you different from them?"

"My determination to strive for the best and my loyalty to those who trust me."

"Around here trust is earned, not just handed down. Tell me, why should I believe anything you say? Men would sell their mothers to have an opportunity to be here."

"You're right, you don't have to believe a word I say, and quite frankly I am not going to stand here and kiss your ass either; you read my file, you know my past, you already knew whether you were going to accept me or not before I came here this morning."

"What do you want to do for the Legion?"

"Kill."

The tap on the shoulder brought Karsten out of his daydream and back to reality.

"Ten minutes to the D.Z." The jump master yelled. Karsten yawned and put a grape jolly rancher in his mouth.

"Alright Wolves, we're nine minutes out, check your weapons, gear, chutes, and get information on the ramp. And for Christ sake someone please get rid of that fucking head, it stinks. I ain't gonna ask who bagged it, just get rid of it now!" Karsten yelled as he made his way to talk to the pilots, "Crazy superstitious motherfuckers," he mumbled underneath his breath.

Tonight the wolf pack was high in the sky, cruising at thirty-thousand feet in the air in a re-modified C-160 Transall transport. They were getting ready for an H.A.L.O parachute jump (High Altitude Low Opening) into Cameroon. H.A.L.O jumps are considered one of the feared and hardest jumps in every Special Operation outfit throughout the world. They require specialized training, gear, chutes and above all, a pair of brass balls doesn't hurt either. The fact that they were doing this at night made the pucker factor even higher.

"Five minutes!" The jumpmaster yelled. Everybody was in formation in the back of the plane. Each man checking the man in front of him to make sure his gear and chute was in order and secured. "Three minutes!" They heard.

The ramp in the back was lowered. All of a sudden the temperature dropped from a cozy cold as hell to a Jack Frost holding your nuts while bear hugging you freezing cold. Everyman was in his own thought as they waited for the green light-go time. They had made these combat jumps before together as a team, but each time it felt new. H.A.LO. jumps were something one did not get use to.

"One minute!" Karsten was in the back of the formation, the last to jump. He always made sure his men exited the plane correctly. If not, it could mean the death not only for the jumper but the team as well. "Alright Wolves, howl at the moon and grab your nuts!"

Karsten yelled. "Everyone have their coordinates, see you on the ground." Right then the jump signal went from red to green as the jump master was yelling, "Go, go, go, go, go!"

****

"Karsten you are a pussy, you don't belong in the legion, how you made it this far is impressive."

"Merci Corporal Chief Sprazzo!" Shouted Karsten.

"I was not congratulating you, you dip shit. It appears you're so stupid you don't know when you're being insulted."

Karsten was standing at garde-a-vous with the rest of his twenty-five-man platoon on the parade grounds, in the middle of the night, in the middle of a thunderstorm.

"You know why I don't like you Karsten?"

"Oui Corporal Chef," was the reply.

"You don't uh, well why don't you tell me why, as a matter of fact, tell the whole platoon why." Karsten knew that no matter what he said the Chief was going to find a way to punish him either way. And if he wanted to stay in the Legion he would have to put up with the sketch and man-up. "The Corporal Chief doesn't like me because when the Chief saw my dick in the shower this morning it made him feel like he was a twelve-year-old boy all over again," Karsten replied. There were a few small under breath laughs heard through the platoon.

"Does the platoon think that was funny?!" Asked the Chief.

"No Corporal Chief!" The platoon replied in unison.

"Well Karsten allow me to retort, I don't like you because," and before the Chief finished his sentence he punched Karsten square in the nose. Blood immediately started gushing from the sudden impact. And as Karsten hunched over to put his hands to his face the Corporal grabbed him by the back of his head and pushed it down to meet his knee.

Suddenly, Karsten's mouth filled with blood as well. "Who told you to get out of formation Karsten!" The Chief yelled, "Back at garde-a-vous pussy." Karsten did as he was told. "As I was saying before you interrupted me Karsten; the reason I don't like you is because you're a bleeder. Look at all of this blood, all over the ground and your uniform. You should be ashamed of yourself. It's like your menstruating, are you on your period Karsten?"

"No Corporal Chief," Karsten replied with a half closed mouth.

"You see Karsten, you are weak and I am strong. You are the sheep and I am the big bad wolf. Your pathetic life is mine, and mine to do with as I like. I am going to break you Karsten; Break you so hard you are going to put a bullet in your brain and save me the trouble. This first week of basic was nothing; I have you for four more months. That's four more months for me to make you eat that bullet Karsten, which will be a real treat for me. And do you know why smart-ass? Because it would make my twelve-year-old boy dick real hard, probably the hardest it's ever been in my life."

"Well, ain't that just grand chief, you be sure to tell the misses that it was because of me you no longer need that damn pump," Karsten sounded off in a cynical tone. Then he closed his eyes because he knew what was next. At that moment the Chief took out his truncheon and hit Karsten on his legs buckling him, and then proceeded to beat Karsten on the back, arms, legs, and stomach, everywhere but his head. The chief was rumored to give brutal beatings without leaving a mark. The platoon watched and listened in awe as the Chief beat Karsten to a pulp. It was hard listening to a grown man cry. When the Chief tired he dismissed the platoon back to the barracks, leaving Karsten in a puddle of mud and blood. And before the Corporal walked away he bent down and whispered into Karsten's ear, "Your kind doesn't belong in the Legion, you can quit anytime or have a training accident that might paralyze you." With that said the Chief kicked Karsten on his chin knocking him out, then straightened his uniform and walked away towards the N.C.O. barracks, he was good on his promise.

"Next!" yelled the clerk. Karsten had been waiting outside the Captain's office for more than two hours. "Name, asked the clerk.

"Karsten."

"The Captain will see you now, that way." pointed the clerk.

Karsten walked about twenty-feet toward an open door, he knocked anyway.

"You Karsten?" Asked the Captain.

"Oui Mon Captain," came the reply.

"Come in and have a seat," the Captain pointed to a gun metal gray chair that was positioned in front of his desk.

Karsten did what he was told. The chair was hard and uncomfortable with a stiff back. Probably the way the Captain like it to show his dominance Karsten thought.

"Comfortable?" asked the Captain.

"Very," replied Karsten.

The Captain gave a slight grin before his face went straight serious again. "Karsten I reviewed your file from basic. Your I.Q. is off the charts, above average fit-reps, 3rd top rating in your class. Suffered from a training accident I see; a bullet found its way into your shoulder during a live-fire exercise. All of your instructors say you are Legion material but one, a Corporal Chief Sprazzo. He say's and I quote, *'Not motivated or driven, lacks discipline to become a leader. Has a poor attitude toward authority?'*

"Any idea why?"

"Absolutely not," replied Karsten.

The Captain looked him straight in the eyes and they were locked into a staring contest for about two minutes before the Captain continued, "I see, it says here that your first request for assignment is for the 3 R.E.I (Regiment Entranger d' Infanterie) in the French Guiana. You like the jungle Karsten?"

"Oui Mon Captain."

"Well there's plenty of that down there that's for sure, along with snakes and spiders the size of infants. It also says that you want to go to P.M. school as well. With your scores from basic I don't see that assignment being a problem for you."

"Pardon me Captain, but if it is not a problem I wouldn't be talking to you right now," Karsten stated.

"Speak what's on your mind huh Karsten, so let's cut the formalities shall we? I have good news and more good news for you. The good news is that you won't have to deal with Corporal Chief Sprazzo anymore." Karsten smiled. "The better news is that you're not getting your placement in the 3 R.E.I. It was felt that you could do more good for the Legion in the 2 R.E.P. (Regiment Entranger Parachutuiste). Hell Karsten, you should be rejoicing, most men will prostitute their sisters out to join that outfit. Anyway, your orders are to report to Camp Raffala in Calvi, Corsica within the next twenty-four hours.

Your transportation details are in the packet my clerk will give you when you leave this office. You are to report to your Commanding Officer," the Captain grinned before he spoke the next words very slowly, "A Sergeant Sprazzo."

Karsten tried to protest as he was standing up. But the Captain stood up from behind his desk, his 6'4 frame towering over Karsten's 5'10. "I said dismissed Legionnaire!" the Captain roared.

Karsten saluted smartly and with a perfect about face marched out of the Captain's office.

Once outside the buildings Karsten stopped and took a deep breath and looked up into the sky and yelled, "What more do you want from me?" When he didn't get an answer he looked at his watch, he had a transport to catch.

Kribi, Cameroon

The air was cool and the smell of the sea was heavy in presence. Karsten was pulling in and tucking his chute away when he heard a faint sound of the movement in front of him. He immediately stopped, dropped to the ground and brought up his H.K. G11 Assault Rifle.

"Whoa Sarge, it's just me," Rone whispered loud enough so he could be heard.

"Rone, what's the sit-rep?"

"Angels have landed and awaiting your heavenly presence. We're tucked away about fifty-meters from here, East." Rone pointed to the dense jungle to his left.

"Ok, let me finish gathering my shit then lead the way." Karsten replied.

"Yeah sure boss, take your time. We were hoping to catch the sunrise over this nice lovely ocean."

"Move out smart ass." Was the answer to Rone?

"Glad you could make it Sarge." Mclean said as Karsten and Rone pulled up in the thicket to meet the rest of the team.

"Listen up Wolves, you all been briefed and know the mission, so I am going to spit this for you quick. Some powers to be decided it would be nice if Omar Shaka was to leave this planet and never return. Who makes these decisions and why is above our pay grade, we just do what were told? To get this op off right, the best line of attack is to snipe Mr. Shaka and coordinate a diversion from this area north of the compound," Karsten pointed to a spot on a map he had laid out in front of him on the ground, "We do not want to engage the rest of the rebels if it could be avoided, so we are going to set up some decoys here and here." He pointed to another spot, "Our extract is here, by boat to sea for a rendezvous with a support helo. If our plan goes F.U.B.A.R. (Fuck up beyond all repair) we will rendezvous here, that's eight miles from the original location located in the middle of the jungle, and await further instructions. Everyone still with me?"

"Oui Sarge." They all said in unison.

"Ok here's the makeup, Nordeen, you will head to the extract point and set us up for our journey out to sea. I want that boat in the water as soon as the first man radio's that he is on the way. Tiekert, you and the mad bomber need to be in position here," Karsten pointed to a place on the map, "this is directly north-east of the compound. There you two will set up some decoys and pray the rebels will bite and draw their fire further into the jungle. If not, need I say it's going to be a long morning for all of us? Not to put pressure on you two, but yours is the hardest jobs of all. It needs to be convincing that the initial shot came from that direction. Mclean I will be here, just north of the compound on a small ridge overlooking the diamond mine. From there we will coordinate and I will take the shot. Ok ladies, the time is 22:42, the camp is located about five miles from our current location. That's plenty of time to be ready to go at 01:15. Intel says our boy is a late night drinker; let's hope they get it right this time uh? We go radio silence until go time unless there's an emergency, any questions?" Karsten looked around, there were none, "Splendid, let's move out, we ain't getting paid overtime."

"Damn this jungle is thick; I can't see ten feet in front of me, even with night vision. Do you think there are any tigers or panthers in here on the prowl? I sure would hate to go out like that." Tiekert was speaking softly.

"Will you please shut the fuck up," Rone said, "I can't concentrate with you yapping in my ear; you do want to be in the right location, don't you? Then leave me the hell alone and let me navigate, ok.

"I was just asking…"

"Zip it, not another word out of your mouth or I swear I am going to let that tiger who's been stalking us for the last mile take a bite out of your ass."

Tiekert looked back, "Is there really…?"

"Ssshh, just keep moving." Rone said with a wide grin on his face.

****

"This ain't a ridge, it's a fucking hill," Karsten said in a disgusted tone, "These Intel boys are like weathermen, just take a wild guess and pray that they come close. Mclean, range this for me will ya?"

Mclean took out a high powered spotting scope and made some adjustments. "six-hundred and twenty-one meters, with the wind at 6mph ssw, an elevation decline at nine degrees Sarge."

"Copy that. What's the time?"

"It's exactly 0:32 Sarge."

"Let's hope Tiekert and the mad bomber has some goodies set-up on time. You see the target yet?" Karsten asked as he was looking through his night vision scope attached to the Sig Saur SSG 3000 Sniper Rifle he was cradling.

"Affirmative Sarge, three o'clock, second shack next to those two ton trucks."

"Copy that; let's keep an eye on him. And would you look at that, for once the Intel boys were right, he is a late night drinker." Karsten zoomed in on his scope to get a better look, "And apparently he has a little taste, that's a bottle of Woodford Reserve he has in his hands."

"Well I be damned; how come you can't buy us something that nice when we go to town Sarge?"

"I don't know, probably because when I do go to town it's to pick you ducks up from the jail, stinking and hammered. And besides you guys already had your fill on cheap beer and whiskey, you wouldn't know the difference between good whiskey and cat piss."

"Don't judge me Sarge. "Mclean said as he grinned and was thinking about all the times Karsten had to bust his ass out of jail.

"Say Rone, where did you get that rocket launcher from?"

"Oh, this old thing, I picked it up a couple miles back."

"Of course you did, what was I thinking; they practically grow R.P. G's in the jungle nowadays, them crazy kids."

"I found it in one of those crates on the plane."

"Found it uh, why was it lost? Why the hell were you looking through those crates anyway?"

"Well, I was looking for some reading material for a shit I had to take."

"Right, why not break open a random crate and see if it's full of number one titles from Barnes and Nobel."

"He, I need something to do when I take a shit."

"How about just take a shit and be done with it."

"I could, but then it will have me felling like I didn't accomplish anything."

"Why do I even waste my breath talking to you? What time do you got?"

"01:00, now give me a hand with these trip wires will you?"

Tiekert and Rone had spent the last hour setting up claymores and other small booby-traps throughout the north-east side of the rebel camp. They were also rigging some ammunition belts at the jungle's clearing to stimulate an attack coming from the brush.

"What's the time?" asked Rone.

"We have three minutes until go time, you ready?"

"As ready as a forty-year-old virgin on her wedding night."

01:15 A.M.

Karsten keyed his throat mic, "Ares to Dragon Fly, over.

"Dragon Fly here, we are a go and awaiting your mark."

"Copy that, Ares to Bishop, over."

"Bishop here, extract point looks good Sarge, the love boat is ready to go."

"Copy that, stand-by for further instructions." Karsten then looked at Mclean, "Mclean you ready?" McLean nodded his head yes. "Alright quarterback this shit for me then!"

"Target is around six-hundred meters out, wind at four miles now, two mil hold left, one mil hold high." Karsten made adjustments to his scope, "check." was all he said.

"Target is motionless, fire on my command; fire, fire, fire." Crack! the sound echoed for a half a mile. The report sounded like a tree snapping in half on Gods knee.

"Target down; repeat target is down, nice shot Sarge."

Almost immediately after Karsten fired the shot he and Mclean watched as an R.P.G came rushing out of the jungle heading towards one of the two ton trucks that was next to the shack and the target. It exploded the vehicle and flipped over on its side, and as on cue Tiekert and Rone set off the ammunition belts to make the brush explode in gun fire. The rebels re-grouped and were firing towards the direction the R.P.G. came from. A small group was slowly advancing towards the brush were only seconds ago Tiekert and Rone were at.

"Ares to Bishop, over."

"Bishop here, over."

"Bishop start getting our ride ready, eta about fifty minutes, over."

"Bishop copies."

"Say uh Mclean," Karsten said, "Where do you suppose Rone got that R.P.G. from, because he sure in the hell didn't have it when we left the base?"

"Fuck, I don't even know Sarge, maybe he had it hidden in his ass the whole time. Karsten shrugged, "I wonder sometimes about this outfit. Let's go, we have a boat to catch."

"Hey Sarge, don't you want to check on Tiekert and Rone?"

"Not really but what the hell." Karsten keyed his mic, "Ares to Oxford, over."

"A little busy here Sarge." Tiekert sounded winded.

"What's your sit rep?"

"Let's see shall we, I am currently running through a jungle as thick as my dick being chased by a pissed off mob, bullets are flying past my head and grazing my ears, my ass is puckered so tight I am going to need an operation to remove my boxers. So really not much else to report Sarge."

"Copy that, over. See Mclean they're fine, you worry too much," Karsten said as he and Mclean disappeared in the jungle.

"You have the easy job Nordeen; just make sure the boat is ready. Oh and by the way I forgot to tell you that you will have to manually inflate such said craft when we radio in. And let's not forget, drag that beast of a craft two miles through a fucking jungle to the beach that by the way has more rocks than sand. And please try not to pierce the fucking thing either, uh. Why do I put up with this shit job?" Nordeen was talking to himself as he trudged along the coastline.

Mclean and Karsten were about one-hundred and fifty meters out from the extract point looking through night vision goggles. "Please tell me that ain't our boy still lugging that fucking boat toward the water." Karsten said to Mclean.

"Alright I won't tell you, but take a wild guess Sarge."

"Damn, come on, let's go help his ass."

"Ares to Bishop, over."

"Bishop here, go."

"Bishop I am coming up on your black six so don't shoot me; you can shoot Tin Man though he won't mind, I think he wants some time off anyway."

"Thanks Sarge, just when I was beginning to think I have something to live for."

As Karsten and Mclean approached Nordeen from behind to catch up with him, Karsten said, "Well I was just praising those Intel Winnies and it looks like it was premature. Smooth white sand beach my ass, damn beach has more rocks than a corner dope dealer."

"A little help here please guys." Nordeen pleaded.

As they were approaching the surf they heard faint voiced in the distance coming in their direction. "Shit who the fuck is that?" asked Mclean to on one in particular.

Karsten was already lying in a prone position, loading a round in the chamber of his sniper rifle, while looking through the scope. "Looks like five tangos, I don't see any visible weapons," Karsten zoomed in closer, "Fuck me, it looks like a family out on a fucking stroll. One adult male, one adult female, and three small children. What the hell are they doing on a beach at three in the morning?"

"Don't know Sarge but I'm willing to bet they are going to be asking that same question when they spot us. What do you want to do?" asked Mclean.

"Shit if they spot us were fucked, we don't know whose side they're on. And even if they are on the right side we ain't supposed to be here. What you want to bet they can't keep a secret?"

"Probably not, the question is still at play Sarge, what do we do, they're getting closer." Nordeen asked.

Karsten's mind was racing, no killing of innocents and take no prisoners. These people could mean a success or failure of this mission. Not to mention possibly the life of one of his men. "Mclean finish helping Nordeen with the boat, I'll be back." Karsten got up from the sand and started walking towards the group to intercept them. He took out his Glock model 36 (.45 Cal) pistol and a silencer from his tact vest. He screwed the can on the barrel and put the gun behind his back. As he approached within twenty-five yards of the family he started to wave at them to get their attention. They saw him and responded slowly, but were waving back. The adult male said something to Karsten but he couldn't understand it, nor did he want to. When he was within twelve meters he could see the

expression on their faces change when they saw his black painted face. He didn't hesitate; he withdrew his weapon from behind his back and fired five shots, one for each person. He dropped the whole family in less than two seconds. Karsten ran to the bodies to verify the kills. Four of them were dead; a little girl who couldn't have been more than seven years old was still alive and looking in Karsten's eyes. Karsten put the gun to her head and pulled the trigger. Just then his radio cracked, "Oxford to Ares, over."

"Ares here, go,"

"Coming in at your green four, repeat green four."

"Roger."

When Tiekert and Rone came closer to Karsten they saw the bodies.

"Help me drag them in the bushes; we can't leave them in the open." Karsten growled.

With that done all three of them meet up with the other two team members who already had the boat ready in the water.

"Grab paddle ladies, were going on a cruise." Karsten ordered.

As the Wolves paddled out to sea to meet the helo, all was quiet. Nobody had spoken a word, and nobody would until the sun rose over the horizon.

Chapter 5

"So Mr. Lomas, would you like to tell the group what happened?" asked the counselor.

"Well I got thirsty one night, so I went into this Mom and Pop liquor store."

"Ok, then what?"

"Well I asked the old man at the register for a pack of Lucky's and a fifth of Wall Street."

"And?"

"He did not want to give them to me. So I had to persuade him a little, you know, change his mind."

"Ok Mr. Lomas, how did you persuade him? Did you use force or was it just verbal threats?"

"Um, I guess you can say it was a gun."

"What did the police call it Mr. Lomas?"

"A gun."

"So you stuck the place up is that right?"

"That's what the judge said I did."

"Thank you for sharing that story with us Mr. Lomas. Is there anybody else...?"

"Oh bullshit, give me a fucking break, hey doc why don't you ask him what happened next," yelled Diamond.

"Mr......."

"Shut up bitch, that was not a question, I ain't done talking yet. You see Mr. Muthafuckin rapist over there conveniently left out the part where he shoots the old man and then rapes and kills his wife in the back of the store. And then let us not forget how he stole the security tapes and was sitting in a $10.00 a night roach infested motel room, ass hole naked jacking off watching the crime when the police kicked in the door.

Is that all or did I leave something out you piece of shit?"

"Mr...."

"Bitch if you interrupt me again I swear I'm going to... You know, never mind doc, how rude of me to disrupt your class like this, but unlike you I am not getting paid to sit in a circle to listen to this shit. Bad enough I have to live with some of these child molesters and rapist. So I tell you what, fuck you, fuck this bullshit class and fuck half the people in this room right now. Yall know who I am talking about, eat a dick faggots, I'm out of here." Diamond got up to leave then turned around to the counselor, "Oh yeah doc, could you sign this pass for me please, thanks.

"Dam cuz, I thought you were at group?" Tony asked as Diamond came into the cell.

"Yeah I was but it ended early."

"Early my ass, you got kicked out huh?"

"I can't do that shit man, sit and smile at pedophiles, it ain't in me."

"Who gives a fuck, if it helps you get parole, do it."

"Man these people ain't parole me yet, and I'm really beginning to think that it don't matter what classed I took or not; they already know who they're going to set free, and believe me I ain't one of them. The fucking justice system is a joke, give drug dealers and bank robbers ten plus year sentences, but turn around and give child molesters probation before you send him to prison. Then when he gets to prison it's only a two-year sentence, and then let him go because he did a so-called treatment program where he expresses he has a problem. All of that just to see the prick on the ten o'clock news three months later because he's been showing his pink willy to grade school children. Then their crying in court saying they have a disease, and of course they find some fucked up therapist who agrees with them and convinces the court he didn't mean to do it. Yeah, if it's a disease then I surely have the cure, it's a called a forty-five hollow point. Take one and see you in, Hell in the morning."

"Damn Diamond, you seem to have a lot on your chest, anybody else you don't like?"

"Ya, seals, Catholic Priests, and Sara Jessica Parker, bitch looks like a foot."

"Sorry I asked, look why don't we smoke a little something to calm your high octane ass down for a minute?"

"Shit playa, what you got?"

"Some of the finest green pimp, cat I know had his hoe bring it in yesterday, you can still smell her pussy on the bag; here take a whiff."

"I'll pass; I've seen some of these guy's bitches. What you can do is hand me that Bible, would you?"

"You know Diamond I don't think God likes us to be smoking weed from the pages of his Bible."

"Non-sense, it helps us absorb the word better. Just look at this passage I am about to use.

Hebrew 12:10 – 13, now tell me that ain't some cold shit. Jesus punishing us because he loves us, so we can see the correction of our ways."

"You're going to Hell you know?"

"Yep, and I got a feeling I'll be seeing some familiar faces, but not today son. Hey look out that door to see if the man is coming while I light this shit."

"Damn playa, that was some good shit." Diamond said.

"I told you, the finest green, I'm supposed to get some more next week, you want in?"

"Man, hell yea I want in, how much for a cap?"

"Thirty-five beans cuz."

"What the fuck, that's robbery. It's good but it's not that good, and they call me a thief."

"Yeah but this prison is drier than Ann Coulter's pussy, supply and demand cuz."

"Oh I get that, but still, you know how hard I have to work on the poker table to win that much from these penny pinching drug lords just to blow on a sack?"

Tony laughs, "Yeah that's if you can find someone to play with your ass first."

"Man ain't that the truth. All these gangsters and ballers always talking about how many houses and cars they had on the street, and don't forget how they were moving more keys than grand pianos. But not one of them has more than ten dollars a month state pay on their books. Hell, from the entire kilo's they were moving you'd think they would've been retired on an island by now."

"You know the saying, ain't no such thing as half-way crooks." Tony said.

"Oh shit look what I found on the idiot box, I ain't seen Rad Girls in a minute. Damn you looking all confused, you've never seen Rad Girls before?"

"Nope, what is it?"

"Man these bitches are the female version of Jackass, plus they're super-hot. Fuck it's a re-run though; these hoes go out on a crowded street asking random people if they can fart in their mouth."

"Now why in the hell would I want to let a bitch fart in my mouth huh? How much sense does that make Diamond?"

"Shit, are you not looking at these hoes, they fine as hell yo. I tell you what, fuck a fart, that fine ass white bitch Clementine could drop deuce on my face for all it's worth. Just so I can get a whiff of that fire ass pussy I know she got."

"Diamond, you sick ass mothafucker, you probably got off watching the viral video Two girls and a Cup didn't you?"

"Did I ever, that shit was crazy playa. What was not to like, two bad bitches, naked, taking turns shitting in a cup. Man my dick was instantly hard. You trying to tell me you didn't love that video?"

"I threw up after watching them eat it."

"Not me, I think I came in my pants."

"Dam cuz, I sure hope it's the weed that got you talking crazy right now, if not then you my friend have some serious problems."

"Yeah ok, judgment coming from a guy who when we were fourteen persuaded me to help him stick the wide end of a forty bottle up that bitch Mimi's pussy inside Byron's garage. Yes, I can see how I am the one with a problem."

"Hold on now, it fit didn't it? And you sure weren't complaining after you busted a nut in her mouth."

"Actually I was, because if you remember, I wanted to fuck the shit out of her. But after that big ass forty bottle, King Kong could've stuck his dick in her and she wouldn't have felt a thing." Tony and Diamond started laughing hard.

"Shit Diamond, we were only kids then, didn't even know what pussy was."

"Now look at us Tony, grown ass men stuck in a fucking prison cell, talking about forty bottles and bitches shitting in a cup, what's the world coming to."

"Damn this is some good weed." Tony said.

"Hey Tony, you want to hear the best joke of all time?"

"Enlighten me sir," Tony replied.

"Why is six afraid of seven?"

"Why?"

"Because seven eight nine." Diamond laughs.

"No more drugs for this man." Tony said as he walked out the cell shaking his head.

"Hey man where you going, you about to miss the part where all three of these hoes shave their pussy hairs and put it in a burrito." Tony gave Diamond the number one salute, "Suit yourself, I'll probably take a bite just for G.P." Diamond said to no one.

****

"That's eight, come on two more, that's nine, one more baby, ten. Now that's how you're supposed to hit that shit. Push that fat bitch off your chest." Tony said.

"Maybe I want her sitting there, gives me a great view." Diamond laughs.

"Nasty motherfucker." Tony replied with a grin on his face.

"How many sets was that Tony?"

"Our last one number eight. My chest is sore as hell already. All we got left is cardio and we're done for the next two days."

"Cool, let's make it quick; say two miles in eleven minutes sounds right?"

"Oh hell no it don't sound right, you ain't in the Marines anymore cuz. I was thinking more like one mile in ten minutes."

"Quit being lazy Tony."

"Lazy my ass, hell not too many people here can even hang with you working-out, and I just did so I ain't trying to hear shit from you."

"Ok, ok, how about we rock, paper, scissors for it? If I win, we run two miles, if I lose we don't run and call it a day."

"Deal, you cheating ass fucker."

A high pitched sounded from the prison's P.A. system then, "Inmate 97441 report back to your housing unit, inmate 97441 report back to your housing unit."

"You just got saved Tony; let me go see what these faggots want, later."

"Who are you?" The guard asked over the speaker at the slider to get into unit two.

"97441." Was the reply.

"So?"

"So you faggots called me, believe me I may be in prison but I have better shit to do with my time than talk to your inbred ass."

"Hold on," the guard said, "The L.T. wants to see you in his office."

'Of course he does' Diamond thought. Twenty seconds later Diamond walked into the L.T.'s office, "What can I do for you L.T.? Now before you answer that, I have to tell you sorry, I'm not gay, but there are all sorts of wonderful candidates for you to choose in the yard right now." Diamond said with a sarcastic tone and smile.

"Still have that smart ass mouth huh boy? That's alright I am not going to let you ruin my good news for you. You see after months of hard work, I finally got our boy 'Ham' moved back to the facility. As a matter of fact, he's on the other yard right now. That is until I pull some more strings to have that segregation hold lifted against you two, then we'll be able to pick-up where we started from, uh boy. And by the way Ham's dying to get another chance at seeing you, since how he only has one good eye left from your last encounter. I still believe it was pure luck that you were able to take Ham down. But I do believe he will be playing for keeps this time. Now doesn't that news just bring joy to your day boy? Now don't go checking in on me now, I will be very disappointed."

"You really are a prick, uh L.T.? I can only imagine how many dicks you had to put in your mouth to pull this one off. But then again I don't think you mind at all, being you do it for the taste if no other reason at all. Oh what's this, not so smiley and happy no more uh? I see, you don't like the way I speak to you, fair enough, I don't give a fuck though. I'm willing to bet you think you're racist; redneck ass could take me down huh?

Oh yea, by the way your knuckles are turning white right now along with your flushed face, you believe you can do it. Well L.T. nothing would turn about my spirits than stomping a hole in your sorry ass, but I am not going to make the first move, you ain't worth adding more years to my sentence. But you on the other hand, all you have to do is make your move, so I can claim self-defense and grant your wish. But you won't, your little dick ass don't have the balls, that's why you set people up." Diamond rose from his seat, "Now if we're done here, I do believe your wife, uh I mean the shower is calling my name." Diamond started to walk out of the office.

The L.T. got up, "Hey just one fuck-up and your sorry nigger ass is mine. And when that time comes, there will be no cameras to save your ass for what I have in store."

"There you go again L.T. this fixation you have about my ass, let it go man." Diamond said as he walked out of the office towards his pod.

As Diamond walked into his pod, he saw two people walking out of his cell. They were a couple of Tony's boys, so he didn't pay it no mind.

"What they want with you pimp?" Tony asked as Diamond walked into the cell.

"That fucking L.T. has a hard on for my ass, he's back up to his old tricks again. Asshole got Ham sorry ass back in the facility, on the other yard at that. Apparently Ham's holding a mean grudge because I left him with one eye. The L.T. is going out of his way to get that seg lifted between us. When he does it ain't gonna be pretty Tony."

"Fuck his ass, you beat the shit out of him last time, just take out his other eye. I'll bet he'll leave you alone then."

"Nah man, you ain't getting it, if we go at it again, only one of us coming out alive. You best believe he is going to try his hardest to kill me, so that means I have to take him out."

"That nigga ain't worth doing life for playa."

"You think I don't know that, but I be damned if I check in or not fight back."

"You know I got your back D." Tony said.

"I know, I know."

"Well fuck it; don't let that piece of shit L.T. bring you down. I just got the July issue of Butt Man. You might be wanting some cell time so you can enjoy."

"Yeah, why the hell not, I need to rub one off anyway before I hit the water."

"Oh yeah, page thirty-two might be something you like cuz." Tony said as he left the cell. *'Thirty-two uh, well let's see what surprise page thirty-two holds shall we'* Diamond was talking to himself, '*Damn ass like that should be illegal. Fucking bitch ass is so phat it might take two hands to rub this one out.*' Diamond said as he was reached for the Vaseline.

Chapter 6

They were sitting in front of Keri's house in Daryl's Lexus parked in the driveway. The night was cool and the stars were shining bright. Daryl had the moon roof open, and the heat was on low. "Thanks for calling Keri, I was beginning to think you maybe thought I was crazy or something." He smiled.

"Oh, I still haven't made up my mind yet on rather you're crazy or not."

"Sure you have; you gave me the address to your house did you not?"

"I've been drinking too." Keri smiled.

"Well it's a start, you can call me anytime during your drunkard sorties, it's nice to be thought of."

"Who said I was drunk? I had a long day so I drank two beers and remembered I had to call a crazy guy who already knew my name. So how did you know my name?"

"I paid one of your co-workers fifty bucks to divulge the secret."

"Uh, and that's not crazy at all, paying someone fifty bucks for a name. Hell, if you had asked me, I would've only charged you forty bucks." Keri said in a cynical tone.

"This is a nice house you got."

"It's ok, look what do you want from me Daryl? I'm not a whore if that's all you want. I am thirty-nine years old, I have two kids who mean the world to me and who come before myself."

"Keri, do you believe in love at first sight?"

"It's not impossible if that's what you're asking."

"Fair enough, I am not looking for a one-night stand Keri. To tell you the truth I do not know what I am looking for; but I do know whatever it is it's with you."

Keri sighed, "There are so many things you don't know about me Daryl, and you probably won't like the things you find out."

"Ok, try me then."

"Alright, I have herpes."

Daryl sat motionless never taking his eyes off Keri.

"So now that you know you can leave anytime and you'd never have to see me again." Daryl rubbed his chin in mock thinking, "Ok, I can live with that, but do I have to tell you now though, I have a small dick. It's not tiny or anything like that, but it's about the standard. Nothing impressive like King Kong you know."

Keri grinned, "So that doesn't bother you then?"

"Nah, why should it?"

"It does almost every man I meet."

"Their loss and my gain I guess."

"So how come you're not married Daryl? You seem to have your shit together."

"Well I've been holding out for the right person. Plus, I travel a lot for the company I work for. I'm gone about two weeks out of every month."

"Are you seeing anybody right now?"

Nope, and if I was I would've broke it off the minute you called."

"You can cut all of that flattery out; I'm not as pretty as you think I am."

"The hell you're not, you're gorgeous Keri. Anyone with common sense can see that and if not, they're blind as hell."

"If that's the case, then why do I end up attracting jerks and unemployed men?"

"Well that's simple to see, you've just been killing time waiting for me is all. And now that I am here, you're stuck with me."

"A little arrogant aren't you?"

"Absolutely."

Keri looked up out the moon roof then looked back at Daryl who was staring in her eyes.

"So what exactly do you do for a living? It says consultant on your card, what do you consult, that you can wear jeans to work?"

Daryl laughed, "It's a little more complicated than that, but I'll try to explain it to you the best way I can. In a nutshell, I do work with various governments, police agencies, and military from all over the world. I am more of an instructor than a consultant. I train these organizations in the latest counter terrorism techniques and set them up with companies that will make all sorts of cool high tech toys for them to succeed."

"So you actually train them in hand to hand combat, stuff like that?"

"A little, what I do is set-up real life scenarios. For example, if a certain police force wants to learn how to storm an airplane that's been high jacked; more efficiently and with virtually no civilian casualties. I will set –up a mock high jacking on a real airplane on a closed course and play the terrorist. And I will let them see if they can come in and get me without anybody getting hurt. Then I will review with them their tactics and training, and make suggestions. Then we will do it all over again until they get it right."

"What makes you an expert?"

"Um, I got more than fifteen years' worth of military training underneath my belt, with twelve of those in special operations. Plus, I have a great tendency to think outside the box in certain situations where others may not. But trust me I am far from an expert. The truth is you can never really anticipate every detail that is going to happen in any circumstance, all you can do is plan ahead and hope you're ready."

"I see, are you sure you're not seeing anyone?"

"I can assure you Keri; you are the only person I want to see."

Keri looked at her phone to check the time, it was 20:30. "I have to put my kids to bed, they have school in the morning. But I do have about thirty more minutes before I do.

Want to tell me more about yourself?" She asked.

"Sure, I give you the thirty-minute tour of Daryl's life. It all started when I was a young warthog, the world was not ready for me yet...." As Daryl continued talking about his life, Keri was genuinely interested in what he had to say. Forty – five minutes later he escorted her to her front door and told her goodnight as he kissed her hand, then driving away leaving her guessing who he really was.

****

"Dude is your phone broke?" Gary asked as he walked into Daryl's office, carrying a large file folder in his right hand. There was no response, "Hello, did we go deaf overnight?"

Daryl was staring out the window behind his desk, sipping on a Red bull watching the sun rise higher in the sky. He turned around to look at Gary with a smile so wide it would've made the Joker sad. Gary looked back at Daryl, he knew that look. He immediately said, "My man finally took my advice and got a piece of pimple pussy last night didn't you? Ok, ok, what she look like? Was she a blonde? You know I like blondes. Did she have a phat ass? Was it soft? Was the pussy tight? Did it smell like pee? You got it on tape don't you? You sly ass dog you, you did record it uh? Where's it at? Let me see, let me see man, don't have your boy beg all morning."

"Daryl put up his hands, "Slow down horn dog, it's nothing like that."

Gary sat down on the chair in front of Daryl's desk looking disappointed. "Well what the hell are you so happy about? What, did you find out the world is round after all?"

"I met and chatted with someone very interesting last night."

Gary sat up in the chair, "Now we're talking, please continue."

"Anyway, we were in my car."

Gary interrupted, "So she blew you uh, did you record it? Can I watch it?"

"Will you shut the hell up? Let me finish. So we're in my car talking. I'm telling her about myself, and she's telling me about herself. Had some Keith Sweat playing in the background; the moon roof was open so we could see the stars. And the night ended with me kissing her hand goodnight."

Gary looked at Daryl like he was crazy, "What type of pathetic story is that? Are you gay? You've been gay this whole time haven't you? And you chose today to come out the fucking closet. That was the sorriest story I have heard in my adult life. Please next time instead of wasting my time, just kick me in the nuts and kiss me on the cheek uh?"

Daryl was looking at Gary grinning, "Oh I see," Gary said, "You want me to play along uh? Ok, who was this mystery man or woman, who seems to have you whipped like a runaway slave?

"Her name is Keri." Daryl said.

"Ok where did you meet Keri at?" Gary asked.

Daryl just sat there looking at Gary without saying a word, Gary got the silent message.

"Are you serious? You can't be serious. Damn you're serious aren't you? Dude what's wrong with you? You're fucking your way towards the bottom. The fucking cleaning lady from next door, the short white one with the long black hair? The one you're always watching like a stalker?"

"Yeah, she be the one."

"I don't understand you sometimes man, you can have any woman you want. Hell, half the women that work in this building have been eyeball fucking you for years now. And in the end all you want is the janitor. Did I sum that up right?"

"Pretty close, yeah."

"Geesh," Gary took a deep breath, "So when you taking her out?"

"I don't know yet, she works nights, plus she has to find a baby sitter for the kids."

Gary shook his head, "I see. This just keeps getting better and better every time you open your mouth. Kids, she had kids? Can you be even more of a sucker?"

"Yeah thanks for your support asshole." Gary handed him the large folder he was carrying.

"What's this?" Daryl asked.

"That my friend is a proposal from the Venezuelan government. I need you to read it through and see if it is something we can make happen. And if we can I am going to need you to type a report giving an outline of such said operation."

"No problem pal, first you talk shit about my future wife, and now you want me to do your work for you. Let me ask you this, what are you going to be doing all day while I'm slaving?"

"First of all, I was just expressing my concerns. Secondly, it's a team effort here. And third, since you must know, I will be at the testing site with a couple guys from HK playing, uh I mean testing some new goodies they brought all the way from Germany just for us."

"How come I can't go and you stay and do your own work master?"

"Ain't it obvious, they want a man who can handle these weapons, not a school boy who day dreams about getting it on with the janitor." Gary laughed as he ran to open the office door before Daryl could hit him with the letter opener that he had threw.

****

"So where are you taking me?" Keri asked. They had been driving to the south of the city for almost twenty minutes now.

"It's a surprise."

"A surprise huh, well how about you spoil it for me a little?"

Daryl looked at her, *'damn she's so beautiful',* he thought. "Ok, ok, without giving away too much, I thought that maybe I might introduce you to a couple of my friends, followed by a modest dinner, depending what's on the menu tonight, then for desert, a little ice cream under the stars."

"Why aren't you the romantic?" She said in a cynical tone, "Do you really think I should be meeting your friends on our first date though?"

"Well actually yeah, to be honest with you I value their opinion a lot. Over the years they have helped me make choices in my life I wouldn't have otherwise made."

"So you're basically looking for a confirmation from them to see if I am worthy to date you, is that it?" Keri asked in a mildly irritated voice.

Daryl laughed, "Not at all, I already know they'll love you, the question is, would you like them?" As he finished saying that he pulled up to what looked like an old Victorian house, "This is it." he said.

Keri looked out the window and said, "Are we going to a house party, all your friends stay in one house?"

Daryl smiled, "All my friends stay here, let's go." Daryl exited the vehicle and ran over to the other side of the car to get the door for Keri. "I can get that myself you know."

"You could but it would be very rude to the gentleman who's offering to do it for you."

As they approached the house they hear voices of small children in the background. Keri asked, "So I take it your friends have kids huh?" Daryl just smiled and didn't say a word. As they reached the front door Daryl asked, "Are you ready?"

"Do I need to be ready?" Keri said in an irritable voice. Daryl pulled out a key card and opened the front door and gestured Keri in first. "You have a key card for your friend's house? What type of friends are these?" But before she could get an answer back from Daryl, what she saw next made her smile. There were five kids running through the hallway with newspaper pirate hats and swords. As Daryl led the way through the hall they came upon a living room where even more children were playing a variety of video and board games. When the children saw Daryl the room exploded with yelling of his name. Most of the kids stopped what they were doing just to come up and hug him.

Daryl looked at Keri, "Keri, these are my friends, friends this is Keri."

The voice of a middle aged woman sounded from another room in the house, "I've told you kids keep it down in there." Five seconds later an older woman with gray hair entered the room wearing an apron. That's when she noticed Daryl standing there with Keri. "Should've known it was you," she smiled, "Well just don't stand there come over here and give me what's mine and introduce me to your friend." Daryl walked up to the woman and lightly kissed her on the lips and gave her a big hug.

"Miss Mary this is Keri; Keri this is the lovely Miss Mary."

She gave Daryl a play smack on his cheek, "I'm old enough to be your mother young man," she said to him, then to Keri, "What a nice treat meeting you Keri," She looked at Daryl, "So do we have two more for dinner then?" Daryl nodded yes. Then Miss Mary yelled, "Tonya, add two more plates to this party," then she looked at both of them and said," Spaghetti is what's on the menu tonight kids." She smiled and hurried off back to the room where she came from.

"Daryl, Daryl," A small voice sounded from down below. Daryl looked down to see an eight-year-old boy by the name of Jake pulling on his pants leg, "I want to show what I made at school today, come on." With that being said, the little boy was dragging Daryl off. He looked at Keri and mouthed the words, "I'll be right back." A few seconds later as Keri was standing there by herself in the living room, a small six-year-old girl came walking up to her. "Excuse me Miss," the young girl said, "Are you Daryl's girlfriend?"

Keri blushed, "No sweetie, we are just friends." The little girl smiled then said in a matter of fact tone, "Good let's keep it that way missy. When I grow up I am going to marry him." Before Keri could say anything else the little girl kicked her in the knee and ran off.

They were sitting in a long dining hall with four long tables in the room. Each table sat about fifteen people. But tonight there were only thirty-seven total. Keri, Daryl, and Miss Mary was sitting next to one another, along with another twelve kids.

"That spaghetti was delicious Miss Mary," Daryl said and Keri agreed, "What's on the desert menu tonight?" He asked, but already knew the answer to his question.

"Well once we clean up some of this mess and get the dishes in order, I do believe the menu called for ice cream under the stars." Daryl looked at Keri and smiled.

"Ok, kids, whoever is on kitchen duty tonight, let's get these tables clean and everything taken to the kitchen. The rest of you please wipe the tables and sweep the floor. The sooner we get done, the faster we can eat ice cream."

All the kids started yelling in delight. And as she excused herself from the table Keri stood up and said, "Please allow me to help you," as she started to take away Daryl's plate and then her own, and then she walked toward the kitchen. In the kitchen she asked Miss Mary, "What kind of place is this?"

Miss Mary looked around and said, "This is a group home for children age's four to twelve. All of them are looking to be adopted. Most of them have been in the system their whole life. For others their parents abandoned them or they were removed for one reason or another. As nice as this place is, most of these children will end up growing up in the system. The lucky ones won't end up in jail or become junkies.

Keri looked around at all the kids who were smiling and laughing like they hadn't a care in the world. "How do you know Daryl?" she asked.

Miss Mary stopped what she was doing and dried her hands on her apron and sighed, "Oh Daryl, well he just showed up one day about two and a half years ago wanting to volunteer. He has not left since. He remembers all of the kids' names and birthdays and always buys them a present. Once a month he arranges field trips for the kids. Everything from swimming to horseback riding. Things that we don't have the funds to do ourselves, he pays for everything himself, out of his pocket. The kids love him and I truly believe he loves them back too. He tries to visit once a week if he's not out of town working. He even stops at our other facility for the kids ages thirteen to seventeen and helps them with everything from homework to finding a job. You know to this day we don't know why he does it, and after all these years we quit guessing."

She turned to face Keri, "In all these years he spent coming here, he never brought anybody with him; you're the first. Do you know why?" Keri shook her head no. "Sure you do child, all you have to do is accept it, come on." She lightly grabbed Keri by the arm, "If we don't get outside to the backyard in time all the ice cream will be gone." They walked toward the back of the house and walked out the screen door to enter the back yard. Some of the kids were lying on the grass, others had telescopes set up looking in the sky. Keri looked around and saw Daryl lying on the grass laughing, and sharing an ice cream with the little girl who had kicked her earlier that night.

Chapter 7

"My name is Sergeant Sprazzo, welcome to the 2nd R.E.P. ladies. This is the most prestige outfit in the Legion. All of you pussies should consider yourselves honored that you are standing here right now. But make no mistake ladies, you ain't made it yet. This is your 'indoc', your basic training all over again; to see whether you belong here. Fifty percent of you will wash out and be assigned to another unit. For those of you that make it, you will be selected to go in one of the five specialized units we have here, where you will learn the art of war, and the craft of killing. I will not accept anything less than the best of your abilities. To put it to you simply, if I think that you are not giving me your all, I am going to put my foot so far up your ass that you will taste my Rangers for the next three days. Do we understand each other?"

The platoon sounded off in unison, "Oui Mon Sergeant."

The sergeant came down from the top stairs of the H.Q. building from where he was speaking and began walking through the platoon. He gave out random punches to the gut for those recruits he thought was weak, too skinny, or cocky. Then noticed Karsten standing in the last row. The Sergeant smiled, "Well, well, well, what do we have here? Karsten how the hell did you make it to this outfit; this is where the best come to get better, and believe me you ain't one of the best. Matter of fact you may be the absolute worst Legionnaire here. So tell me Karsten, what made you think you belong in the 2nd R.E.P.?"

"Sergeant, this June Legionnaire did not request this assignment."

"You didn't, then why are you here then?"

Karsten thought to himself, *motherfucker you know damn well why I'm here.* And he knew it didn't matter what he said the Sergeant had it in for him. "I am here because God hates you and he wanted to punish you by my being here."

"Indeed, indeed, he does." replied the Sergeant. And at that moment the Sergeant swung a right hook and hit Karsten on the side of his jaw, causing him to lose balance and go down on one knee. "Why Karsten, since you're so eager to start some P.T., why don't you start giving me push-ups until I get tired."

"Oui Mon Sergeant," was all Karsten could say, "Un Mon Sergeant, deux Mon Sergeant, trios Mon Sergeant..."

The Sergeant continued talking to the platoon, "Now for the rest of you candy asses, if think that I am going to tolerate any disobedience, think again. This operation is mine, for the rest of your 'indoc' I will be your God and you my children. If I tell you to run across the street and fuck a goat, your little peckers had better already be out and you working the spit from your mouth around the head of your dicks before the goat see's you coming. I am not here to see you succeed, I am here to make sure you fail, and fail you will, ain't that right Karsten?"

"Oui Mon Sergeant."

"Am I tired of doing push-ups yet Karsten?"

"No, Mon Sergeant."

"I'm not uh, well you may be right. Maybe I'll get tired from a petit footing, eh?" The Sergeant turned to face one of his Corporals, "Corporal Chief Desta, would you please as to be so kind to get in that jeep over there and show Mr. Karsten the tour of the island?"

The chief smiled, "Oui Mon Sergeant."

"Karsten on your feet; the chief has agreed to show you around the island, ain't that grand?"

"Oui Mon Sergeant."

"Outstanding," shouted the Sergeant, then he went close and whispered into Karsten's ear, "If the chief tells me that your sorry ass fell more than eight feet from behind that jeeps bumper, I will personally see to it that you have another training accident, but this time it will be fatal. Do I make myself clear Karsten?"

"Oui Mon Sergeant."

"Then move," shouted the Sergeant, "What are the rest of you pussies standing there for, go follow the chief, now!" The platoon moved frantically as everyone struggled to put down their gear and catch up to Karsten who was already about twenty meters ahead.

****

Karsten had just left the recreation building after a forty-five-minute session of lifting weights when he came across the Wolfpack who were all creased up and looking sharp in their pressed uniforms. "Hey Sarge," Rone said, "We as in all of us was wanting to know if you want to do a little drinking, and whoring tonight? That is if you don't have anything planned for this long overdue R&R we finally got."

Karsten looked at his watch, it was only 18:45 and the sun was still high. "I got some other things to do first fella's, but save me a Kronenbourg will ya? I'll catch up with you guys in a couple of hours."

"Well take your time in a hurry Sarge," Tiekert said, "Otherwise you may have to bed down the fat chick instead of Rone this time, uh?"

Rone snapped, "She wasn't fat, just a few extra pounds."

"Yeah a few extra pounds from eating that whole elephant by her damn self." Replied Tiekert. The whole group burst out laughing, even Rone who was now pink in the face.

"Look guys," said Karsten," It's about to be 19:00, do you think you men could maybe, even possibly, not get into any shit before I get there?"

Every one of the Wolves put on a hurt expression on their face. "Sarge, do you really think that our intentions in town are anything but noble?" Rone asked. Karsten raised an eyebrow. "We promise Sarge." They all agreed but kept their fingers crossed behind their backs. Karsten shook his head in disgust and started on the three-mile jog back to the unit's barracks, which was by its lonesome on the south side of the base.

Karsten returned to his quarters ready for a shower until he saw a large brown manila envelope lying on his rack. He sat down at the end of his rack and opened the envelope. He pulled out a packet containing approximately ten sheets of paper, and started to read. His heart almost jumped out of his chest when he was halfway through reading the first page. It was papers saying he was now officially a French citizen. He didn't finish reading the rest; he lay down on his rack and thought to himself how it only took eight miserable fucking years sweating blood to finally get what he wanted. He felt like screaming at the top of his lungs for joy, but decided instead he would go out after all and celebrate with the Wolves tonight. They were the closet thing he had to a family for the last four and a half years. They've trained together, lived together, drank together, and chased pussy together. Theirs was a one of a kind unit in the Legion; they operated outside the Legion norms. Hence why their barracks being located on the other side of the base, next to the airstrip, so they can come and go without anybody knowing their business.

'Fuck it.' He thought, *'Tonight I am going to get shit face drunk with the boys and fuck on that fat chick so Rone won't have to.'* He laughed to himself as he got up off the rack and headed for the showers.

****

Sergeant Sprazzo went on shouting," This is your final practice jump ladies. Tomorrow you will do six consecutive jumps, four in the daylight hours and two at night. Then and only then will your sorry asses be considered for a placement in a unit. Make one mistake tomorrow, just one and your whole time in 'in doc' would have been a waste of Legion time, and when I ship your lousy asses out of here to a base in Africa where you will become an officers' bitch and he'll make a playground out of your ass, you'll have nobody to blame but yourself. Are we clear?"

"Oui Mon Sergeant." The platoon sounded off.

The 'in doc' had started with sixty-two men strong, but only after eight weeks it was down to twenty-one, including Karsten.

"Karsten on your feet, at the double."

"Oui Mon Sergeant."

"Take off that chute and put this one on." The Sergeant said as he handed Karsten a new rig; Karsten stood motionless. "I was not asking god damn it, that was an order asshole."

"Oui Mon Sergeant." Karsten took of his chute and put on the new one. It was plain to see on his face that he didn't want to.

"I packed that chute myself Karsten, consider yourself lucky." The Sergeant said. The platoon was on their way to the D.Z. for their last static line jump before the test tomorrow. As every man got into formation and hooked up, Karsten's heart was racing.

He knew that the Sergeant was giving him a fucked up rig, one that was probably not going to open, let alone the reserve working. At one-thousand feet about time your main canopy doesn't open the reserve is only going to slow you down just enough to let you know you're going to break some bones on impact.

'So what do I do? Karsten thought to himself as the jumpmaster yelled, "One minute!"

"Fuck it, I ain't endured eight weeks of the Sergeant for nothing, he can kiss my ass before I bow down and quit, the racist son of a bitch; I don't have shit to lose anyway."

As Karsten jumped out of the plane he felt his static line yank and nothing happened. His heart stopped as he looked up and saw there was no chute deployment. He cursed himself for about three seconds, then he felt a small tug as his drag caught and deployed his reserve chute. Karsten looked up and over at the plane overhead shaking his fist. "It opened, you sorry sack of shit!" He yelled knowing he could not be heard.

Back in the plane Sergeant Sprazzo watched as Karsten's chute opened and thought to himself, *'Well I be damned, it opened,'* as he walked to the front of the plane to speak with the co-pilot.

****

Karsten felt refreshed after an hour long hot shower. He had returned to his room and was in the process of ironing his uniform when the phone rang in his office across the hall. He sighed, looked at his watch and noticed it was 20:30, as he put the iron down and walked next door to pick up the phone. "Building W." Karsten said as he picked up the receiver.

"Yes Mon Captain…" But the phone on the other end had already hung up.

"Shit, shit, shit!" Karsten cursed as he hurriedly put on his jungle green B.D.U.'s and rangers and rushed out the door to the already waiting vehicle that would take him to the Captain's office. He arrived at the base H.Q. seven minutes later and was standing in front of the Captain thirty seconds after that.

"Karsten," the captain yelled, "I am fed up with the bullshit and recklessness of your unit. You men are supposed to be the elite of the elite. You are expected to hold yourselves to a higher standard, hell you men are supposed to be ghosts, but this whole rock we call Corsica knows who you are because your men can't control themselves when they go into town."

"Mon Captain, if it means anything, the men have not had any R&R for the last nine months, their due..."

The captain cut Karsten off, "It doesn't mean shit, and shut the fuck up. I don't remember asking you a goddamn thing, if it was up to me, I would've already had your so called Wolfpack disbanded years ago. But it ain't up to me; hell no one knows who's running this cloak and dagger operation of yours." Karsten smiled. "You find something funny Sergeant?"

"No Mon Captain."

The captain stared at Karsten for twenty seconds before he continued, "I don't know who you think you are Sergeant, but I will throw you and those sociopaths you call a unit in the Silo so fast you'll receive your speeding ticket in the post a week from Monday. Now, the powers to be have already made the necessary arrangements for you to go get your men out of the city jail. You will be polite and professional and say all the nice ass kissing things you need to say to the police commander so he will think it was his decision not to bring you men up on charges. And Karsten when I say kiss his ass, that's exactly what you are going to do. As a matter of fact, when you come back on base tonight, I will be waiting at the front gate. And if I don't see any French shit smeared around your mouth I will personally make a hand puppet out of your ass. Are we clear Sergeant?"

"Oui Mon Captain, you want me to stick my tongue so far up the Commander's ass he'll think I'm French kissing him."

The Captain looked at Karsten with an evil smirk, "The Corporal out front will drive you into town. Now get the fuck out of my office."

Karsten saluted him smartly and left out the same way he came in. Out front the Corporal who had given him a lift over was patiently waiting for him. "Hey Corporal, you got any rope?" The Corporal nodded and inclined his head toward the back seat of the jeep. In the back seat Karsten saw about two-hundred feet of rappelling line. "You're a good man Corporal." The Corporal just gave a wide grin and started the engine.

****

"The Legion appreciates your generosity and your patience you have with our soldiers. Without your continuing support to work with us, we would have failed to incorporate relations with the citizens of your lovely city." Karsten was speaking to the police Commander.

"Are you done cleaning my ass Sergeant?"

"No sir, the Legion would also like to thank your country for the wonderful selections of wine and women, uh I mean cheese sir."

The Commander snickered before he spoke, "You know Sergeant, I received a couple of phone calls made to me tonight from my superiors demanding I release your men, free without charges at that. Now in all my years as a police Commander I've never, not once had any such request made to me until now. I don't know who or what you are, and I really don't care to be honest with you Sergeant. I don't like you, I don't like the Legion. You foreigners come to our country and disrespect our people and our way of life. Hell, you don't even respect yourselves. You are not wanted in your own country because all of you men are liars, cheats, murderers, thieves, and pedophiles."

"Uh excuse me sir, I hate to interrupt you but that last part about being a pedophile; I can't speak for the whole Legion, but sir I swear she told me she was fifteen going on sixteen." Karsten added.

The Commander glared at him. "You people are a disgrace to the human race, I hope you all burn in hell when judgment day comes." The Commander rose from behind his desk and straightened his tie, "Now the booking officer down the hall will handle your request. Is there anything else the city can do for the Legion Sergeant?"

"Uh, just one more thing sir, I know it's late but do you validate?" Karsten asked in a serious tone.

The Police Commander looked as if he wanted to strangle the shit out of Karsten. "If you will excuse me Sergeant, I have more pressing matters to attend to, good day." With that said the Commander stormed out of his office down the corridor.

"Ok everybody out of the jeep!" Karsten shouted. He had the Corporal pull over on the side of the road once they were out of the city. "Look at you men, your Legionaries for Christ sake, get your asses in order. Tuck in your shirts, stand tall, and put that Kepi Blanc on the proper way!" Karsten was yelling, "You smell like moldy ass and throw up." And they did too. Each man looked as if he was hit with an acne safe by a crazy wild coyote. "Not even two hours and you fuckers were arrested, two fucking hours! I could've swore you told me that you were going to be on your best behavior tonight, or was I mistaken you for some other highly trained, highly disciplined, covert operations team?" Every man looked at each other, but did not say a word.

"Ok who wants to be the first to lie, uh?" Karsten asked the group, nobody responded.

"No takers eh, that's alright, I was hoping for that. We have a long way… Hey Corporal how far back to base?"

"Around twenty kilometers Mon Sergeant." The Corporal replied.

"Excellent, as I was saying we have a long road ahead of us on this beautiful warm night." Karsten looked around, "Now everyone strip the fuck down to your boxers." There were groans and protest. Karsten began shouting, "I said strip the fuck down now before my foot makes a home in some one's ass! And fold those nice uniforms, wouldn't want them to get dirty now, would we?"

While the men were undressing, Karsten took the rappelling line from the back seat and proceeded to cut four segments about four meters in length each. He then went around to the front of the jeep and attached each end to the front bumper. When he was satisfied with his work, he summoned the unit to the front of the vehicle. "Damn, would you look at that me, the Corporal here is having engine problems, ain't that right Corporal?"

The Corporal begin laughing, "Oui Mon Sergeant.

"Fortunately for us Corporal, we have four highly capable bodies that stay in great shape who has just volunteered to tow us the rest of the way to base." Karsten looked at the Wolves, "what are we waiting on ladies, and invitation? Tie yourselves to one end and start pulling."

The men did what they were told as Karsten got back in the jeep with the Corporal.

"Please feel free to ride the brakes and anytime you feel like it Corporal." Karsten told him. "Sure is a nice night ain't it Corporal?" Karsten asked as he sipped his bottle of beer, "Would you like another round Corporal?"

"Why certainly." replied the Corporal.

Karsten reached down on the floorboard and handed the Corporal another beer. "I don't hear anybody laughing, having a good ole time like you were having in town fellas." The men started mock yelling and laughing for about thirty seconds.

"I do say Corporal, I believe I am a little tipsy, how about you governor." Karsten stated in a bad English accent.

"Indeed Mon Sergeant reminds me when I was a young lad at Oxford." The Corporal replied in his own bad English accent. They both started to laugh uncontrollably. When they got their grips back, Karsten asked, "How far have we gone so far Corporal?"

"Almost five kilometers Mon Sergeant."

"Alright Wolves, take a five-minute breather, I have to piss." The next thing you heard were the sound of two men throwing up on the side of the road, while the other two were dry heaving, they were exhausted. The Corporal was having his jollies riding the brakes hard.

"Ah that feels so much better." Karsten said as he walked back to the jeep and opened another beer. "Now my merry men, who wants to tell me the first lie, um?" Nordeen, Tiekert, and McLean all looked at Rone. "Well Rone, you just volunteered, and do make it quick. The Corporal is off duty in another two hours and we have a long way back to base."

Rone stood up off the ground, "It's a little embarrassing Sarge."

"Cut the shit, you have no shame, now out with it. What did I miss on this fine summer night?"

"Well, me and the guys met up with some Brazilian women who were on holiday."

"And?" Karsten persisted.

"There were five of them, and we told them that you'll be joining us shortly. So we started drinking, having a damn fine time. They were kiss all over us, and I was feeling on some tits when I suggested to the one I was with that we go outside for some fresh air. So we're outside getting fresh air and she takes me around the corner to give me a little action with her tongue, if you know what I mean. Anyway, she's kissing on my neck, rubbing her hands all over my body, and then she starts rubbing in mini me."

"Karsten interrupted, "I ain't got all night Rone, how about you skip to the part where you clown's got arrested."

Rone looked back at the others, they all nodded. "Well Sarge, to make a long story short, it turns out that they weren't women, they were transsexuals." Karsten and the Corporal looked at each other, using superhuman strength trying not to smile. Rone continued," As you can figure we didn't take too kindly to being lied to, so we, uh, kind of kicked the everlasting shit out of all five of them. Maybe stripped them naked and left them in the ally."

"So how did you get caught?"

"The mad hatter over there thought it would be fun taking turns shitting and pissing on them."

"Ah I see, you assholes are damned lucky that charges were never filed, especially since two of them are in critical condition in the local hospital." Karsten sighed, "One question Rone, did you find out it was a man before or after you got your rocks off?" Karsten couldn't control his laughs anymore. Rone was silent. "Ok, I guess it ain't important than is it? Wolves, get your clothes back on and get in the jeep, my beer is getting warm." When everyone was packed in the jeep like a can of sardines, Rone asked, "Hey Sarge, this stays between us, the unit I mean right?"

"Of course it does Rone. Corporal you heard that right, not a damn word of this to anybody, that's an order."

"Oui Mon Sergeant." The Corporal said as he looked at Karsten. They both were crossing their fingers.

Chapter 8

"So what are you going to do when you get out?" asked Tony. Dee was hitting the joint they had rolled earlier; 1st Corinthians 6:14.

"I don't even know, maybe go club a baby seal."

"Say what, maybe you better pass that back down here, it's clouding your mind."

"No, I'm dead serious Tony."

"Why in the fuck would you want to go club a baby seal?"

"Let me ask you, how many people do you know that ever club a baby seal?"

"Can't say I know any." Tony replied as he was inhaling the weed smoke.

"That's my point, it's a conversation starter. For example, let's say I was at a charity auction or something…"

Tony interrupted, "Why were you there? Were you planning on robbing them nice rich old folks?" Tony laughed.

"No, I am there to pick up their daughters." Anyway, let's say I was at this auction and some random people comes up to me and started making small talk and telling me how they went to the country club and had drinks with the Abbot's last weekend."

"Wait a second, with whom?" Tony asked.

"The Abbots, you know from the Young and Restless. So their telling me how much they adore the Abbot's and how Jack is a great golfer. Then they notice I have not said a word in more than five minutes, because they've been doing all the talking. So I get asked, "What did you do over the weekend?"

I look at them in both of their eyes and say, "You know what Jim, I flew to Norway, had a few drinks with some beautiful women, broke a few hearts, took in an Opera, and did a little ball room dancing. And oh yeah, while I was over there, I clubbed a baby seal for the fuck of it. And when I tell them that, the Misses grasps for air as she grabs for her pearl necklace and the husband coughs up his champagne unable to speak. And for those tense five seconds they stare at me. And I look back at them with a cool and calm composure.

Then they look at each other and start laughing; the husband puts a hand on my shoulder and says, "That's a good one son, you sure know how to liven up a party." And of course I smile and say "Thank you Jim." That's when he gets himself back together and says, "You know what young man, I want to introduce you to my daughter, she has a crazy sense of humor like yourself." And that's when I say, "I would be delighted Jim." Knowing all the time I was really telling them the truth is what makes it so much better."

"Damn Dee, you really thought this one out huh?"

"A little, yeah, why? Did I rush it?"

"No, it was good. But let me ask you something, do you think it'll work?"

Dee shook his head, "You know I was just asking myself the same thing. You see if I didn't have bad luck I wouldn't have any luck at all. The moment I do go to Norway and find, not to mention befriend a baby seal, and gain the trust of its mother over a few days by bringing them some fish. The moment its mother turns its back for one second, out comes the good ole Louisville Slugger. Nothing like a good old fashion wooden bat for a proper beat down. Anyway, here comes the bat and I start to crack the shit out of that baby seal. Well mother seal see's what's going down and she don't like it, so I have to crack her on the side of her head, so she realized who's the boss. So while I am doing all of this, and this is where my bad luck comes in at.

A fucking National Geographic film crew comes running out of the bushes screaming at me. Apparently they have been filming this one particular baby seal since he was born' even named him Oshi. You see my problem now don't you? I got my fresh kill getting cold on me on the ice, mother seal has come back to her senses after the crack on the head and she's madder than ever, and on top of that I got a fucking film crew of three who's yelling at me, taking pictures of me, and trying to take away my Louisville Slugger. Now you try explaining that to the non-English speaking concierge at the hotel when you go back and all of your clothes and bat have fresh blood on them. Next thing you know, I'll be stuck in a Norwegian prison cell with a skinny Norwegian trying to explain to him the difference between a hooker and a whore, that's my luck."

Tony passed Dee the joint, "I wasn't talking about beating up a seal, I meant do you think that you can go to a charity auction and pick up some rich guy's daughter?"

"Oh that part, man I don't even know. This weed got me thinking all sorts of crazy shit right now. Hell, in about five minutes I'll probably come up with a mathematical formula for going faster than light speed." Dee said as he passed the last few hits of weed back to Tony.

It's hot as hell out here, and it ain't even noon yet." Dee was speaking to Tony. They were walking on the rocky track of the prison yard.

"That's because we're surrounded by concrete cuz, concrete walls, concretes sidewalks, concrete benches, shit even concrete water fountains. Motherfuckers got us up in here walking around this track like cows going to the slaughter house."

"Man you ain't never lied. Check this out Tony, I know I am about to break a prison faux pas, but I've known you since we were twelve, so fuck it. You said you were in here for dope, what the fuck happened?"

Tony stopped walking and turned to look at Dee, "Man, me and my bitch rolled up to Denver for my sister's B-Day party. We were up there kicking it and shit, doing a little drinking, sniffing a few lines of coke, having a good time. These five busters come to the party who was a friend of a friend of my sisters and started acting crazy, calling every woman up in the house a bitch and shit. Well this one buster started yelling at my sister, up in her face calling her a bitch because she wouldn't give him no play. So I step in and tell the punk to back the fuck off. Next thing I know I got hit upside the head with a bottle and two guys were kicking me. I'm telling myself I be damned if I get stomped out. So I pull out my .380 and let a few go in the air. That got them busters off of me. So I point the pistol at the motherfucker who I think hit me with the bottle and pistol whips his ass until he's out cold. At this point I am ready to redrum all them mothafuckers. Then my bitch comes rolling in yelling at me for always ruining a good time. I tell that hoe to shut the fuck up and go get in the car. So she acts like she doesn't hear me, so while I got the burner pointed at these suckers I grab the heifer by her arm and put her in the whip.

So now we're in the car driving on the interstate and all of a sudden she starts slapping me and yelling talking about how we can't go nowhere without me starting shit. I try to tell the bitch what happened, but she keeps cutting me off not listening. Then the hoe had the audacity to punch me in my eye while I'm driving. I don't know what made me do what I did next, maybe it was all the coke I was sniffing. But I give the bitch a right jab to her chops, unbuckle her seat belt and start smashing her head into the dash. Well, as I'm doing this I guess I'm swerving all over the road. You already know what comes next. Fucking Jake pulls me over, see the hoe all bloodied and bruised, takes me out of the car, starts searching the car and found my heat and a quarter key in the trunk. Twelve fucking years I got for that shit cuz, twelve fucking years, can you believe that shit?"

"Oh I believe it alright; these judges are handing out time like its holiday fruit cake."

"What about you Dee, all I saw on the news was that you pulled some serious scores hitting banks and bread trucks."

"Yeah, something like that, you know me; I was out there trying to reach that coke number, one over Jordan. I would have got away with it too if it weren't for those meddling kids and that damn dog. Nah, the one guy who I thought was a true friend dimed me out so he can save his own ass. And the cold thing about it is that we never got caught pulling those licks. I called it quits because I was still on Federal Parole for those weapon charges.

This shaky dog ass nigga thought it would be fun to go on a home invasion spree with one of his minions. Cat didn't even need loot; he was set from all the banks we hit. Dude was just an adrenalin junkie. Anyway, so he and his partner are kicking in doors all over town. Well they in the wrong door, literally. They thought they were about to rob the D-Boy but the clowns got the wrong house. The problem was, the house they planned on robbing was actually owned by a couple of cops. Seriously, the owners of the house were cops and they had their cop friend's downstairs watching the Denver Broncos game. It still amazes me how they didn't get killed that day. So the cops got them down at the station telling them they have them linked to ten home invasions and they're going down for life. So this idiot gets all scared and tells them he has information about a few bank heists, so he can get a deal.

To make a long story short he turns Kings Evidence against me. Remind you, I'm already on parole at the time. The Fed's and Swat raids my pad, disrespects me in front of my bitch. I got booked and my piece of shit public defender tells me she can't win at trial and I should take this great forty-year deal. I tell her to go suck an Aids infected dick and die; I ain't taking no forty-year deal. I might as well try my luck at trial, lose and get the sixty – four max. In the end, on the day of my trial; I ain't going to lie, I pleaded out to a bullshit robbery and felony possession of a weapon and get two ten year sentences running concurrent.

Punk ass co- defendant got a two year bid and a pat on the back from the D.A. for snitching." "Damn cuz, sounds like you got fucked too. What's that nigga's name who ratted you out?"

"It ain't even important anymore Tony, I already let that shit go." Just then a verse from an old 'Nas' song popped in Dee's head, loves changes, a thug changes, and best friend's become strangers.

****

"Five dollars."

"I call."

"I call."

"And I raise ten more dollars back, fifteen plays gentlemen." Dee said as he looked around the table. In the middle of the table four cards were already spread out with a fifth one still to come. The game was Texas Hold Em. There was already a king of clubs, a king of hearts, and ace of diamonds and a two spades.

"I fold."

"Me too."

"I call." Said a man named Jack.

"Is the pot right?" Asked the dealer. Everyone nodded, then the dealer turned over the fifth card, it was a seven of diamonds.

"Another fifteen dollars." Said Jack.

Dee looked at his stack, he had about fifty-two dollars in front of him; and then he looked at Jack's stack, he had about forty-five dollars to his name. "I push all in." Dee said. Jack almost had a heart attack as he called so quickly and turned over a pair of aces which gave him a full house. "Damn that sucks." Dee said to himself and Jack started to rake in the pot, "Hold on a minute playa, I ain't called my hand yet."

"You just said it sucks." Jack said.

"It does suck, sucks to be you right now." That's when Dee turned over his hand to reveal two pocket kings, giving him four of a kind. Jack was frozen stiff; his mouth dropped, and he was speechless. All he could do was sit- down. As Dee started to rake in the chips Jack yelled, "You're a fucking cheater!"

"Look Jack, I know you're a little upset right now, so I am going to let that slick shit slide right now, ok."

"Let it slide my ass, what are the odds of you having pocket kings when I have pocket aces and two fucking kings flop on the board?"

"It's poker Jack, that's the way the cards hit sometimes."

"Yeah right, you just cheated me…"

And before he could finish speaking Dee reached across the table and slapped the shit out of Jack, right in his mouth. "I told you, I'll let it slide the first time but not a second. Now if you feel like you need to redeem your pride after that bitch slap you just received, I have an open door policy at my cell. Otherwise, sit the fuck down and shut the fuck up." Jack rose up from the table and went across the pod to talk to his Aryan brothers.

"Damn Dee, you know those white boys ain't about to let that shit ride. But fuck it, I'm due to give a good ass kicking right about now." Tony said.

"Glad to hear that Tony, cause I think that's what their plotting right about now. Hey house man, cash me out; I'll collect when I come out of the S.H.U. alright."

The house man nodded. Dee got up from the table and walked towards his cell. Dee and Tony took off their shirts and rubbed baby oil all over their chest, neck and back.

"Won't be no wrestling tonight boys." Tony was laughing as he was applying the oil to his body.

"Hate to drag you in this shit Tony." Dee said.

"Man, as many times as you had my back over the years, it's the least I could do cuz." Just then three guys came running into the cell. Two of them had socks with combination of locks inside of them and was swinging for the fences. By the time the C.O.'s came with their Tasers and pepper spray paint balls, Dee and Tony had knocked two of the three out, with their own locks and was taking turns stomping the third. As they were sprayed, tased, and handcuffed, being escorted to medical they both looked at each other and started laughing. They were laughing so hard that the C.O.'s sprayed pepper spray in their mouths to shut them up.

Chapter 9

Prague, Czech Republic

"Damn Daryl, that blonde has been eyeball fucking you all night."

"Yeah she's cute."

"Cute my ass, the broad is superhot. But that's beside the point, why you ain't over there is what I want to know."

"Come on man, you already know."

"Seriously man, because of Keri? Look around man, the toilets are clean and she ain't around. As a matter of fact, she's more than three-thousand miles away, she ain't going to know."

"Can't do it brother, I love her."

"Love her? Shit man, feelings are for women, it comes from their ovaries. You're killing me man, I live vicariously through you. When you bang a broad I feel like I am actually there."

"Could it be because you are there Gary, holding the camera straight if I remember correctly?"

Gary laughed, "Man that ain't the point, the point is you'd be a fool if you don't go over there and say a little something. You know like, hi my name Daryl, can I offer you another drink, how about we go back to my room to get more comfortable? Oh what's this; well it ain't going to suck itself, and don't mind him he's just my camera man."

"If you want to see her on film so bad, how about you go talk to her, uh?" Whoa their buddy, now hold on. I am a married man, and married men don't talk to women like that, because they won't be married afterwards. And besides you already know I'm scared of Casey. If she knew I was with you right now looking at another woman, she'll cut my dick off and feed it to the dog. I think I'll pass."

Daryl chugged the half of bottle of Beck's he was drinking, "You know, you're right, a little conversation never hurt nobody. I am going to go over there and talk to her."

"That's my boy, hey if I can't be your camera man on this one, can I at least watch it afterwards? I'll be up in the room, if not wake me up ok."

"It's not like that Gary."

"It's not? Then why are you going over there then?"

"Good question, I am going over there, to introduce myself, make small talk, walk her to her room at the end of the evening, kiss her on her cheek goodnight, go back to my room, jack-off, shower and take my ass to sleep. We have to be up at 04:00, remember?" After saying that, Daryl walked away leaving Gary at the bar by himself. Gary raised his voice a little, "You have no nuts." Daryl just kept on walking and put his hand behind his back to remind Gary he was number one.

The morning was chilly and windy. A fog had developed overnight and was a little thick in some parts of the area. It was an overcast day with temps only expected to reach a high of 35 degrees. The training exercise was taking place in an abandoned industrial district outside the city. The police force had sent some of its best men and women from surrounding cities as well as locals. They totaled about sixty people. Forty of which were armed with sub-machine guns and assault rifles spread out over the entire industrial area looking for a lone sniper, who had at this point had been pretty elusive for more than three hours now. The sniper had shot nine targets total from all over the complex. Each shot getting closer and closer to the Major who was overseeing the operation. Gary was standing next to him.

The Major spoke, "Who the hell is this guy? And why has he not been found yet?" But the Major was not looking for an answer, he was talking to himself as he was looking through a pair of high-powered binoculars. He picked up his radio and began speaking Czech, "Bravo team, movement at the second south-west building to your left, third floor window. Alpha team, move in to intercept, assist, and surround the building," The Major smiled. "We got your boy now Yank, there's nowhere for him to go."

Gary smiled, "I wouldn't count on it Major."

"Ah, shall we wager a little something then Yank? Perhaps that nice warm overcoat you're wearing?"

Gary looked over at the Major who was eyeing his jacket, "Ok, but when I win I want to drink what's left in that flask in your inside left pocket Major."

The Major smiled then nodded, "Deal." Five minutes later the radio cracked, "Well do you have him?" The Major asked with a strained voice.

"That's a negative Major, but he was here we know that for sure. And by the looks of it we missed him by a couple minutes' sir." The voice on the radio responded.

"And how did you come up with that deduction?" The Major asked.

"Well sir, he was eating breakfast here; he left a half of bacon and cheese sandwich that's still warm and a bottle of beer that's still cold sir."

But before the Major could respond, a bullet flew overhead, spinning a steel target that was five feet over the Major's head. "Crazy son of a bitch," the Major said in Czech, then taking out his silver flask and handing it to Gary.

Gary chugged the alcohol, "Sure does make you all nice and toasty, doesn't it Major?" Gary said while wiping his lips.

"Daryl, these are my kids. This is my ten-year-old daughter Melody and my nine-year-old son, Devin."

"Nice to meet you both," Daryl said.

"What do we say kids?"

"Nice to meet you too," They both said together. Then ran off to finish playing video games downstairs.

Keri led Daryl to the kitchen, "have a seat, can I get you something to drink?" She asked.

"Sure, what do you have?"

"Let's see," she replied as she opened the refrigerator, "I have Kool-Aid, orange juice, water, milk, and some funky looking brown stuff."

"I think I'll just have a cup of water please." She poured him a tall glass of water, and handed it to him. "Thank you for inviting me over for dinner Keri."

Keri had her back facing him as she was focusing on the food on the stove, but still responded, "I figured why not? You gave me a home cooked meal last time; just thought I'd return the favor."

"Awesome, what are we having?"

"Mac and cheese, salad, and baked lamb chop."

"It does smell good; I give you that. Say uh Keri, let me ask you a question," Daryl said in a serious tone. She turned to face him. "Who's under the table smelling my crotch?" He smiled.

Keri turned red, "Venus No!" Out from under the table came a gray, short haired dog of medium height. "Oh yeah, this is Venus. She's part Pit Bull and Rottweiler. Don't worry she won't bite, too hard anyway."

"Yeah, I'll tell that to my crotch, I'm quite sure he won't mind. So will she come to me if I call her?"

"Maybe, I doubt it though, she was badly abused as a puppy and she is cautious of strangers. But try and find out."

"Ok, Venus come here Venus." Daryl called. Venus looked at Daryl then back at Keri, then Daryl again. She ran toward Daryl, tail wagging furiously and semi jumped on him with her two front paws in his lap. Daryl laughed, "I seem to have that effect on women, must be the cologne."

"Yeah must be, I wanted to hop in your lap the minute you walked in," Keri said in a sarcastic tone, "She probably thinks you have food for her."

"I will if your cooking ain't good." He grinned.

"Sorry baby." Keri was talking to the dog, "Since that's the case, you might as well go lay down, there's not going to be anything left on his plate for you." As if Venus understood what Keri said, she got off Daryl's lap, looked him in the eye, and walked out of the kitchen.

"So mom says you're a teacher." Melody said with a mouthful of lettuce.

Keri looked at her irritated, "Please chew your food before you speak."

"Well, kind of," Daryl responded, "I help people with certain problems."

"What do you teach?" Asked Devin as he was picking at his salad.

"Um, let's just say I help the good guys fight the bad guys."

"Do you carry a gun?" Asked Devin.

"Not always, but I do sometimes if I have to for my job."

Then Melody asked, "Do you have any kids?"

"No I don't sweetie."

Melody continued her line of questioning, "Do you want any?" She asked.

Daryl was looking at Keri, a bit uncomfortable about the question. "Actually, I do one day, when I find somebody special."

"Do you play video games?" It was Devin this time.

"Of course, who don't?"

"What's your favorite game?" he asked.

"Let's see, I would have to say Call of Duty Black Ops."

Devin got all excited, "That's my favorite too, you wanna go play!?"

"Maybe after dinner if your mom lets me, ok."

Keri said, "Only if you quit picking at your food and clean your plate."

"Ok mommy." Devin said as he started shoving lumps of food in his mouth.

There was a silence at the table for about five seconds when Melody asked, "Do you have any secrets?"

"Yes I do Ms. Melody."

"Can you tell me one?"

"Well if I tell you sweetie, it would not be a secret anymore, would it?"

"Maybe you can tell me a secret only me and you would know."

Daryl thought about it, and then he got up from the table and walked over to Melody and whispered in her ear. When he finished, Melody let out a loud gasp and put her hand over her mouth. As Daryl was walking back toward his chair, Melody asked, "You promise?" Daryl shook his head. Melody was all smiles and had nothing else to say.

"What did you tell my daughter?" Keri asked with a fake concern in her voice.

Melody blurted out, "He can't tell you mommy, it's our secret."

"Can you tell me a secret too?" Devin asked.

Daryl leaned over to his side and cupped his hands around Devin's ear and whispered. Devin looked up at Daryl and smiled and then said, "Ok."

Keri feeling left out, jokingly said, "Since we're telling secrets, what's mine?" She was grinning.

Daryl scratched the side of his head pretending to think. Then he leaned over and told Keri, "I've been looking for you my whole life." But before she could respond, Devin yelled, "Finished," and jumped up from the table grabbing Daryl's arm saying, "Come on, come on let's go play."

Daryl rose up from the table and allowed himself to be pulled by Devin as he looked into Keri's eyes. Melody hopped up too, "I wanna come." Then she raced out of the kitchen after them leaving Keri sitting at the table by herself.

Thirty minutes later after Keri cleaned up the table and dishes, she went downstairs to where Daryl and the kids were playing video games. "Alright kids from Satan, go upstairs and finish playing so Daryl and I can talk."

"Oh man, we were in the middle of a good part." Devin said.

"I don't care boy, move your narrow behind and take your sister with you. This man did not come all the way over here to play video games, now go." The kids were reluctant as they obeyed their mother, "Bye Daryl." They both said as they walked slowly upstairs.

"Sorry about that, those kids have way too much energy sometimes."

"Nah, it's okay, if I had known you had Black Ops I would've suggested we skip dinner and play games all night." Daryl said as he went to go sit on the love seat next to Keri.

"So tell me, what are the characteristics you look for in a man?"

"Honestly for starts, good looking of course, a job, living in a place of his own, no roommates or living in the parent's basement. A sense of humor, someone who's not a player, he has to get along with kids, someone who I can trust and who will be there for me when I need someone to turn to."

"Have you been reading my Facebook? Because what you just said matches me completely."

"You have a Facebook?"

"Actually no, I have a shitty ass My Space account. What about you?"

"Yeah, I try to stay in touch with friends back in the U.S. from time to time."

"So how did you end up in Canada of all places in the world?"

"You know the story, girl meets boy, thinks she's in love, boy leaves girl for another girl, and then she realizes he didn't really love her. So how about you, you're a long way from California."

"Pretty much my job, I thought it was a good choice at the time for opportunity, growth, and career diversity. Ok, so not exactly, it was the money. They made me an offer I couldn't refuse. And I've been there for about three years now and actually love it, especially now that I've met you."

"You keep saying that, but is it true, or do you just want to sleep with me that bad?"

"Both actually, Keri look, I know it sounds strange, especially after the way I introduced myself to you, mainly stalking you at your job. But everything I've ever said to you, I meant it. You are a remarkable woman, you're smart, sexy, know how to have a good laugh, independent, and have a lovely ass to add. What you have here, you don't need a man in your life and I respect that. But as I already told you before Keri, it was love at first sight when I saw you. You can try as you may but it will take an Army for you to get rid of me. I want to be with you Keri; I want to be a part of your life."

Keri was looking in Daryl's eyes, "Did you write that speech or did you just make it up?" She was smiling.

"Kind of both, why did it work?"

"Don't know yet, I'll guess we'll see in the future, won't we?"

"So I am going to take that as you plan on going out on another date with me then, right?"

"Something like that." Was all Keri said.

Daryl's cell phone began ringing, he ignored it.

"Do you want to get that?" Keri asked.

"No, not really."

"It might be important."

"The only thing that's important is right here, right now."

"It's ok, I won't get mad."

"Alright, let me just see who it is real quick."

Daryl took out his cell phone from his pocket and looked at the screen, it was Gary. "It's just Gary." He said as he pressed ignore on the phone again.

"Who's Gary?"

"Gary is a close friend and a guy I work with for over two and a half years now. More like a partner in crime."

"Are you sure you don't want to take it? It could be work related."

Daryl shook his head, "Let's see, it's a Saturday night, around nine p.m. on a warm spring night, it ain't work related." The cell phone stopped ringing. "His nosey ass just wants to know what I'm doing. He's married, so he always wants to know how the single life is living. Plus, he's a horn dog. He wants me to go out every night and sleep with random women, says it makes him feel more of a man when I tell him a story of a wild adventure, instead of feeling like a slave with a ball and chain on his leg."

"So do you sleep with random women often?"

"Nah, but I tell him a wild story once a week to keep him at bay."

"I see." Keri said.

Just then Daryl's phone rang again; he looked down and saw it was Gary again.

Keri said, "If you don't answer it, I will."

"Be my guest." Daryl said as he handed her the phone.

"Mayor Keener's office." Keri said in a sexy voice.

"Yeah, is Daryl there?" Gary asked.

"Yes he is, may I ask whose calling?"

"Tell him it's Gary." Gary said in mild irritated voice.

"Hold please." She waited five seconds, then said, "I'm sorry Mr. Gary, but the Mayor is a little busy right now, he seems to be tied up right now, if you know what I mean. But after his spanking, I'll tell him to call you immediately ok, bye." But before Gary could say a word Keri hung up the phone.

Daryl was staring at Keri, "What?" she asked in an innocent voice, "At least now you have a damn good story to tell him for the week." They both laughed.

Chapter 10

His hands were zip tied behind his back, his feet zip tied together as well. He was on his knees, soak and wet. His head had been underwater for about two minutes now in a horse trough filled with ice cold water. His body shaking and squirming, as he was trying to get up; but he was being held down by two large men who were laughing. Finally, they brought his head up out of the water, Karsten started coughing up water that he had swallowed, and then there was a smack across his face with an open palm.

"I do believe Karsten that you are a liar, and I hate liars. In your file it says you could hold your breath for three minutes, it's barely been two. What do you have to say about my accusation Karsten?" But before Karsten could answer, the Sergeant gave a nod to the two men who were holding him and they dunked his head back in the water. This was Karsten's fifth dunk in the freezing water. Two and a half minutes later he resurfaced again, this time not putting up any resistance at all. The men let him fall to the ground on his side where he began coughing up more water, vomit, and some blood. The Sergeant continued his speech, "Liars get men killed in combat. They care about nothing but themselves, ain't that right Karsten?" The Sergeant looked down. Karsten mumbled some words. "What was that Karsten, speak up. Here let me help you with that water problem." The Sergeant pulled back his right leg like he was about to kick a field goal in the N.F.L. and let Karsten have it right in the gut. More water and blood came forth.

"You were saying Karsten?"

"Oui Mon Sergeant." Karsten replied.

"Outstanding Karsten, admitting you have a problem is the first step to correcting the problem." The Sergeant looked around the group, "I thought you 2 R.E.P. boys were supposed to be tough?" Then he looked down at Karsten waiting for an answer.

"Oui Mon Sergeant." He mumbled.

"You are huh, well off to the next exercise then, shall we." The Sergeant signaled the two large men, "Drag his sorry ass over to the chair. Cut his hands and feet loose, strip him naked and strap him in."

The Sergeant waited impatiently while this was being done. When he saw that the work had been finished, he spoke, "Pay close attention men, you get two small elephant clips like these," he put up his hands to show the group, "You put one on the subject's ear like this," he demonstrated, "And the other one on his little bitty toe like this. "He placed the other one on Karsten's toe. "You then put a piece of wood or towel in the subject's mouth. After that you take the other two ends of the clips and clip them to an electrical source. Today we are using a small bike battery. You attach one clip sternly to one prong, and then when you are ready to begin, you simply touch the other clip to the other prong of the battery and viola."

When the Sergeant touched the last clip to the battery an electrical current flooded through Karsten, causing him to shake uncontrollably. His eyes and jaw set on the piece of wood that was in his mouth. The Sergeant held the clip for about eight seconds then released it. He then waited about five seconds and did it again, this time for about eleven seconds. "Un-strap him," The Sergeant told the two men. They did what they were told. Karsten immediately fell to the ground in a semi-fetal position. He had shit and pissed himself. The Sergeant came toward him and bent down on one knee and whispered to Karsten, "Courtesy of our mutual friend Sergeant Sprazzo."

He then got up and spoke to the group loudly, "The Legion does not interrogate because there is no one to interrogate. The Legion does not take prisoners. What you witnessed here this morning is what lies ahead for you if you are ever caught and prodded for information. No matter how tough you think you are, everyone has a breaking point, everyone," The Sergeant paused before he spoke again, "Welcome to the N.C.O. / Corporal training course maggots. Now drop and give me my five-hundred push-ups before my nice shiny Ranger finds a new home!" The Sergeant then looked at one of the two men who was holding Karsten underwater, "Chief, I don't want a man standing before evening chow." With that said the Sergeant walked off, he had a strong urge to go wash his hands.

****

"There was this white rabbit hopping through the forest without a care in the world. Until he came around this bush and ran smack into a bear who taking a shit. The rabbit was so scared and shocked that he couldn't move. The bear looked down at the rabbit, the rabbit immediately said, "Please Mr. Bear, please don't eat me, I didn't mean to disturb you." The bear looked around, then said to the rabbit, "Look, calm down, accidents happen, I am not going to eat you ok." The rabbit relaxed a little bit and said, "Thank you Mr. Bear." The bear said to the rabbit, "Hey, let me ask you a question, do you have a problem with shit sticking to your fur?" The rabbit thought about it and said, "No." That's when the bear nodded, then picked up the rabbit and wiped his ass with him." The table started laughing.

The Wolfpack was seated around a gaming table playing cards. They had been at it for about three hours now, and everyone had glassy eyes. The unit had already consumed six1.75 liter bottles of Rain Vodka, four bottles of Sailor Jerry's Rum, two bottles of Hornitos Tequila, and was at present time working on finishing their second case of Kronenbroug. They were playing 'shot poker'. Instead of chips, everyone had shot glasses for money. At the beginning everyone had ten shot glasses in from of them. Before every hand was dealt, everyone must take a shot to ante up just to get dealt cards, then proceeded to play whatever game the dealer chooses. They bet with the shot glasses, the winner of the hand got to divide the shot glasses amongst the losers and watch them drink.

"Where did you hear that joke at Rone?" Tiekert asked Rone, who was barely able to sit straight.

Rone said, "I don't remember, I think it was that damn unicorn who's been following me all damn night to the bathroom asking me if I need a towel to dry my hands with." Rone was dead serious, which made it funnier to everyone else at the table. Once again they all burst out laughing.

When they had quieted down a little, Karsten said, "So this guy walks into a bar and asks for a beer. The barkeep gives him a bottle of Corona and moves to finish wiping down the bar. Well the guy starts looking around the bar and notices a horse stall at the very back of the bar. He also notices that there is a huge see through foot locker sitting behind the bar that's full of cash. So he asks the bartender, "What's with the cash?" The bartender tells him, "It's a contest, you put in ten bucks and then walk over to the horse back there and try to make him laugh. If you can get him to laugh, you win it all." The man asks, "So all I have to do is make this horse laugh?" "That's all." The bartender says. So this guy is sitting there thinking, sipping on his beer, then he finally says, "Ok, I want in." So the guy gives the bartender ten dollars, then walks over to the horse and starts whispering in the horse's ear. He stops halfway and asks the bartender, "can I have free drinks all night if I can get him to cry too?" The bartender shakes his head yes. So the guy went back to whispering into the horse's ear for like another ten seconds.

Then all of a sudden the horse starts laughing his ass off. I mean really laughing so hard people passing by on the sidewalk could hear him. The bartender is silent; he can't believe someone actually made his horse laugh. They guy who made the horse laugh started whispering into the horse's ear again for about another ten seconds. The next thing you know the horse was in tears. Crying so hard he couldn't stand anymore. So the guy walks back to the bar and tells the bartender that he can put the money in an all-black trash bag. The bartender who is still in shock asks, "How in the hell did you make that horse laugh?" They guy replied, "I simply told him my dick was bigger than his." Well, how did you make him cry?" asked the bartender. "That was simple," said the guy," I showed him." The Wolves couldn't stop laughing for a straight four minutes. When they came to their senses that the joke wasn't that funny, McLean asked Karsten,

"So Sarge, how long you got left on your contract?"

"A few years' baby, and then I'm out of here, time to move on to other things."

"You ain't gonna re-list for another five?"

Karsten shook his head no.

"Shit Sarge you should, five more years and then you can retire and be paid for life; not much money to live like a king, but enough to get drunk and fuck cheap whores until you croak." Nordeen said.

"Yeah I'm ranking in the dough now boys, Viva La France," Karsten said in a tart tone, "Once I put in my ten years and my contract is up, that's it, no more Legion for me."

"What do you plan on doing afterwards?" asked Rone.

"Really never thought about it, maybe I'll just roam the earth like Cane from Kung-Fu getting in adventures and shit, hell I don't know. What I do know is that I'm done, Legion sketch is fucking maddening. What about you boys, who's here for life?" Everyman at the table raised their hand, "I don't have nowhere to go Sarge."

"Neither do I." Nordeen said.

Then Rone spoke up, "Don't none of us have nothing to go back to Sarge."

"Neither do I," said Karsten, "I'm taking my new hard earned French Citizenship and making a home for myself somewhere, away from the Legion. How I made it this far boggles my own mind."

"So if you leave, who's going to lead the pack?" Rone asked.

"I'm presuming you, hell you're all Corporal Chiefs; one if not two of you will make Sergeant."

"Speaking of which, we all have been taking bets on how you made Sergeant so fast. It normally takes at least five to six years at best, and you did it in a little less than four.

What gives?" asked Rone.

Karsten sipped his beer, "I was a Corporal Chief when I asked to start a training program for a special project. The powers that be skipped me right to Sergeant when we went online four years ago."

"Lucky son of a bitch." Tiekert said. Everyone at the table agreed.

Rone continued, "Which brings me to my next question, how did we all end up here? I mean look at us really, were the black sheep. And all I can remember is you pulling me out of commando training and asking me if I had sold my soul to the devil yet. I remember saying yes and you saying that you were there to collect."

Karsten smiled as he remembered that day, "I remember that day, you were gung-ho-Legion, a fucking virgin. All of you were, but now look at you. You got a taste of that combat pussy and now you're all fiends."

"Here, here." Said Nordeen, and everyone began howling then chugged their drinks.

After a couple more poker hands, Tiekert said to Karsten, "Sarge, you never answered Rone's question." Karsten looked confused. "How did we all end up here? Whose idea was it to make a suicide unit? Because that's exactly what we are, ain't it? Take the missions that have a five percent probable of success, out the plane we go as the monkey flips the switch?"

"Hell guys," Karsten said," You're all barking up the wrong tree. As I know it, we weren't supposed to make it this far. It was supposed to be an experimental thing. But somehow, some way it became reality. All I know is this…"

There was a knock at the door, "Come," said Sergeant Sprazzo. Karsten walked into the Sergeant's office and stood at attention in front of his desk.

"Karsten, how did you make through the N.C.O. training course? That course was designed for leaders, people who know how to give and receive orders without question." Karsten took around three seconds before he answered," By being a sneaky bastard Mon Sergeant."

The Sergeant gave Karsten an evil appraisal before telling him he could stay standing for the rest of the meeting. Karsten glanced to his right and noticed another person in the room whose back was facing him as he looked out the window. He was wearing civilian clothing. The Sergeant brought Karsten back to attention, "So you think you're a leader now huh Karsten?"

"Oui Mon Sergeant."

"Bullshit, you're a weak link Karsten, a bad apple, a fucking splinter in my palm that I can't get out until now." The Sergeant got up from behind his desk to retrieve a short file box with about one-hundred files in it from behind him, and sat it down in front of Karsten. "You are hereby as of now being re-assigned to Headquarters." Karsten didn't say a word. "Orders from the brass in that the 2 R.E.P. is to come up with an experimental, secret, and unconventional specialized unit. This clandestine unit will consist of five men, one to include you."

The Sergeant smiled a mischievous grin, "In the box are eighty-eight men who currently fit the basic requirements that the brass is looking for. It's your job to weed out four men, four men that you will personally lead and train for the next nine months. You will be given an old building by the airstrip to accommodate yourselves. You will have priority over training facilities and/ or weapons at your request, of course with my approval first. At the end of those nine months, the brass will come down here and throw every test they can think of at you to see if you have wasted Legion time and resources. And when you fail Karsten, and you will fail, I will have the authority to bust your ass back down to June Legionnaire and kick your sorry ass all around this base before I ship you off to be a groundskeeper in Africa."

Karsten finally spoke, "But why me Mon Sergeant, there are more qualified, combat tested soldiers out there?"

"Why you, because I want this experiment to fail, and I want you to fail with it, the 2 R.E.P. already has the best Commandos in all of France, we don't need any more. This so-called experiment is a waste of my time and Legion money, others agree. Why you, because you couldn't Karate kick your ass out of a paper bag Karsten. You're a fucking joke; you don't deserve to wear the Kepi Blanc. Technically you should've died years ago with that training accident. But no, you're like a fucking disease. And the only cure is for you to blow your brains out or the Legion to kick you out. And let's not forget the main reason, I don't like you Karsten, never have and never will; that's why Corporal." The Sergeant said in a crisp irritated tone.

"Well thank you for your confidence Mon Sergeant." Karsten said.

"Dismissed Karsten, and don't forget your box." Karsten saluted smartly and started to walk out of the office. "Corporal," the Sergeant said, "No need to go back to the barracks, while you were here I took the liberty of having all your personal belongings moved to your new home by the airfield." Karsten glared at the Sergeant, the Sergeant smiled.

"So now you know what I know. That's what happened. And we weren't even supposed to make it this far, but for reasons unknown to me, we're still here."

"So we're the rejects, the fuck-ups uh Sarge?" asked Tiekert.

"Not at all, I personally chose each and every one of you men because of your performance and attitudes. The Legion chose us because we have no family and will not be missed if we didn't come back from an op. But never forget, we sweated blood, busted our ass, and sold our souls to get where we are now Wolves. The Legion says we don't have family, but they're wrong. As I look around this table at each and every one of you, I consider you all my family. And I would die for each and every one of you." Karsten turned over his cards and revealed a pair of ten's. There was a pair of three's, one ten, and ace, and a jack in the middle of the table, "Full house ladies, let's down some drinks uh?" Everyone threw in their cards and was moaning and groaning as Karsten filled up shot glasses and handed them out accordingly. "Oh yeah boys I forgot to tell you, we have a five a.m. eight mile run on the beach tomorrow, you might want to slow down on those drinks." Karsten said smiling while sipping his beer.

What Karsten did not know himself was the conversation held in the Sergeant's office after he left. "So that's our guy?" The man in civilian clothes asked.

"Oui."

"How can you be so sure; he doesn't look like much?"

"This is true, but drop him off in the South Pole wearing nothing but bikini underwear, he'll show up at your doorstep the next day with a million-dollar smile and a handful of pesos. He's the Patron Saint of the impossible. I've been grooming him since his first day in the Legion. He's a natural leader, and has a smart head on his shoulders. If any reason why he will succeed is just to prove me wrong sir."

"You picked him out; now give him the tools he needs. I want this combat operational in nine months Sergeant. The Ministry of Defense has a lot riding on these young men, make it happen." The man in civilian clothes said as he walked out of the Sergeant's office. The Sergeant stood up, "Oui, and thank you sir for…" But his ass kissing went unheard, the man was already gone.

Chapter 11

Dee walked into the visiting room and saw Sabrina. *Damn! She looked even more gorgeous than he remembered,* he thought. Her blonde hair was in a long ponytail dropping past the small of her back. She stood there and watched as Dee approached her. When he was five-feet from her, he said, "Really?" Then he looked at his watch, "Only took you a year and some change for you to come rolling up here huh? Hell and I thought this whole time you forgot about me."

As he sat down Sabrina said, "Well if that's the attitude you're going to have I might as well leave now, I don't even know why I came."

"Why did you come Sabrina, huh? What prompted you to get off your ass, and drive two-hundred plus miles to some nameless one horse town in NE Colorado? Was it to show me you still have a phat ass?"

Sabrina looked at Dee with daggers. "I felt bad about the way our situation ended."

"You do, don't ya? Well was it the way you quit coming to see me in the County jail only after two months? Or maybe it was the whole not writing me, not accepting my phone calls, or the part where I waited almost two years for you to come and see me?" Sabrina was getting angry, "You're the one who lied to me or you don't remember that?"

"I didn't lie to you Sabrina; I just left out some parts of my life that I thought were irrelevant."

"Yeah, like the part of you being a felon, or how about the part that you were on parole, and indeed let's not forget the part where you're a fucking bank robber Dee!" Dee folded his arms in front of him, "Yeah sorry about that, when we met you said that whatever I did in the past was not important, I tried to tell you everything if you remember. And for the record I never lied to you once."

"You didn't huh, what about the bank robberies?"

"What about them, you never asked me if I was robbing banks did you?"

"Would you have told me the truth if I did?"

"Yes Sabrina, I would've done anything for you. I was in love with you Sabrina, and even after all this time my dumb ass is still in love with you, you realize that don't you?" Sabrina's eyes started to tear a little, she wiped them with a piece of tissue, "Well, it's too late for all that now. That's the reason I came down here today," she stated with new found confidence, "I just wanted to let you know it's over between us."

"Shit I figured that out a long time ago honey, you're a little late."

"Well, I only think that it's right for me to tell you in person. That and I am also pregnant."

Dee's face was drained of life. "It's Ali's." She added.

Dee took a moment to compose himself, then he said in a low angry voice, "Bitch, you have the nerve to visit me in prison to tell me that you're pregnant, by your ex-boyfriend. The man who use to beat the shit out of you? The man you put in jail for breaking your jaw? The same man who cheated on you by fucking your best friend, that Ali?" All this time I thought you were intelligent Sabrina, but I was fooled. You truly are a stupid white, blonde hair, blue eyed bitch, aren't you? I sure hope when we get to Oz, the Wizard has two brains to give out.

Sabrina looked at Dee with disgust. "He says he loves me, and he's a changed man."

"Of course he said that, what you expect him to say, that he's going to continue bashing your head in? And of course you believe him; you were fooled by every disguise by the Trix rabbit."

"He was there Dee. There when you decided to get locked up. If you really loved me, you wouldn't have done what you did to go to prison."

"Are you serious, you are, aren't you? Listen to yourself Sabrina, you're making excuses to why you're back together with this woman beating asshole."

"Don't judge him, you don't even know him!"

"Oh I do Sabrina; I'm in prison with his type. Glorifying how they put their hoes in check by smacking them around all the time."

"Look, I didn't come here to argue with you, I just wanted to clear things up between us."

"Oh you did that part nicely, to believe that I would've done anything in the world for you to make you happy. I guess your stupidity was rubbing off on me."

"If you're just going to talk shit I can leave you know!"

"No, allow me to excuse myself." Dee yelled, "C.O. this inmate's visit is over," he turned to Sabrina as he stood up, "I hope you have damn good medical insurance at your job, you're going to need it when that nigga starts kicking your head in bitch."

That was three years ago Dee thought as he looked at her picture in his photo album. He only had six pictures in the damn thing and three was of Sabrina. He was still daydreaming when his celly 'Bama' walked in, "What's up pimp?"

Dee looked up, "Shit, just sitting here thinking about the complexities of life."

"I feel ya, who's that sexy bitch?"

"My ex actually."

"Damn Dee why in the world did you let a piece of fine ass property like that go?"

"I didn't, you know how it is when a nigga gets locked down. She left me to be back with her woman beating ass ex. Talking about she can't put her life on hold while I do this bid.

And here's the crazy shit, she writes me a letter about two years ago, telling me how she lost her baby because that sorry excuse for a man was kicking the shit out of her because he lost his job and got drunk one night. I must've read that letter twice before I taped it back up and put return to sender on it and dropped it back in the mailbox."

"Bitch got what she deserved."

Dee looked a Bama and laughed, "Yep, those are the same words I told her."

Dee put the photo album away back in his locker box and looked over at Bama who had a mischievous grin on his face. "You wanna get fucked up?" Bama asked.

"Is pussy pink? Hell yea, do you need me to roll it up I got a good bible verse all picked out and ready to go.

"Nah, not that; I got about forty Zoloft pills." Bama reached into his pocket and pulled out a handful of pills, "Twenty for you and twenty for me. We'll be high for two days off this shit."

Dee rubbed his stomach, "Nah, I'm good playa. I don't dig that type of high. And besides the last time I took those with you I was shitting for four hours straight, had to put my intestines back up my ass when I was done."

"But you were fucked up though, weren't you?"

"Oh no doubt, I was plenty high, but it wasn't my type of high. When I get high in here it's for a reason and I want to enjoy it."

Bama looked confused, "Then why you get high then?"

"When I get blazed in here, I feel as if I cheated the state on a day they have control over my ass."

Bama grabbed a cup of lukewarm coffee off the desk, "Then let the cheating begin," he said as he took about a third of the pills in his hand and downed them with the coffee,

"You sure you don't want any?"

"I'm aight, I got to go to the yard and meet up with Tony." Dee said as he walked out of the cell and to the slider that lead out to the yard.

****

"Hey Tony, Tony!" Dee yelled.

Tony was on the basketball court in the middle of an intense game. When he saw Dee he pointed to one of his boys, "Hey cuz, fill in for me for a minute, I got business to take care of." Without waiting for an answer he walked over to Dee and embraced him with a half hug, half handshake. "Just the man I wanted to see. Come on let's walk this track." Tony said as they moved away from the court.

"What's up sweaty ass?" Dee asked.

"Yo, can I borrow around one-hundred and twenty-five stamps? I want to get this tatt of my kids on my chest?"

"Hell no you can't borrow them, but I'll give them to you. You ain't got to pay me back, considering you did take a lock to the jaw for my ass over that white boy shit last year."

Tony smiled, rubbing his chin, "Yeah, what are friends for huh?"

"Come out on first yard movement and I'll have them ready ok." Dee looked down at his watch.

"You got somewhere to be?" Tony asked.

"Got to go over to medical and refuse this punk ass psych appointment."

"Refuse; why in the hell would you want to do that?" Tony stopped walking and looked at Dee, "Have you ever seen that psych bitch?

Dee shook his head no.

"Hell I go once a week just so I can look at that woman's ass. She be wearing tight ass skirts and slacks to show off that phat ass and I be looking. That bitch be knowing what she be doing. I'll give my left nut just to stick the head of my dick in that tight asshole of hers, and I mean that literally."

"Man ain't no bitch that hot playa, I love my balls too much just to be giving one away; we make a great team."

"Ok, when I see you later tonight, I want you to say what you just said again and mean it."

"I will, I gotta go, wouldn't want to be late to lose my nuts, now would I?" Dee said grinning. Tony didn't say anything, he just made a hand gesture of scissors cutting.

****

Dee walked into the psych office. The doctor stood up and gestured for him to have a seat in front of her desk. Dee was mesmerized; *yep he'd give both his nuts and one kidney to stick his dick in her ass;* he thought. She was outstanding; standing at around six feet-two, long curly auburn hair that went down her back past her ass, a caramel skin complexion, a small waist but with hips and an ass so phat that he had him thinking she had to have used a pair of pliers to put on her pants. Her name was Daisy Sanchez P.H.D. it said sitting on a name tile on her desk. Dee approached the desk and sat down. "Hi, my name is Daisy Sanchez, but you can call me Daisy or just Mrs. Sanchez if you like." She picked up a file, "And how would you like me to address you?" She asked. Stuttering for words, Dee said, "You can call me Dee."

She nodded, "So I see this is your first time you have come to a scheduled psych appointment. It says here in your file that you always refuse, what changed your mind?" *To see if the rumor of that phat Mexican ass was true,* he thought. He shrugged, "Nothing else to do, so I said why not."

"Okay, well at least you're here. So tell me why the nickname Dee?"

"It stands for Diamond, but since I ain't gay and some guys are uncomfortable about calling another man Diamond, it was shortened to Dee."

"How did you get the name Diamond?"

"Um, you can say it was given to me back when I was in the Marine Corps."

"Why is that?"

"Dee thought about telling her a lie, but then again she probably wouldn't believe the truth anyway, so he told her the truth. "It's because I have a Diamond dick."

The doctor looked up from her notepad with wide eyes. She put the pad on the desk and said, "Okay, explain to me this so-called Diamond dick."

"Well for starters it's not so-called, it is what it is. When I was in the Corps a group of female soldiers gave me the nickname because they said my dick was a woman's best friend; and for the record they were telling the truth. You see doc, a woman can go get dick anytime, anywhere. But just because a woman gets some doesn't mean she was satisfied. You hear men talk all day long bragging about how they made a woman scream or how sore she is when he was done. But the truth is, ninety-five percent of men do not know how to fuck. And sadly only three percent of men in this world can truly satisfy a woman, I mean completely satisfy her just by using his dick. No tongue, no hands, no mind games, just a dick. And fortunately for me, I am in that three percent population." The doctor paused before she spoke, she looked a little flushed and flustered at the same time, "So let me get this straight, you have a gift and it is to please women; and these women call you Diamond?"

"You listen well doc."

"Do you think that maybe you're a little egocentric?"

"Absolutely doc, but I like to go farther and use the word narcissistic if you ask me."

"I see and how is your relationship with your mother?"

"Doc please, how about you quit trying to analyze me and talk to me like a human being and not a test subject, uh? And for the record, I hate the bitch."

"Well I have to ask, how one goes from the Marine Corps to..." She looked at his file, "Robbing banks?"

"Had a bad upbringing; is that what you want to hear? Look, I robbed those banks to help a friend who was in a financial boggle. I didn't do it because of the music I listen too, or the neighborhood I grew up in, or because I had a troubled life growing up. He asked for a favor and I said yes, it's that simple."

"Okay, so you want me to treat you like a human being and not a patient, I will. Why did you really come here today? You been here for years and never came before. And don't give me that sorry ass lie about not having anything to do."

"Honestly, I wanted to see that phat ass everyone on the yard has been talking about for years. Word around the yard is that you're the hottest chick here. I just wanted to see and try to confirm it for myself."

"And?" The doctor asked.

"And what?"

"Is it confirmed?"

"Oh most definitely doc, a perfect ten." Dee used his hands to make an outline of her body.

"Now since that is out of the way, let's talk about your future. Where do you see yourself in two years?"

"Still in prison doc."

"When you get out of prison, what are you going to do?"

"To tell you the truth doc, I don't know. Ain't nobody trying to hire a felon these days, that's one of the reasons why the recidivism rate is so high. Eight out of ten people will be back in prison within three years of their release. Don't leave any room for mistakes, does it?"

"Do you want to come back to prison?"

"Now what kind of fucked up question is that doc? That's like me asking you if you want to go home and find Mr. Sanchez in bed with your brother Raul, who by the way is wearing your lipstick and perfume. Hell no, I don't want to come back."

"Well what steps are you taking to succeed in that?"

"Hey doc here's the deal, I don't have anybody waiting for me when I touchdown. No bitch, no family, and no friends. All I got is a bus ticket and a hundred – dollar gate money the prison is going to give me. How far do you think that's going to get me huh? When my P.O. starts telling me to find a job, find a place to stay, take these drug and alcohol classes, which by the way I have to pay for. Not to mention U.A.'s, clothes, food, and personal hygiene items that I am going to need. One-hundred dollars don't pay for all that, and contrary to the public's knowledge there ain't a single fucking program out there that's worth a fuck on trying to help a felon stay out of prison. Shit, I'm better off spending that money on a dirty motel room, with a cheap dried up hooker and a bag of dope, telling my P.O. to suck my dick."

"You still haven't answered my question, but we'll move on. What do you want in life?" Dee looked up at the ceiling and cleared his throat, then looked back at the doctor, "I want a Roth I.R.A. I can start tapping at sixty and not have to work. I want a career, not a job. I want to never see the inside of a prison again. I want to be happy whether I am rich or poor. I want a God to show me how to do things his son did, and I wouldn't mind some of that Nazi gold either."

They sat in silence for almost five minutes, each in their own thoughts, and then Daisy asked, "What did you do in the Marine Corps?"

"What do you think I did doc, I killed people."

"Not all Marines are killers; most of them will never fire their guns in combat."

"True that, I was in a special unit. And to answer your future questions, I don't have nightmares or wake up with chills. I don't see ghosts or the faces of the people I've killed, and I don't have any remorse for the things I've done, next question please."

"What is your life motto, what words do you live by?"

Dee thought about it for twenty seconds, "There should always be at least one thing in life for which one would sacrifice everything for." With that said Dee got up from the chair and walked toward the door.

The doc asked, "If I scheduled you for another visit will you come?"

Yep, come right in that phat ass of yours bitch, he thought to himself, "Don't think so doc, I got what I came here for. It was a pleasure meeting you doc." He turned the knob to open the door. He was halfway out when the doctor said, "Hey in your file it says you have a B.A. degree from San Diego State, what is it in?" Dee turned to look at her and grinned, "What else would it be in doc, Clinical Psychology." He was already gone before she could say anything else.

Chapter 12

"Where are my clothes?" Keri asked as she rolled over in the bed to face Daryl, she was naked underneath the bed sheets. Daryl looked at her strangely, "Your what?"

"My clothes silly, where are they?" Keri looked over the edge on the bed, nothing. "What did you do to me last night, um?" She was smiling.

Daryl was not, "What did I do to you; you have nerve for being a rapist. Have you forgotten about you raping me last night? And now you have the audacity to ask me what I did to you last night. Seriously you have some nerve."

"Oh yes, I didn't rape you."

"You didn't uh? then why is my eye swollen?" Daryl pointed to his left eye.

"Hello, you were drunk when you came over last night; maybe you hit it somewhere and forgot."

"Oh I hit it somewhere alright; I hit it on your fist." Keri started laughing. "This shit ain't funny Keri, you need help."

"Please, save me the bullshit this early, I didn't touch you."

"Oh no," Daryl sat up in the bed, "Let me refresh your memory of last night's events, shall I? So I'm leaving the poker tournament I was at. I give you a call to let you know I'm coming over. I hear voices in the background; you say its Kelly and Janelle. I asked what you were doing and you said drinking, and watching videos on YouTube. Then you asked me if I could stop by the liquor store and buy you guys some cheap ass Burnett's vodka. I told you that I already had a bottle of Goose in the freezer, but you told me you don't want to drink that, so I say alright. So here I am driving drunk, which I should know better, pulling up to the liquor store down the street. I am tearing up every aisle looking for that damn vodka that I never heard of before. Finally, I give up and ask the Arab at the counter does he have Burnett's. To my surprise, he reaches down behind him and pulls a fifth from the bottom shelf next to some McCormick's. I'm thinking to myself, why is my baby drinking this cheap ass rot gut shit. So the camel jockey asks me is grape ok. I didn't know so I said, sure. He bags it up and I am out the door.

Only because of God's help, my drunken ass makes it to your place. I walk in and see Kelly and Janelle sitting in the kitchen at the kitchen table. So I make my way to the kitchen, say 'Hi' to everyone, give you a kiss, squeeze your ass a little and hand you your cheap vodka. I look on the floor and I see a cardboard box with about sixteen empty forty-ounce Mickey's bottles in it. From my deduction, you were all fucked-up. I go to the freezer and pull out the Grey Goose, you three finish off the rot gut and about two more forties' a piece. By now my head is spinning, I excuse myself and tell everyone I'll be back in about an hour, I have to go lay down. Kelly and Janelle says cool, you walk me downstairs into the bedroom and I flop face first on the bed, shoes and all. You ask me if I was ok and I say, 'yeah baby, come get me in an hour ok.'

You leave and go back upstairs; ten minutes later I feel something on my back. Naturally, I think it's Venus so I yell at Venus to leave me alone. Sure enough Venus comes running into the room on the side of the bed because she thinks I called her and starts licking my face. I turn over and there you are with a mischievous grin on your face rubbing my back. So I say, 'baby, I'm good, go back upstairs and keep your friends company, I'll be up in an hour.' So you leave, and a few more minutes after that I feel a hand under my shirt rubbing my chest. Surprise, there you are at it again. I say, 'Keri baby, your friends are here to see you, go back upstairs, I'll be up in a few.' So you leave again, now I don't know how much more time goes by when I wake up the next time. All I know is that I was naked, lying on my back and you were on top of me, riding me so hard I thought you were trying to win the Triple Crown."

"Oh yes." Keri said.

"Shut – up, I'm not done with the story yet. So anyway, I'm shocked, I don't even remember you undressing me. So I say softly, 'Keri', you tell me, 'shut –up'. Now I'm really confused, so I say again, 'Keri', this time a little louder. That's when you sock me in the eye and said, 'I said shut – up.' At that point I'm scared."

"I didn't hit you, now you're making things up." Keri said smiling.

Daryl looked at her sideways, "Like I was saying, I was scared, I didn't know who this Keri was. So I just laid there while you did your thing. Twelve minutes later after you done drained every ounce of man out of me; you roll over and start snoring."

"I don't snore."

"Snoring like I said, I laid awake for thirty minutes, scared to move a muscle. Finally, after a small cry I fall asleep. And now you have the nerve to ask me what I did to you. I should be pressing charges, that's what I should do." Daryl got out of the bed, found his boxers and put them on. Fortunately for you, I like you. I'm going to let Venus out. You want something from the kitchen; perhaps a knife to put to my throat or maybe a used dish cloth to stuff in my mouth, hmm?"

Keri shook her head no, and slipped her whole body back underneath the covers. Two minutes later Daryl comes back in the bedroom, "I found your clothes rapist."

"Where were they at?"

"Let me see, your T-shirt and pants were in the living room, and your bra and panties were on the kitchen floor. How do you suppose they got there?"

"You just put them there."

"Yea, I grabbed all of your clothes when I left here just two minutes ago and spread them around the house, damn Sherlock you solved the case."

Daryl got back into the bed. Keri grabbed his dick and started stroking it. Daryl pushed her hand away, "Don't touch me; there's nothing left for you to take."

Keri started laughing at the same time her cell phone rang. She rolled over Daryl to the night stand and picked it up. It was Janelle, Daryl could hear her voice. The first thing Janelle said was, "So did you rape Daryl last night?" Before Keri could answer, Daryl snatched the phone out of Keri's hand put it on speaker, then asked Janelle, "What do you know about the rape?" Janelle started to laugh and went on telling her version of the story, "When you went downstairs, Keri came back up giggling telling everybody how horny she was and that she was going to rape you. We all thought she was playing. But then she kept going downstairs to mess with you. Next thing I know she was pushing and kicking me and Kelly out the front door. Looking all crazy saying how she was about to take some dick from you. After that I don't know what happened because I was kicked out on the streets. Why, did she do it?" Janelle asked with a humorous voice.

"Hell yeah, she got what she wanted, the thief."

Janelle started laughing uncontrollably as Daryl handed the phone back to Keri. "Girl I have to call you back, ok." Keri told Janelle as she hung up the phone and threw it on the floor. "I'm sorry baby; you know how I get when I'm drunk. I'm really, really sorry baby." Keri said in a seductive voice as she started kissing Daryl on his lips then moved her mouth down to his chest, while she was using her hand to make him hard.

"Unhand me you harlot." Daryl said as he pushed Keri off of him.

"How about I make it up to you; you can do whatever you want to do to me, hmmm? Will that make us even?"

Daryl looked at her with a raised eyebrow, "Anything I want huh?"

Kerri nodded. Daryl leaned over and whispered in her ear. Keri's face changed to a surprised but curious expression at the same time, "You're nasty." She said.

"No." Daryl said as he got out of bed and grabbed Keri yanking her out of bed as well, "Actually, you are, going to let me do it." He finished saying as he led Keri into the bathroom and shut the door.

****

It was an indoor rock climbing venue. Daryl had rented it out for half a day. Together there were around seventy-six kids present. Everything were from the two foster homes that he volunteered at. The venue didn't just have rock climbing, but zip-lining, a ropes course, an arcade, a go cart track, and a black light miniature golf course. Kids were running around wildly, having a good time. Daryl had just got done losing a game of air hockey to an eight-year-old. Mrs. Mary was watching and waiting for him to come over to her. Daryl sat down next to her, "Hello Mrs. Mary, can I interest you in a game of air hockey to an eight-year-old who I believed just somehow, someway hustled me?"

She smiled, "Oh no, the last time I played him, I was out of five dollars." They both started laughing. "So how's Keri?" She asked.

"Keri is good; we make a great couple. And I think I love her kids as much as I love her already."

"You really love her don't you?"

Daryl looked at Mrs. Mary, "I feel as if I have been waiting for her my whole life. It's like I know deep down that we were made for each other. I know it sounds stupid, but that's how I feel. I've been feeling like that since I first saw her over a year ago. And it seems like every day my love for her just gets stronger."

"I see; how does she feel about you?"

"Well, she first told me that she loved me about four months ago. I believe her, but I know deep down she's worried that I might hurt her. She's been with some scumbags over the years that have treated her like shit."

"Come on Daryl," the eight-year-old air hockey hustler yelled at Daryl, "One more game."

"Not a chance you hustling hoodlum." The boy smiled.

"Don't worry about it sweetie, Keri will wake up one of these days and realize who you are." Mrs. Mary finished her conversation with Daryl.

"That's just it Mrs. Mary, sometimes I wake up and don't know who I am. Sometimes I feel as if I am in a dream."

"That's rubbish and you know it. You know exactly who you are. I see it in your face every time I look at you. You need to quit living in the past and live for today. You've found someone that makes you happy, what more do you want?"

Daryl took a deep breath, "Keri is all I want Mrs. Mary."

"Well now that you got her, what are you going to do?"

"Show her she can trust me and that I'll never hurt her or the kids."

Mrs. Mary just nodded her head and smiled. Daryl got up and kissed her on the cheek. "Now there you go flirting with a woman who could be your mother young man." She slapped him jokingly on his face, "I'd give Keri a run for her money you know." "Um, might be kind of fun to watch the two women I love duke it out to the end for little ole me." Daryl said as he was being pushed by a little girl who wanted him to play golf with her.

****

"Gary!" The kids yelled as he walked into Daryl's office. Gary was a little stunned at first, then told the kids, "Hi." He turned to Daryl, "What's this?" He pointed to the kid who were playing Call of Duty on the X-Box 360. "Oh, the kids didn't have school today, Keri couldn't find a sitter and she had a few medical appointments to go to, so I told her that I'd watch the kids for a while." "That's nice Daryl; let's just bring the kids to work." "It's only for a few hours at the most. Besides its Friday, not too many corporate guys are working past noon anyway."

"You know this is how it starts right?"

"How what starts Gary?"

"The losing of the nuts, first it's here watch the kids for a few. Next thing you know you're wearing an apron cooking and cleaning the house. A little later on the physical abuse will come as you walk into the house and Keri is sitting on the couch with a beer in her hand asking you what's for dinner. That's when you try to explain to her that you had a long day at work and you just stepped inside the house. Well, she ain't trying to hear that shit, and the next thing you know, she's screaming and pushing you, telling you to get your shit together or she's leaving you. Poof, off go's the nuts."

Daryl asked, slightly amused, "Where do you get this crazy shit at Gary?"

"Experience my friend, experience that's how. Say what happened to your eye?"

"I fell and hit my head."

"Fall my ass, that's from a fist; a tiny fist at that. She's already kicking your ass huh?" Daryl remained silent. "I knew it; see it's already begun. Get out man, get out now why you still can."

Daryl smiled, "Anyway, what do you want Gary, I know it's not to look at my handsome self?"

"Yeah about that, you see, I just got off the phone with the wife. She got this crazy idea that Keri, you and her kids, and of course my wild bunches should go out to a fancy restaurant for dinner."

"So?"

"So she wanted it to be like a two family outing. She really likes Keri. Can't stand you, but likes Keri."

"I don't know man I really can't stand your wife too much either, love your kids, really hate your wife. And besides, I don't know what Keri has planned anyway."

"Yeah, I hear you, but I already told her you said yes, so she will leave me the hell alone." Gary put up his hands to block his face, just as Daryl threw his pen.

"Gee, thanks friend; just leave me in the trenches taking grenades uh?"

Gary turned to leave, "I owe you one Daryl, you're a life saver."

"Sure, no problem; I'll just add it to the other eight-hundred and twenty-two favors you already owe me anyway." Daryl mumbled to himself, as he checked his watch, 12:45 p.m. He picked up his phone at his desk and dialed a number.

"I.T. supervisor, this is Tim."

"Tim, this is Daryl from Field Office."

"Oh yeah, what's up man, what can I do for you?"

"Tim, when was the last time you had a Mo's bacon bar?"

"I'll say probably like about four months ago, why?"

"Loser buys two bars for every person in their department."

"Is this what I think it is Daryl?"

"Oh yeah."

"Well, war it is then, we didn't start it, but we'll finish it."

"Yeah, yeah, sounds good, we'll see who surrenders by five this evening."

"Get your white flag ready, you field office boys think you're all top shit. Today we'll put an end to it." And with that being said Tim hung up the phone. Daryl got up from his desk to walk out of his office, "Kids I'll be right back."

"Ok Daryl." They both said.

Daryl walked to one of the secretary's desk, "Could I use your phone real quick please Stacy?" She nodded; Daryl pushed a button so he could be heard over the intercom system throughout the department. "Ladies and gentlemen your attention please. I've just been notified that the I.T. boys on the twenty-second floor have a quarrel with us. You all know what that means, office wars!" All of a sudden there were shouts and screaming throughout the department. Someone killed half the lights and mysteriously a red strobe light came out of nowhere and began flashing. The excitement was in the air.

"Calm down, calm down, now you all know what's already at stake here. I want that bacon, and we will not lose to a bunch of pocket-protector wearing nerds. So I need you to be sneaky, dirty, and ruthless toward our common enemy. We have four hours' people, let's make it happen, that is all." As soon as he hung up the phone, the lights came back on, the strobe disappeared, and everybody went right along with their normal business.

Stacy asked smiling, "How do you still have a job?"

Daryl knocked on the glass window; he was signaled to come in. "Well this is a surprise, what do we have here?"

"Amanda, this is Melody and this is Devin. They are my girlfriends' kids. Kids this is the nice and lovely Amanda. She is one of our company accountants, she and the government work together so they can take all of my hard earned money away from me."

Amanda smiled, "Kids don't believe him, he's known for making up stories."

"So that story about you and Bigfoot was made up?" asked Melody.

"No baby, that was true." Daryl looked down and told her.

"So what brings you up to the forty-second floor?" asked Amanda.

"Oh nothing really, just wanted to see how good the living was up here." Daryl said as he was glancing around the room, "Say you think I could use your office fax machine for about twenty minutes?"

"Don't you guys have a fax on your floor?"

"Yeah, but they're kind of indisposed right now, the I.T. boys are working on them right now as we speak."

"All of them huh?" Amanda asked suspiciously. Daryl nodded his head. "This wouldn't have anything to do with the office war games would it?"

"Office wars, that's absurd. You mean to tell me people really do play that?"

"Yes, and of course you wouldn't know anything about that huh?"

"Why heavens no Amanda, I take my job seriously."

Amanda pointed to the back office, "Over there." she said.

"Mucho gracias senorita."

Daryl walked over with the kids to the fax machine, and pulled out four sheets of all black construction paper he had in a manila envelope. "Alright kids, here's your first lesson in becoming a "Phantom faxer." He looked over at Amanda who was smiling and shaking her head. "Ok here's what you do; first we tape three pieces of this paper together on the ends, like this. Then we insert the first page in the machine, and then we dial those stupid I.T. boys and girls main fax number." There was a beeping sound and then the paper started to go through the machine. "Ok see how the first piece is going thru?" The kids shook their heads, "After the first paper comes completely thru, then you take it and tape it quickly to the third piece of paper like this. So now we have a loop of continuous paper going through the fax machine. So you're probably wondering why this is so special. Well, because the people on the other end are receiving black pieces of paper, which in turn is using up all of their toner and is tying up their fax machine so nobody can use it or receive anything. Even if they turn their machine off, when they turn it back on the paper will continue coming." Melody and Devin was staring at Daryl with confusion on their face. "It makes the other people very mad kids, let's go down to the cafeteria and get a snack, ok." They both shook their heads furiously, "Amanda, I'll be back in about fifteen minutes to retrieve any evidence." She didn't even acknowledge him.

Forty minutes later when Daryl returned to his floor, he was approached by Gary, "Dude, don't open any e-mail attachments. Those damn I.T. guys dropped a bomb on the system. It already shut down half of the computers on the floor. People are losing their minds trying to figure out a way to get their shit done. I think you ought to throw in the white flag on this one buddy, they were prepared this time."

"You must be out of your mind. We ain't quitting, I want that bacon. I got a few more tricks up my sleeve that will have those boys begging for mercy." Daryl told the kids, "Let's go kids; we have a dirty bomb to make." Back in the office, "Ok kids, dirty bomb making 101." Daryl was looking inside his office mini fridge. "Alright Melody and

Devin grab four of those one-liter soda bottles, all six cans of those sardines, both cans of tuna, that bottle of mustard, and let's not forget the Tabasco sauce. Now follow me into the bathroom. "Ok put all that stuff down in the sink. First thing we have to do is take those sodas and drank less than half of each one." They all began drinking, "Now what we do is open all the fish, divide it up and put a portion in each soda bottle. Then we do the same thing with the mustard and hot sauce ok." The kids nodded, "Ok, I'll be right back, while you guys finish doing that." Daryl left the bathroom and walked over to his desk, opened a drawer and pulled out a brand new roll of Mentos candy and smiled. He went back to the bathroom were the kids were hard at work at their new task.

"Good job Ms. Melody and Mr. Devin, here come over to the sink and wash your hands so we can get rid of that fishy smell." The kids did what they were told. "Now you're probably wondering why we did all of this and how these bottles that are filled with food are bombs." They shook their heads yes. "Ok, I'll break it down for you. You see these Mentos in my hand? These are the detonators. When the time is right, we drop these into the soda and create gas. As the pressure builds up in the bottle it has nowhere to go. That's when the bottles explode and create a big nasty tuna mess. And you don't want to be around when that happens. Do you understand a little?" The kids shook their heads yes and no. Daryl repeated everything from the beginning about three more times.

Daryl picked up his phone, "Stacy can I see you in my office for a second please?" Two minutes later came a knock on his door, "Come in." It was Stacy. "Hey Stacy, could you do me a favor please?"

"It depends; does it involve payback on those I.T. guys? My computer is down and I have to finish a cash out report before I can leave for the weekend."

"As a matter of fact, it does. Ms. Melody and Mr. Devin have volunteered to end this war so everyone can get back to work."

"How are they going to do that?" asked Stacy.

Daryl grabbed a soda bottle off his desk with one hand and the pack of Mentos in the other hand, we dirty bomb them."

"And what's my role in this?"

"Well my face is known down on the twenty-second floor where the I.T. guys are at, but yours is not. All I need you to do is escort these fine young soldiers of ours to their conference room, the break room, and the restrooms."

"That's all?"

"That's all my lady; the kids will do the rest. They know what's at stake."

"Ok, but don't forget this when I need a favor from you."

"I won't." Then Daryl turned to the kids, "Here, you take two bottles Melody, and Devin you take the other two." Then he opened the Mentos, "Keep these in your pockets until you're ready to put them in the soda ok. And remember you have about thirty seconds to get as far away from them as possible, alright?" They shook their heads yes. "Alright, go with Stacy and show them boys we mean business, good luck."

Fifteen minutes later while the kids were playing video games and Daryl was typing a report on his laptop, his desk phone rang. "This is Daryl."

"Damn Daryl, it smells like a dirty whores' ass down here."

"Whatever do you mean Tim?"

"You know what I'm talking about you, son of a bitch, that shit stinks. Call off your dogs, we wave the white flag."

"Is that official Tim?"

"Yeah, it's official; I'll make the announcement, now get your guys down her to clean this shit up."

"No problem Tim. Be sure to send your boys up here to fix these computers and we have a deal."

"Fine."

"And oh Tim, that will be ninety-six Mo's Bacon Bars by next Friday champ."

"Kiss my ass Daryl, I hope you choke on them." and then there was only a dial tone.

Chapter 13

It was only a rumor that it still existed in the Legion, many have heard the stories, even few believed, in the Silo. The Silo consisted of a funnel shaped hole in the ground, broad at the top and pointed towards the bottom; your basic funnel. In this hole, used as punishment for solitary confinement, the assailant would be thrown in, dressed only in a thin pair of worn fatigues clothes or an orange jumpsuit. No blankets or any other protection against the sun or rain, at the pity of the heat by day and the freezing cold by night.

The wrong doer would be left for days in this posture. Laying down was impossible, for the bottom part of the hole was only about one square foot. He spent all day and night alternately standing or crouching, in the pouring rain or the hot baking sun. The prisoner soon became ill from foul vapors. When the sentence was served he was taken out of the Silo, he could neither stand nor walk and had to be carried into the infirmary. Every once in a while a Silo prisoner would die in the hole. Karsten had been in the ground for twelve days now, his crime, breaking the record at the Commando course at Mount Louis by four minutes and twenty-three seconds.

Un-Disclosed Location

The prisoner was 'snatched' less than fifteen hours ago from his heavily fortified home. Now he was hanging by his wrists, handcuffed, and attached to the ceiling. His clothing was fully removed; he was naked. He had been in this position in a pitch black, sound proof cell for about nine hours now. Rone and McLean was standing guard outside the cell; holding fully automatic FN P90 Assault Rifles at the low ready. They straightened their pose when they saw Karsten approaching. He was carrying a large black duffle bag which by obvious looks seemed heavy. He approached his men and stopped at the entry way to the cell, "Hey Rone, when Tiekert and Nordeen comes to relieve you two, would you mind bringing me back down a large cup of black coffee? I have a feeling I am going to be in there a little while.

"You sure you don't want me to cook you up a little something while I fetch your coffee Sarge? Perhaps an omelet or some blueberry pancakes." Rone said in a sarcastic tone. Karsten just stared at him for about three seconds, and then used his security pass to let himself in the isolated room. As he entered he reached to his left and turned the over headlights on, they were extra bright. The prisoner immediately looked at Karsten, who was putting his duffle bag on top of a gun-metal gray table, that was in one corner of the room. He took out a digital recorder and sat it down next to the duffle bag.

Karsten walked towards the prisoner and stopped about five feet in front of him. The man stared at Karsten with the look of defiance in his eyes, Karsten smiled before he began speaking in Arabic, "Well my friend, I have good news and bad news for you. The good news is my God tells me that I am going to make it out of this room alive. The bad news is, that it's not looking so good for you. As you have probably figured out, I am going to torture you. Not because I want you to tell me what you know or don't know, I can really care less. My superiors on the other hand might entertain the words you speak, but not me. What they fail to realize is that a tortured man will say anything to make the pain stop.

"No my friend, you see I am going to torture you because I find it amusing to torture a piece of shit like yourself." Karsten let his words sink in for about three minutes before he spoke again," You're a seemingly smart man, you do realize that I am not wearing anything to hide my true identity, which can only lead to one conclusion; and I think we both can agree what that is, right?"

The prisoner spoke for the first time, "You are a coward, and infidel who will be cursed by Allah. I will tell you nothing. My death will make me a martyr, stories will be told about me, songs singed."

Karsten clicked his tongue, "No, I don't think so; your death will be just that. Nobody is going to know your dead and nobody is going to find your remains. No my friend, your death is going to be either very painful or very painful, it's your choice really."

The man spat in Karsten's face, "May the great Allah curse you and your offspring."

"Yes indeed may he," Karsten said, "But while I wait for that to happen I am going to walk over there to that table and dig inside that bag, get out a notebook with various questions that are meant for you. Turn on that recorder and casually walk back over here to you and see if you would like to answer any of those questions. Now I am a betting man, and I am betting that you are not going to be very corporative with me, at first that is. So while I am over there digging around in that bag, I am going to get out my very trusty straight razor blade, never leave home without one you know what I mean? Also I am going to get my handy butane torch and some ammonia packets for when you pass out on me." Karsten again let his words sink in as he went over to the table and did exactly what he said he was going to do. He walked back to the prisoner who now instead of the look of defiance in his eyes had the look of fear. Karsten smiled at him, and then opened the notebook and read the first page quietly to himself, then looked at the prisoner when he was done.

"Ok Bob, may I call you Bob?" Without waiting for an answer Karsten continued, "Ok good Bob, first question, where did you get the VX gas from that you used in a dirty bomb that blew up two train cars, and killed one-hundred and twenty-one people; thirty-nine of them were children."

Bob just stared at Karsten with hatred in his eyes. When he did not respond, Karsten said," Great, I was hoping you'd say just that." That's when Karsten grabbed the man by his testicles and in a swift move sliced them off with one stroke of his razor blade. Bob began to scream erratically as the pain shot through his body. He watched as Karsten held his balls up for him to see, then dropping them on the floor as he smashed them with his Rangers.

Then Karsten lit his butane torch and applied the blue flame to the man's bleeding wound to cauterize it. Bob passed out. When Karsten turned the torch off, there came a knock at the door. He sat the torch down on the ground, walked to the door and opened it. It was Rone with a big cup of steamy hot coffee and a bagel. Karsten took the items without saying a word and shut the door just as Rone was trying to get a peek of the chaos that was happening inside.

Karsten casually walked back over to Bob eating his bagel and sipping his coffee. He stared at the man while he finished his bagel. Then reached into his side pants pocket and pulled out a little ammonia packet. While still sipping his coffee with one hand he opened it and put it under Bob's nose; Bob immediately came to. Karsten dropped the packet on the ground, picked up the notebook that was lying next to the torch and quietly read the second page. Bob, who was now fully coherent, was moaning in pain. Karsten snapped his finger in front of him, "Hey Bob, don't go acting like you're hurt now, I need you to stay focused on the task at hand, ok? Now the people who wrote these questions would like to know how far your network spreads. Who's involved, what's their involvement, who they have working for them, etc.? Pretty much your whole operation in a nutshell, and let's not skimp on the details alright Bob."

Karsten waited for about two minutes for an answer, "Still not talking huh, that's alright you'll change your mind soon enough, I promise." When Karsten was done speaking he took out his razor blade and while still holding his coffee in one hand, he walked behind Bob, took his razor and started from Bob's anus he sliced a deep two and a half inch gap all the way up the crack of Bob's ass to his tail bone. Blood began to flow everywhere, dripping down Bob's legs and gushing out in random spots. Once again Bob started to scream uncontrollably. This time Karsten waited for three minutes before he fired up his torch to seal the gaping wound.

An hour and a half later when Bob woke up on his own Karsten was sitting at the table with his feet up reading a file on Bob. Karsten turned to look at him and then turned the recorder back on. Not getting up from the table he spoke, "Hey, so glad you could make it back to the real world. You weren't dreaming about those seventy-two virgins I hope, who really wants a virgin anyway? I know I don't, they just lay there like dead fish, not knowing what to do, praise Allah." Karsten stood up from the table and began to walk across the room.

"You see, I truly believe no matter how much pain I inflict on you, you're not going to answer any of these questions I have in that notebook over there, but as I stated before I don't really care. It's the people I work for that care Bob. Everyone had a breaking point, everyone, including yourself. Clearly yours is not pain to your physically body, especially when you know you're going to die anyway. I admire that, shit I have to be honest with you, if I got my nuts clipped and a new asshole made, I would've been telling you about the time I stole a nickel from my grandmother's purse when I was eight. But no sir, not you Bob. So I am at a dilemma, a pickle if you might say. You see my bosses expect results, results that I have to produce at all cost."

Karsten walked in front of Bob and looked him straight in the eyes, "Pay attention now Bob, I've been doing some interesting reading while you were taking a nap. You're a real family man huh?" At the sound of the word family Bob's eyes went wide and his head up; Karsten had his full attention. Karsten gave a wider grin, "Oh, you were listening; hell I thought you were ignoring me. So about this reading I've been doing over there in that file. It says that you have two daughters' ages twenty-three and twenty, a son who is twenty – eight, and a wife who is I believe forty-nine, is that correct? Oh yeah and both of your parents are still alive as well ages seventy-eight and seventy-six, if I read that right."

Bob spoke through gritted teeth, "You will leave my family out of this."

"No Bob, I won't, you should have thought about that before you went into the terrorism business."

"It doesn't matter, I went through great lengths to protect them, and you have a better chance of finding your Waldo before you find them."

"Oh non-sense Bob, we found you didn't we?" After Karsten told him that he walked toward the door and gave it two good bangs with his fists. Twenty seconds later the door opened fully and Bob's parents, son, and daughters were all slowly escorted in, lined up and put on their knees. They all had blindfolds over their eyes and their hands were handcuffed behind their backs; they were also stark naked. Bob begin to curse at Karsten, and then he spoke to his family, telling them that everything was going to be ok. Rone and McLean looked at Karsten who gave them a slight nod, and then they left, shutting the door behind them.

"Uh Bob, let's not lie to them shall we. They are not going to be alright, not as long as you keep this little charade of not answering questions that need to be answered up. We are going to give this another try, ok Bob. Now before we start, let's get a few things straight. As you can see they are wearing blindfolds because I want to keep them alive. This location and the identity of my men cannot and will not be compromised. Now whether they live or die is up to you."

Karsten went over and kneeled down in front of one of Bob's daughters. Karsten began groping one of her breasts and squeezing it. He then smacked her and told her to shut up if she wants to live and squeezed her breast even harder; she was moaning. He then put her other breast in his mouth and began sucking and biting it. Karsten kept this up for about two minutes or so and then continued talking, "I sure would hate to see a piece of fine Iranian ass like that go to waste. Bob."

Bob began to lunge at Karsten, trying with every effort to break loose of the restraints. "Now Bob before you start giving me false answers, know that your family will only be released un-harmed if everything you say checks out. And yes I mean everything Bob, so you best be telling the truth, uh?" Karsten walked back over to the table, turned the recorder back on, picked up the notebook and walked back to the center of the room.

"Shall we begin at the top Bob?" For the next seven hours Karsten got all of his questions answered in detail without any pause. Bob had told it all. When he was done, Karsten walked over to the door, opened it and handed the recorder to Tiekert, then shut the door.

Bob spoke, "Now let them go, let them go!" There were tears in his eyes.

"Not so fast Bob, the powers to be have to verify all of that Intel to make sure you were being honest. For your sake you had better be or else your daughter and I are going on a little date right in front of you, if you catch my drift." Karsten winked at him.

"You animal!" Bob screamed.

"No doubt Bob." Karsten replied then looked at his watch, "Well Bob, they are probably going to be a while with that Intel, what do you suppose we do to kill the time?" Karsten waited for a response. "Nothing uh? If you don't have any ideas, I surely do." Karsten walked back over to the table, reached into his duffle bag, grabbed a portable drill and some extra drill bits, a battery operated medical saw, an apron, a cattle prong, and a dull butter knife. He looked back at Bob, "Don't worry so much Bob, I am not going to kill you just yet, just having a little fun is all." With that said, Karsten walked toward him with a shit eating grin on his face.

Eight hours and four cups of black coffee later Karsten felt satisfied, he was admiring his work when there was a knock on the door. He went to open it. It was Rone, all Rone did was nod his head once. Karsten shut the door and walked back over to the barely alive Bob, lifted his head and put an ammonia packet under his nose. "Wake up Bob." Karsten smacked him hard. "Wake up now, I've got some good news for you, some of that Intel actually panned out to be true. You should be happy." Karsten waited for a response, but when he didn't get one he went on, "But I also have some bad news for you Bob, you lied to me about some things Bob."

Bob nodded his head and whispered, "No."

"Yes you did Bob, what did I tell you about telling fibs? Now you've forced my hand, I didn't want to do what I am about to do next Bob, but you have to be punished."

"Please no, no please." Whispered bob in a barely audible voice.

"Yes Bob, yes." Was all Karsten said as he took his razor blade out and walked over to Bob's mother; Karsten looked down at her, then walked behind her, put the razor to her neck and cut her from ear to ear, blood spewing everywhere. Bob started to scream until he had no energy left, he could only watch what happened next. Karsten looked at him from across the room and shrugged his shoulders, and then he sliced his father's throat, then his son, and lastly his two daughters. A pool of blood was gathering at Karsten's feet. He walked over to Bob who was crying. "You see Bob, you did that, not me; but hey don't look so sad, you'll be joining them any minute now." That's when Karsten took the blade to Bob's throat and sliced him. Blood sprayed all over Karsten's face and chest.

Karsten walked back to the table in the corner of the room, pulled out a towel from his duffle bag and wiped his face. He then started to gather up all of his tools and accessories and began putting them back in the duffle bag. When he was done, he walked to the door, opened it and let it shut behind him. Tiekert and Nordeen looked at him and his bloody clothes, Karsten looked down at his watch and said, "Let's go boys, chopper leaves in ten minutes."

Chapter 14

"My old man never laid a hand on me my whole life, now my mom was another story. As far back as I can remember, I've known my mom to beat me senseless. I personally think the bitch was bi-polar. One minute she's smiling, and then the next minute I'm getting smacked across my mouth for nothing. My twin sister never got a beat down like I did. In my mom's eyes she was perfect; couldn't do nothing wrong. But for me, she made me feel as if I was Satan's child. My parents end up getting divorced when I was nine. It took that long for my old man to realize the bitch was crazy I guess. Anyway, my sister and I lived with my mom; not by choice that's for sure. My brother lived with my dad. Never saw too much of my dad after that. Every now and then he'd pick me and my sister up and take us to a movie or the arcade. He never stayed with us, just gave us money and picked us up a couple hours later.

I believe I was in the sixth grade when I got fed up with my mom's bullshit. It came to a point that I was getting beat down every day. I remember waking up to the hoe hitting me with a cast iron skillet. Hell, I was not even out the bed yet. She would use anything she could grab onto, belts, shoes, frying pans, bats, fishing poles, horse whips, you name it and I bet you I was probably beat with it. And of course back then teachers at school didn't give a fuck if you showed up with welts and bruises on your body. They already knew you got your ass whooped. So I developed and I don't give a fuck attitude. I knew no matter what I did, I was going to get my ass beat when I came home, so I took my time coming home, sometimes until eleven or twelve o'clock at night. As I walked in or sneaked through a window here comes my mom screaming and hitting me with the day's chosen weapon.

My criminal career started small, I would steal candy and beef jerky from the corner store, catch and kill cats because I thought it was fun. As the years went by, I started growing with my attitude, now I was robbing houses instead of going to school. Smoking weed and drinking every morning on the days I did go to school. All because I thought my life was pointless. At that age there's really nothing to look forward to. I still got the daily beatings from that bitch I called mom, sometimes two in one day. So I took my frustrations out by committing more crimes, because I felt like I had power over something, nothing too major, although I did run a successful purse snatching operation at the age of 15. That was back in the days when mother's use to leave their cars running when picking up their kids from daycare. They would go in and I would go in their car and remove their purse. After that I dappled in check-forging and shit. That only lasted a couple months before I was caught and sent to a juvenile detention center. That was probably the best and worst thing that ever happened to me. My mom told the state that she didn't want me back, so I was put in a foster home. I ended up going to several group homes because I was acting out, thinking I was grown and did not have to listen to anybody.

One summer I ended up getting a job at Taco John's. That was a cool job to have, all the free food I could eat. Things were going decent then, I had my own money, I was not robbing people anymore, and I only smoked weed and drank on the weekends. Then one day when I went to work I fucked around and saw the combination to the safe in the new manager trainee notebook. Well it was back to the old Dee. I was stealing thousands out of that safe every week, and nobody had a clue it was me. So many people got fired over that four-month time period that the higher up decided to make me a fucking manager.

So now I am in school again, working and closing up the Taco joint at night. I ended up getting my boy Tony a job too. Ironically he was my old celly over in unit two. Anyway, we were going hard in the paint. I closed the restaurant at least five nights a week, and then we were officially closed, Tony and I would have all sorts of bitches come through the back door. We use to fuck hoes brains out every night; even threw a couple of parties down in the basement. I thought I was on cloud nine. No more beatings, no more different foster homes, and I was excelling in school. Then one day Tony and I went over to this young girl's house. I think we were sixteen at the time, they were like fourteen or so, but they looked and acted older. So, we over there doing our thing, I was upstairs with one chick and Tony was downstairs with the other one. Well, the girl that Tony was with, it was her house and she didn't expect her mom to come home early.

All hell broke loose, apparently Tony was downstairs playing with the girl's pussy with the barrel of his .45 cal; that's Tony alright, he always was a freak. Anyway, the girl's mom walks in and sees this. As soon as the girl sees her mom she started to scream rape. Well I'm upstairs when I start to hear yelling, I come running downstairs, naked as hell to see what's going on. Mom's turns around and see's my dick, hard, shiny and glistening in the light, then starts yelling at me to get the fuck out of her house. Well you ain't got to tell me twice; I run back upstairs get my clothes and run outside, still naked. Tony was naked as hell too following me, laughing the whole way. We get around the corner, put our clothes on and started walking toward the park to puff an 'L'. So while at the park, Tony is telling me the story about the girl and the gun, and all the screaming rape business. Hell, we both thought it was funny, but that stupid bitch really told her mom Tony tried to rape her so she wouldn't get in trouble. The next day at school when the cops came to arrest Tony, it wasn't funny anymore. Tony ended up getting four years in a juvenile detention center over that shit.

After that, I wised up quick and got my shit together. No more weed, no stealing, and I stop chasing them little hoes who were throwing their pussy at me; I did not want to end up like Tony. I turned seventeen that fall, and went to school every day. That following summer I even went to summer school so that I could get ahead and finish school before I turned eighteen. At the end of the summer I actually graduated, and here I am seventeen years old, and a high-school graduate, still a ward of the state. I say fuck it and went to enlist in the Marine Corps, and forged my foster parent's signature on the release. So there I was seventeen at basic training in the Corps getting my ass kicked. I was beginning to think if I had made a wise decision by joining the military. After basic training, I went into a regular infantry unit, straight grunt. By then I had enrolled in some college courses at San Diego State, go Aztecs baby.

About six months go by and one night as I'm heading back to the barracks on base, feeling like a million bucks, because I just got my dick sucked by the center on the women's basketball team at the college. As I approached the barracks a Gunny Sergeant was outside smoking a fag. As I walked by he asked me who I was, I told him. He threw down his square then stomped on it and told me to follow him. As I got near him I could also smell alcohol. So we get into his jeep, drive all the way to the other side of the base to the long distance shooting range. I look at my watch, it was twenty-two hundred hours, the range is closed and it's pitch black dark out. The Sergeant pulls out from underneath some blanket in the back seat, a M40A1 Sniper Rifle.

He hands me the rifle and says, "Let's go." So I'm following him, not knowing who the fuck he was or what he wanted. We stop near some sand bags, he says to me, "Four-hundred meters out, there's an apple on top of my favorite coffee cup. Now I love my coffee cup, my kids gave it to me on Father's Day about three years ago. I love it so much as a matter of fact, that I will kill someone if any harm ever came to it." When he said that he pulled out a 9mm Beretta and cocked it, then finished talking, "But I do hate apples, would you be so kind as to remove that horrible thing from my coffee cup please?" I tell him, "Look I don't know who he is or what this is and I'm out of here, I'll find my own way back." At that moment, he pointed the Beretta at me and said, "Would you please remove that apple from my coffee cup?" Then throws me one bullet, scared out of my mind, I don't know what to do. So I did the thing I knew would be better than trying to take that gun away from him. I laid down on the dirt, propped that rifle on those sand bags, looked through the night-vision scope that was attached to the rifle, found that damn coffee cup, put that bullet in the rifle, chambered it, checked my windage, hit the safety, then said a small prayer to God and asked him to make sure that bullet finds its mark, and then I fired. The Sergeant seemed somewhat satisfied. I then got up from the ground; he took the rifle back from me, put away his sidearm and told me to follow him.

He handed me a flashlight and we walked downrange until we came onto his precious coffee cup. To my surprise I actually shot the fucking apple. He picks up his coffee cup, takes a big swig and say how lukewarm his coffee is. Then he takes his flashlight and shines it to my face and tells me, "Son, you're going to sniper school." I passed the course and ended up doing other qualifications courses and joined 'Recon.' I did a lot of classified combat missions during my five years in the Corps. So after I got out the Corps, I ran into an old friend whose still in and he asked me if I wanted to make some extra cream. Being that I was un-employed at such said time, I tell him "Hell yeah." He had this scam going with a few guys on the base armory. They would forge the books and sell various weapons to the highest bidder. All I had to do was drive the weapons to a pre-arranged destination, where somebody would pick them up and split, no questions asked. He offered me around three-thousand dollars a shipment, I couldn't refuse that. So I did this about twice a month for about five or six months. Until one day I dropped off a shipment to some undercover N.C.I.S. agents. Bam, federal prison, Lewisburg, PA, where I turned big rocks into small rocks ten hours a day. Did my time, got out, and was still making moves on the low. Then one day my best friend asks me to help him rob a bank, and presto, now I'm here sitting in prison talking to a head doctor. So that's the summary of my life doc, anything else?"

"How true was all of that?"

"Everything was true, except the part of me getting my dick sucked by that center of the woman's basketball team; she was actually the point-guard."

"I see," Sanchez said as she made some notes on the notepad that was sitting on her lap, "So why did you come here today?"

"You know why doc."

"Ok, then why did you share your life story with me?"

Dee rubbed his chin, "You tell me doc, was it because I had a dire need to share a piece of me to somebody, so they can know the struggles I went through? Or was it because I feel I have a bond with you and that I could tell you anything? Yeah, we both know that's not it. I told you those things because it gives me a longer chance to see and day dream about the things I could do to that phat ass of yours. And if I started feeding you bullshit, you would see right through it and throw me out. So I told you the truth, minus what I was day dreaming of course." Dee smiled.

"Seriously, is that all you think about?"

"Look doc, I have not had any pussy in over five years. It takes a toll on a brotha. I walk around here and look at these ugly and fat female guards in here and think about nutting in their ass or mouth. And my thoughts are gentle, try reading some of the minds of these rapist and pedophiles. Point is, I don't do shit all day but work for a lousy forty-eight cents a day in that punk-ass kitchen, work out, watch my back, because everyone wants to test me, and rub one off to Butt Man Magazine, thinking about how I am going to tear up some pussy when these nice white folks let me out."

"Do all men in prison think like this?"

"Oh yeah, unless you're gay, then you daydream about a dick going in your mouth. These fags in here will turn out the holiest of Christians, and turn a Muslim into eating sausage on his knees. They'll forget about those seventy- two white, blonde hair, blue eyed infidel virgins they get when they die."

She laughed, "What's wrong with you?"

"Everything doc, that's why I'm in prison, can't get my shit together."

"So why did you choose a Psychological degree?" she asked.

"You know; I ask myself the same thing sometimes. Part of me did it because I actually wanted to do Psy Ops in the military and go to O.C.S. The other part of me did it because I wanted to know why my life was so fucked-up growing up."

"Did you find your answer?"

"Sure did, God hates me; but the positive end is that I can read people pretty damn good, my secret weapon against the women I pick up."

"Is that right, well can you get a read on me?"

Dee smiled, "You're too easy doc."

"I am huh? Why don't you give it a shot and I'll let you know how close you are?"

Dee nodded his head, "Ok for starters, you work for the state, make about as much as a high school guidance counselor, not nearly enough, if you had your own practice, you 'd make much more. This tells me you feel you have something to give back to society, and you believe in the greater good. And even though you work for the state, you always want people to know you have a P.H.D. so when you introduce yourself to people on the bricks you always put Doctor in front of your name. You're intelligent, and also picky. There is no Mr. Sanchez, even though you wear that diamond on the correct finger and hand. You probably drive an Escalade, or a Navigator, or some other high end S.U.V. because you want to be taken seriously; not be the prissy, pretty, lady who drives a BMW or Mercedes, even though that's what you really want.

You care too much about what people think about you. You have a nice body and not afraid to show it off. Hence the reason you wear the clothes you wear to an all-male prison, you like the attention it brings from the guards and inmates. Most likely on that treadmill every other morning to keep that figure, you like men, but is currently single right now because, hey look at you, you live in the town of Sterling; where the biggest thing in it is the super Wal-Mart. But that doesn't mean that you don't go get some on the D.L., because you do. No kids because that would ruin your Catholic ties with your family and religious community. You have a wild side in you that you unleash when you drink, which is not often. More than likely you have a tattoo on one of your legs of some type of flower or insect like a butterfly.

Your toenails are painted a dark purple or blue although you wear a coat of clear on your finger nails. That's your natural hair color, and you prefer expensive undergarments that you order online and you like wearing thongs instead of panties," Dee sniffed the air, "And I say you're about one and a half to two days away from starting your period. And last but not least, it makes you irate that a convict, who's in prison, who you consider a lower social class than yourself can tell you things about yourself that are true, in less than ten minutes better than any man you've dated in your life. How's that for a shot in the dark?"

Flustered, all the doc said was, "Well you're wrong you know." as she started to straighten up papers on her desk.

Dee got up to leave and was halfway out the door when he turned around and said, "Wrong about what part?"

The doc got up and walked toward Dee and said in a very low tone, "I started my period this morning smart-ass." Then she shuttled Dee out the door.

Chapter 15

Daryl heard screaming as he stepped out of his car and made his way toward the house. It was Keri's voice and a voice he never heard before. He turned the knob to the front door, it was unlocked. As he stepped into the house, the screaming got louder. He turned the corner in the living room, walked toward the kitchen and saw Melody and Devin sitting at the top of the stairs.

"Go to your room kids ok." Daryl said as he walked into the kitchen to see Keri standing face to face with a man he'd never seen before. Daryl immediately got in between them.

"Hold on, hold on." Daryl said as he came between them, slightly pushing Keri back away from the man she was yelling at.

"Hey man, who the fuck are you and why the fuck are you touching up on me man?!"

The mystery man yelled, and then looked at Keri, "Now you got some strange man around my kids, who the fuck is this?" He motioned toward Daryl. But before Keri could answer, Daryl said, "Who am I, I'm the guy who's telling you how it is. Now either you lower your voice and show some respect to Keri in her house or you can find your ass outside talking to the door."

"Man do you know who the fuck I am?" the guy asked Daryl.

"I could care less who you are, now for the last time, lower your voice and show some respect please." Daryl spoke through clinched teeth.

"Bitch," the guy turned towards Keri, "You better tell this fool about me, I don't play."

The guy turned back to face Daryl and stepped back three feet, lifting up his shirt to reveal a pistol tucked in the front of his pants. Daryl looked at the gun, "Yeah not so tough anymore huh smart…" But the guy never finished his sentence. Daryl struck and caught the guy in the throat with the web of his right hand. The man flew back another two feet and was gasping for air with his hands at his throat when Daryl took the gun out of his pants, ejected the clip, cleared the round in the chamber, and then smacked the guy on the right side of his left temple. The guy dropped to the floor and was instantly out cold. When the man woke up ten minutes later, he found himself sitting on the love seat in the living room, while Daryl and Keri were sitting across from him on the other couch.

While the guy was out Keri explained to Daryl who he was. His name was Mark, and he was the biological father of her kids. He was a drug addict and she had not seen him in over six years. Before Daryl had walked into the house, Mark was yelling at Keri because she wouldn't let him stay at her house for a few days and would not give him any money.

Keri spoke, "Mark this is Daryl, Daryl this is Mark."

Daryl spoke next, "Now Mark I don't appreciate people threatening me, especially with a loaded gun, but I am willing to look past that. What I can't look past is you talking crazy, being disrespectful to my woman in her own home. I won't have it Mark. Now I am not going to warn you again, you get out of line one more time, just once, I am going to take this shitty ass pistol of yours and commence to pistol whipping you until all of your teeth are out of your mouth; are we clear? Do you need me to repeat anything for you Mark?"

Mark shook his head. "Excellent, let's see Mark, Keri was telling me that you needed a place to stay. Well, sorry to tell you but you won't be staying here. You see I kind of stay here most of the week myself, and frankly I don't like or trust you." Daryl looked at Keri, "I'm finished he's all yours."

Keri kissed Daryl on the cheek and said, "What do you want Mark, I have not seen you in six years. You have not tried to help me with the kids, and as I recall you left us, chasing every little piece of ass that came your way." She took a deep breath, then finished, "I won't help you, and if you think I am going to give you any money so you can go shoot up then you're already high."

"Keri, I got nowhere else to go." Mark said.

"Good, now you know what it feels like, hurts don't it?"

"Can I at least see my kids; let them know I'm here?"

"Oh hell no, you fucked that up too or don't you remember? Those kids don't even know who you are. I am not about to let you ruin them by showing up and then disappearing all over again. You want to see them, let's see what a judge has to say."

Marks eyes were shooting daggers at Keri, he would've smacked her ass for talking shit to him if it weren't for Daryl being there, he kept his cool. "I quit using," he said, "I ain't about that no more. I'm in the process of changing my life around. All I need is a little help getting started, that's all."

Keri started getting frustrated, "I can't do this. I'm done." She turned to Daryl, "Would you please talk to him and make him understand, I am going to check on the kids." Keri got up and left the living room leaving Daryl and Mark alone together. No one spoke for four minutes; finally, Daryl got up, reached into his pocket and pulled out a wad of cash and counted four-hundred dollars, "If you're serious, find yourself a place to stay." He said as he handed Mark the money. Mark stood up, not even looking Daryl in the eyes and grabbed the money, making his way towards the front door. When he was there he turned around and asked Daryl, "What about my gun?"

"What gun?" Daryl said shutting the door.

"Is he gone?" Keri asked as she came downstairs.

Daryl was in the kitchen helping himself to a nice thick tomato and bacon sandwich. He nodded yes. Keri walked up and kissed him lightly on the lips then sat down at the table.

"I'm sorry about that." she said.

"There's nothing to be sorry about baby."

"I tried to tell you that I came with baggage." Keri gave a weak smile.

"Then I'll be your baggage handler baby, I love you, you do realize that right?"

"I love you too Daryl." Keri looked down suddenly.

"What's wrong Keri, and don't tell me it's nothing either."

Keri looked in Daryl's eyes and says, "I'm pregnant."

****

"What do you mean pregnant?" Gary asked. He and Daryl was inside his garage drinking Corona's and shooting darts.

"That would be the opposite of not being pregnant. You do remember how it works don't you? Egg gets released, sperm goes in, they meet, go on a little date, decide, hey let's make a baby, then attach themselves to the lining of the uterus, nine months later you get a baby."

"So what are you going to do?"

"What do you mean, what am I going to do? I am going to have a baby that's what I'm going to do. I mean, I'm ready, I think I'm ready, no I'm ready, it's time. It's with a chick who I love and I know loves me back. You know before she has this kid I am going to ask her to marry me."

"No, no, don't say that man. Look at me, have you not learned from my mistakes, married men are miserable all the time."

"You're not miserable; you love your wife and kids, nice try."

"That's not the point. The point is that you're going to be carrying the old ball and chain around. Its childhood all over again, you gotta ask if you can go hang out with the boys. Need permission to stop for a quick drink after work. Have to trade in that nice ass Lexus for a minivan. You're going to start going bald, because you're going to be rubbing your head so much, asking yourself why you did it. And worst of all, no new pussy. Did you hear what I just said, no more 'strange' man. You're stuck with the same pussy, day in and day out. There's only so much you can do with the same pussy that's always there. And what about me, do you realize what you're doing to me? No more living vicariously through your whore ass. Man you're killing me, just when I thought I had a little life in me yet, you want to shut the door in my face. Have you no respect for other peoples' feelings?"

"You might want to keep it down; you don't want the wife thinking you're growing your sack back, do you?" Daryl smiled.

"I run the show in here." Gary said hitting his chest. "Me, I bring home the bacon, I'm the H.M.I.C (Head Mexican in Charge) around here. Gary chugged his beer.

"Yeah, coming from the guy who hands over his whole paycheck to his wife every month and then gets and allowance, whoa, go head Mexican."

"Hey marriage is a team sport; I let her do all the hard financial stuff while I kick back. And for the record, it's an allotment of funds." They both started laughing uncontrollably.

"Serious though Gary, I am truly happy for the first time in my life. I think Keri's my soul-mate brother, and I can see myself growing old with her and the kids. And besides, I'm more of a father to her kids than any man before me. I love those bad ass hoodlums."

Gary looked at Daryl, "Dude you're officially a pussy, you'll find the tampons in the medicine cabinet in the upstairs bathroom. Be sure to drop off any remits of your dick and balls in the container marked 'disposable.

****

"This is Daryl." He said as he picked up his office phone.

"Hey baby, it's me."

"What a lovely surprise, I was just thinking about your fine ass, literally."

"Mark came by again earlier today. He must've been watching the house because it was right when I came back from picking up the kids from school. He kept pounding and pounding on the door."

"Did you call the police Keri?"

"No, that's only going to make things worse. He has a violent temper and I don't want him to try and hurt me or the kids on some revenge bullshit. He ended up leaving after twenty minutes or so when he realized I wasn't going to open the door, I don't know what to do Daryl. He just pops up after all this time and expects for me to act like nothing happened between us. And that bullshit about him being off drugs, I don't think that's true. He looked like he was high as a kite, and by the way he was acting, I'd say he was.

I'm afraid to leave the house because I don't know where he is going to show up next." Keri was crying.

"Hey baby," Daryl said softly," I got a meeting in a few minutes, but when I get out, I'm going to make a few phone calls and I am going to try and straighten this out ok?"

"What are you going to do Daryl?"

"I know a few people who dealt with this kind of problem before, I'm just going to ask if they could look into the situation is all."

"Well, be careful Daryl."

"I will baby, I got to go, I love you Keri."

"I love you too, bye."

Daryl hung up the phone and looked at his watch; it was 4:45 p.m. He picked up his phone again and called Gary, "Hey Gary, when you get a chance, could you stop by for a few? Thanks."

"Sure, on my way." Gary said. One minute later Gary came strolling into Daryl's office and sat down in the comfortable chair in front of Daryl's desk, "What's up brother?"

Daryl looked at Gary and said, "I need your help, you can never ask me about it, and we are going to hurt people."

Gary smiled, "Who's car?"

Two and a half hours later, Daryl and Gary pulled up and parked in a Super-Market's parking lot. "It's that motel across the street." Daryl said, "My man said were looking for room 218, it's supposed to be on the back side of the place, which is great for us. And Gary, leave your gun underneath the seat ok, I got our tools in the trunk, let's go."

They exited the vehicle and walked back to the trunk, "Damn Daryl, you gun running on the side? Who drives around in a seventy- thousand-dollar car with five assault rifles in the boot? You know if you're hard up for cash, I could lend you a few thousand, you don't have to resort to this."

"Will you shut up, grab a bat."

As they started walking across the street Gary said, "Does this not look suspicious at all to you? Two men in broad daylight walking across a busy intersection with two baseball bats resting on their shoulders and not a park within four miles of us."

"Nah, just like you said, it's broad daylight; now had this been night time, surely we would've been picked up already. Seriously though, if I was a cop and I saw two minorities carrying bats at night, yeah I'd say they were up to no good, probably would've beat them just for fun. Turn here, and go up those stairs."

"So have you decided on a name for your baby?"

"Not yet, we made an agreement though, if it's a boy, she gets to name him and if it's a girl, I pick the name."

"You should do what I did with all my kids, wait until their born to find out the sex."

"I was thinking about that, maybe I'll give it a shot to Keri and see what she thinks. Let's see, this is 218 right here."

"Are we going to kick the door in or would you prefer to knock?" asked Gary.

"I would prefer to knock if possible."

Gary put his ear to the door, "Sounds like at least one female and two males. I don't know, maybe one or two in the bathroom." "Anybody with guns?"

"Probably, just be sure to dodge the bullets if they start flying."

"Yeah, just call me Neo." Daryl put his hand on the door handle and slowly turned, it was unlocked. They looked at each other. "Would you look at that, maybe they were expecting us after all, allow me to go first, "Daryl said. At that moment Daryl and Gary ran into the small motel room. They were greeted with a picture of two naked men and a naked female. One of the guys was sitting on the side of the bed with the female on her knees between his legs asking for forgiveness. The other naked male was sitting on the other side of the bed getting ready to inject himself with a needle.

Daryl noticed instantly it was Mark who was getting lip service from the naked woman, by the time everyone in the room saw the two newcomers, it was too late. Mark tried to grab for a gun that was laying on the night stand next to the bed. He was rewarded with a broken hand from Daryl's bat. Meanwhile, the man who was about to shoot up, stood up aggressively only to be put back down with a bat to his dick and balls by Gary. Gary then went to check the bathroom to make sure there was nobody in there.

"You broke my fucking hand man!" Mark said obviously in pain.

"Shut-up." Daryl then pointed the bat at the woman, "Bitch get up, get dressed, and get your tired ass out of here."

She started to put on her clothes. When she was halfway dressed, she asked, "What about my money?" Daryl and Gary looked at each other. Gary kneeled down to speak to the man who was still holding himself groaning, "Well don't go cheap on me now, where's your wallet?"

The man pointed to a pair of jeans that was on the floor. Gary walked over and picked up the jeans and pulled out a wallet out the back pocket. He opened it up and saw maybe around fifty dollars or so in bills, he handed it to Daryl. "How much?" Daryl asked.

"Two-hundred dollars." She said.

"Two-hundred my ass, you take whatever this is and be thankful I don't hit women."

She took the money from Daryl.

"Two-hundred dollars my ass, bitch I wouldn't pay twenty-cents for your run - down, titties looking like oranges in a sock, four teeth having ass, get the fuck out of here, and close the door on your way out uh." She did what she was told. When Daryl turned his attention back, Mark tried reaching for the gun again but this time he was rewarded with a smack to his face from the bible that was on the night stand next to the gun. The good book taught Mark a lesson, sending him down on his knees. Daryl picked up the gun that Mark was so anxious to grab earlier.

"A 40. Cal, a step up from that piece of shit nine huh?" Daryl said as he ejected the clip, pocketed it, checked to see if there was a round in the chamber, and then tossed the gun to Gary.

Gary looked at the gun, "It ain't even a real Glock, it's a fucking Chinese knock off man." He was laughing.

Daryl looked at Mark who was sitting on the floor next to the bed holding his hand, "Well what you waiting on brother, get the fuck up, we have a date in the bathroom." On their way to the bathroom Daryl looked down at the man holding his nuts, "Gary quiet this piece of shit, will ya?" Gary nodded as he began smoking a Marlboro.

Inside the bathroom Mark turned around to face Daryl, "You broke my fucking hand man."

"Yes I know Mark, I heard you the first time, now get in the tub and put your hands behind your back." Daryl zip tied Mark's hands together, "Now sit down please." Mark did what he was told to do. "Now maybe I didn't make myself clear to you the last time we met Mark. So there won't be any confusion, I'll make the point clear you ok."

At that moment Daryl took out a Zippo lighter from his front pocket and sat it down on the back of the toilet. He also took out a small bottle of butane and began squeezing the lighter fluid all over Mark's head, face and body. Mark tried getting up but Daryl just punched him in his mouth, and he sat his naked ass back down. "You know Mark, that shit is highly flammable. I wouldn't want to be sitting where you're sitting." Daryl said as he took the Zippo off the toilet and flicked it open and sparked a flame. "Now what do you suppose I do Mark? You show up at my woman's house, yelling, kicking the door, and scaring the kids, after I told you to keep your distance. Hell, I gave you money so you can find a place to stay. Only to come here and see you shooting up dope with a hooker, I thought you said you were clean Mark?"

Mark started to say something was cut off. "Shut up Mark, I didn't ask you anything yet. Now I am trying to be civil here Mark, I really don't want to set you on fire, but it ain't looking too good for you right now. So I'll tell you what, I am going to say this once so pay close attention ok. If you ever show up at Keri's house or anywhere near her or those kids before they turn eighteen, I am going to kill you. Not before I torture you so bad you'll be praying for me to hurry up and end your life. Do you understand what I just said Mark, and before you answer Mark the only words I want to hear out your mouth is yes or no."

"Yes." Mark said through gritted teeth.

"That's excellent Mark; my next advice to you is to leave this city. Don't care where you go, but leave tonight." Daryl took out a wad of cash and put it on the back of the toilet. "That's five grand Mark, use it wisely. I don't want to find out you put it all in that arm of yours. There's plenty for a bus ticket, a cheap motel and more shit to put in your vein when you hit another city. Now Mark, think hard now, are you leaving the city tonight?"

"Yes."

"Outstanding Mark, I'm glad we could have this conversation like civilized men. By the way, you might want to get that hand looked at, I think it's broke." Daryl grinned at Mark as he walked out of the bathroom and back into the main room. "We're done here Gary, let's roll."

Gary was taking pictures on his camera phone of his latest artwork. Daryl looked over to see the other naked man tied down on his stomach, spread eagle on the bed, with a remote control in his ass and a gag in his mouth. "You need a friend." Daryl said. "Yes I do, but I guess you'll do." Gary replied. They were discussing the point as they walked out of the motel room and shut the door. On the way back to the car Gary said, "Damn, now tell me why we don't do that shit more often. That was a hell of a rush, wasn't it?"

Well, Gary as much as I would love to share a jail cell with you, you ain't my type, sorry."

"So are you and Keri going to move in together anytime soon?"

"Crazy you should ask; I was planning on asking Keri that same thing after I propose. But we ain't living in her pad; we'll have to get a bigger house, at least a five bedroom, maybe six."

"Why, you plan on putting another one in her after the first?"

Daryl shrugged, "Stranger things have happened." Daryl and Gary made it back to his Lexus and put the bats back in the trunk. Gary made his way to the front passenger side of the car only to see Daryl heading in the opposite direction, "Hey, where the hell are you going?" Gary yelled.

"Over to that roach coach", Daryl said, "I want a taco."

Chapter 16

Origins:

Lapel Rone- Second in command of the Wolfpack, a Corporal Chief in the F.F.L. German, one-hundred and eighty-five centimeters around 102 kilos, blonde hair, blue eyes. By Legion trade an E.O.D. expert, (Explosive Ordinance Disposal). The man could make a bomb out of bubble gum, a tea cup, some ammonia, and a little bit of rubber from the bottom of a jump boot; that would have Q branch scratching their heads, asking how. Unfortunately, it was his smarts that landed him in the Legion in the first place. He is currently wanted for questioning by German Police Officials for a car bombing, a car that had three people in it, who according to Rone deserved it. When asked why, his reply was, "That fucking rapist and his lawyers had it coming. The man raped a fourteen-year-old girl, recorded it, and sent it to another pedophile like himself; who was under investigation for child porn. The video was intercepted by police and the cock-sucker was arrested. But that cock-sucker was a somebody in the religious world, he spent millions in bribes and attorney fees to only get two years un-supervised probation. To tell you the truth, the fucker actually got off easy. My original plan was to kidnap him and his attorneys, rape them with a hot fire place poker while I tape it, and then send the tape to the girl's family for their enjoyment." Needless to say Rone was an active member of the Anti-Government group known as Shadow Justice. And because of a cheap outside camera in front of the court house, Rone was identified as a suspicious suspect and thus went on the run. Having no place to go, the Legion accepted him with open arms.

Abu Nordeen- A Corporal Chief in the F.F.L. Algerian, one-hundred and eighty-two centimeters even, around 81.6 kilos, dark skin, black hair and brown eyes. By Legion trade he is a Combat Diver, but like the rest of the Wolfpack he is trained in a wide spectrum of specialties. The man could hold his breath for five plus minutes and swim so good he'd make a shark take a remedial swim course. He came to the Legion at the age of eighteen. From a small poor village, he had no proper education, never passing the equivalent of sixth grade; but he's far from dumb. He began working by smuggling opium when he was eleven years old to support his family. His father was a crippled and could not work due to a farming accident. His mother had a nervous breakdown soon after that, and his little sister was too young to work. So he had a responsibility to grow up fast and survive. Nordeen made enough money at first to barely scrape by. But as he got older, the drug runners were giving him a little more responsibility, and he began to make enough money to start saving. When he was seventeen he had enough money save to send his little sister off to a private school in the city. But as fate would have it, he had to 'dump' an opium shipment or risk being arrested. The people whose drugs he dumped was not so sympathetic to his situation. In retaliation they killed his dad, raped and murdered his sister and mother, to teach him a lesson. Nordeen took it hard; he vowed to kill the people who did it. It took him six months to track the four people who were responsible, then buried them alive in the ground with only their head above the ground. He then pissed, ejaculated on them and then poured gasoline on their heads and set them ablaze. Knowing that he would be sought out for their deaths, he joined the Legion.

Thomas McLean-Corporal Chief in the F.F.L. Irish, standing at one-hundred and ninety-two centimeters, 92.9 kilos, red hair, freckled skin from too much sun exposure, and green eyes. By Legion trade, a Heavy Machine Gunner and a damn good one too. McLean once shot a smiley face in a target one-hundred meters away, iron sights, with an American M249. Came to the Legion by bad luck; he was in Marseille working the docks under the table for about two years, until he let his drinking get him in trouble. One night at the bar he got so drunk that he couldn't even remember his own name. He was on his way home when two police officers saw him staggering in the middle of the road. They decided to approach him. As the police approached him, he broke the first one's nose, and then swung at the other one but completely missed. He fell to the ground where he was beat unconscious with truncheons. He awoke the next day naked with one eye closed, a busted lip, and two cracked ribs in an air conditioned jail cell freezing his balls off. He was given two choices from the police commander; go to prison for ten to fifteen years and then be deported back to Ireland, or join the Legion. He chose the latter.

Stag Tiekert – Corporal Chief in the F.F.L one-hundred and fifty centimeters tall; weigh in at 95.2 kilos, dirty blonde hair, and blue eyes. By Legion trade a Combat Medic. The man could perform surgery in a hurricane and not lose his cool. Ended up in the Legion because he was bored with life. He decided he wanted a change from his lifestyle of studying in a prestige college to become a doctor. The only reason he was in college was because he comes from a wealthy family and he was trying to please his father by following in his footsteps as a doctor. After years of schooling he 'woke up' one morning and decided, enough was enough. Fuck trying to please everybody, for the rest of his life and he wanted to do what he wanted, to live on his own terms. He longed for adventure, to travel around the globe and get into mischief. He always wanted to be in the military. When he told his parents that he wanted to drop out of college, they threatened to cut off his inheritance and disown him from the family. So he quit anyway, and instead of joining his own country's military, he decided he had a debt to pay to society and wanted to be pushed harder than he ever had in his life. McLean got his wish granted; he joined the Legion at the age of twenty-three and never looked back.

Daniel Karsten- Leader of the Wolfpack, a Sergeant in the F.F.L. American, one-hundred and fifty-five centimeters, 96.6 kilos, brown eyes, shaved head, with caramel complexion skin; and a hardened killer. By Legion trade a Sniper, but qualified to fly a helicopter, a plane, and drive a tank. He had a mysterious background; nobody really knew how he became to join the Legion. A lot of rumors have surfaced around his past, some say he tracked down his fiancé killer to Spain, and that he butchered the man into tiny pieces while he was still alive. Others say that he's wanted by the Interpol for gun running all across Europe and Asia. Still others say that he killed two policemen in America and that he's wanted by the F.B.I. When asked about these rumors, he neither agrees nor disagrees. But one fact is clear; he is not to be crossed. In basic training he broke a man's back over a stolen can of mutton. And on his first mission as a sniper, not only did he take out the target; he also shot the target's pet dog and the pet goldfish swimming in the aquarium because he thought the fish was looking at him with 'those beady eyes'. Many think he's unstable, the Legion does not.

Wolfpack- The most notorious and most feared special operations unit in the F.F.L. and also the most hated by those who know they exist. They operate outside Legions norms, they don't salute, can grow full beards, do not wear rank insignia, etc. Legion officers hated the Wolfpack because they were envious, others hated them because 'they walked around like they were untouchable'. And in some ways they were technically 'untouchable'. Part of the 2 REP unit base in Corsica, their orders came from top unknown men in France's government. The Wolfpack consists of a five-man unit with a slot for a sixth that is still open at the present time. But one does not apply for the unit, he is recruited. And after a man is recruited he must pass the Qualifications Course, which is run by the other members of the unit. It is sixteen weeks of brutal hell, that would make the toughest of men cry and beg for mercy. Not only do you have to be physically fit but also smart as well. Mandatory fluent in three languages (native tongue is not included), math skills level at calculus or above. An I.Q. of at least 150 or higher, and achieved a rank of Corporal or higher. If selected a recruit must immediately sign a five-year enlistment extension on top of their current contract. The Wolfpack is used for perilous missions that have a 15% lower chance of success, and if failed cannot be tracked back to the Legion or France for that matter; because the unit does not exist. It is a rumor amongst soldiers. Every man knows that he is expendable.

Chapter 17

"Wishing I had a poster of Raquel Welch and a rock hammer right now." Dee said to Bama.

"Man what the fuck are you talking about? Always on some rambling bullshit when you get blazed."

"Shawshank son, you have seen the movie right?"

"You damn well know I saw it, hell we watched it only a million times together in this shit hole of a cell."

"Good, then you know what the hell I am referring to then. Anyway, what I wouldn't give for some lobster right about now."

"Not me," Said Bama, "I wish I had some of that cheap ass fish from Captain D's."

"True that, I do love that cheap ass cod, but the last time I went there, I think I got food poisoning or something; felt like I had Bell's Palsy or some shit. Hey, you ever pay attention to these commercials on TV, the ones where they try to sell you drugs to cure that nasty cough, or high cholesterol?"

"Yeah, why, what's up?"

"What's up? What's up is all those fucking side effects. Correct me if I'm wrong now, let's say I have a chronic cough, I take this magic pill and poof my cough goes away. But, and there is always a but, I have no more cough but I got mad diarrhea, a sore throat, muthafucking pink eye, and a damn weakened immune system. Shit, I'm better off with that cough. How the hell do I win by taking that pill? I end up more fucked up then when I started, and I have to take more pills to combat those side effects, and more to combat those side effects of the pills I'm taking for those side effects. And yet the drug maker insists I'm alright. Man I tell you what; I am obviously in the wrong profession. I should've been a salesman for the big tobacco industry. Telling people how great smoking is and oh by the way there's really no side effects except for death."

Bama started laughing, "Where do you get this shit from man?"

"It's just the truth playa; you need to open up your eyes."

"I can't," said Bama, "The herb got me looking like a Chinaman."

Dee and Bama both started to laugh uncontrollably for about twenty seconds, then Dee said, "Seriously though, I'm higher than eagle pussy right now and the only thing I'm thinking about is little ass Smurfette."

"Who?" asked Bama.

"Smurfette, you know, the only female Smurf in the whole Smurf colony. You already know Papa Smurf was taxing that ass, had to been. I would've if I was him. Why not, I'm head of the Colony, calling all the shots, and got the only bitch in town bent over giving it to her in her blue asshole, literally. Then making the little blue bitch suck it clean, and give her a pat on the back on the way out telling her to have good smurfing day."

Bama was on the floor rolling.

"Real shit though," Dee continued, "Why was she the only bitch in the whole place?

Makes you think, what was the creators of the show smoking when they came up with the concept, had to be some powerful shit. How else would you come up with some fictional characters that are blue, living in a forest inside of mushrooms, and every other word out of their mouth is smurf this or smurf that. That ain't even a fucking word, actually it is, and means to launder money idiots; but that ain't the point. Those fools had to be mushroomed out."

"What about Yogi and Boo Boo?" asked Bama.

"Oh them fools, yeah they the shit. I tried telling the judge I had Jellystone syndrome. He asked me what it was so I told him that I thought stealing was right. I told him that on every episode I watched I saw how Yogi and his sidekick was stealing picnic baskets all around the forest, then running from the law. Think about it, how else where they going to survive? That damn park ranger was putting up signs all around the place saying please don't feed the bears. They weren't hurting anybody, just trying to get by; hustling for a few coins to buy sandwiches. And what better way to get those coins than from a bank?" "That's what I told the judge I was doing."

"What did the judge say?"

"That cocksucker looked me straight in my eyes and told me two ten year sentences to run concurrent."

"What did you tell him after that?" Bama asked.

"To go smurf himself." Dee said laughing.

Dee was sitting on the shitter when he heard the restroom door open and listened as someone in the next stall started to take a piss. He was in the educational building restrooms; he had previously been down the hall in the Law Library. Dee listened as the man in the stall took his piss, flushed the toilet, and ran the faucet to wash his hands. What came next was nothing but a surprise. Dee's stall door was kicked in; he immediately looked up and couldn't believe what he was seeing. It was Ham, with the look of a rabid dog in his eyes, and a metal shank in his right hand.

Ham spoke, "Your ass is mine now bitch." Then he made his way into the stall. Dee with lighting fast speed jumped in the air, each one of his hands grabbing the top barrier of the stall, and using both feet kicked Ham square in his mouth, as Ham flew backwards, Dee not wanting to waste precious seconds pulled up his boxers and pants at the same time. The kick to the jaw only stung Ham because he was back in the stall the second Dee pulled his clothes up. Ham lunged at Dee with the shank, and Dee deflected the blow downwards and was stabbed on his left side, the blade going into him three inches.

Dee felt every inch of the blade but had no time to reflect on his pain as he immediately used his left hand to stop the blade from going in deeper and used his right hand to punch Ham in his only remaining eye. That got the blade out of him but Ham was still inside the stall getting ready to lunge with the shank again. Dee saw it coming this time and used both hands to grab Ham's arm and stop the blade from making contact. Before ham got any ideas about using his free arm, Dee head butted him on the bridge of his nose; sending blood gushing all over the stall and Ham stumbling back.

Now outside of the stall Dee had more room to maneuver around Ham. Dee grabbed Ham's right wrist and bent it backwards until Ham lost grip of the shank and it dropped to the floor. At that moment, Ham's left hand with lighting speed landed a punch to Dee's temple, sending him down on one knee. Ham then cocked back a second time and struck Dee in his right eye, closing it shut instantly, and putting him fully on the floor.

Ham begun kicking Dee in the stomach repeatedly all while screaming, "I told you boy, I told you boy, your ass is mine."

Dee was on the ground fighting to stay conscious as Ham continued kicking him, this time in the face. Dee who was still surprisingly on all fours took three kicks to the face before he felt he was on the verge of blacking out. As he was scurrying on the floor his hand found the shank Ham had dropped. Knowing that he might not be able to take another kick to the face, he used all of his reserve strength to block Ham's foot from contacting his face and jabbed the shank into Ham's balls. Ham was stopped cold as he grabbed for his groin and fell to his knees. Dee used those God sent seconds to move away from Ham's reach and tried to right himself on his feet. But he was too dizzy for more than two seconds at a time.

Ham, who was still on his knees, was starting to stand up. Dee who still punch drunk lunged at him with the Shank aiming or his head but only struck him on his thigh. It was as though Ham didn't feel the blade because he was now standing on both legs. Dazed and confused, Dee watched as Ham two pieced him in the face sending him back down on his back. Ham straddled Dee and commenced to punching him with heavy handed blows to the face. Dee who was on the verge of passing out knew that if he did he was not ever going to wake back up. Dee was still holding the shank in his hand with as much strength as he could muster up and made a one in a million shot and drove the blade of the shank straight into Ham's left ear. The blade, which was about eight inches long, disappeared into Ham's brain. Ham fell in a heap right on top of Dee, not moving. Dee who was barely coherent pushed Ham off of him, and laid gasping for air. He looked over and stared into Ham's one good eye, which was open looking directly at Dee.

Dee rolled on top of Ham, took the blade out of his ear and stuck it to the hilt of Ham's eye; but Ham did not feel it, he was already dead. Dee looked up at the restroom windows to see about twenty CO's watching him. They were trying to get the door open. Earlier, Ham had broken off his room key in the lock and it was jammed. Dee looked back down at Ham, spit on him then rolled off of him and passed out on the floor.

When he awoke nine hours later, Dee found himself handcuffed to a bed at Denver General Hospital with two guards and a nurse standing over him. He tried to speak but the nurse had told him not to. One of the guards addressed him, "Damn boy, where you learn how to get your ass kicked like that? I watched the whole thing twice before we turned over the surveillance tapes to the Sheriff."

The other guard added, "Oh, and by the way the Sheriff is looking to be asking you some questions; after all you did kill a man." The guards waited for a response but did not get one, the guard continued, "Yep, you killed him alright; he ain't coming back for seconds this time, that's for sure."

Dee laid there taking in everything they were saying. All he could think about was the possibility of him spending the rest of his life in prison for defending himself. He passed out again. Three hours went by and he awoke still handcuffed to the bed and a nurse changing his bandage where he was struck by the shank. He looked around the room and only saw one guard, who was sitting in a chair watching a game show on TV. Dee asked the nurse, "What's the damage?"

The nurse looked him in the eye and said, "You're alive, let's leave it at that." She then finished taping the bandage on his stomach and took out a needle. She put it in his I.V. bag and said, "This will help with the pain." she said as she injected the clear liquid into the tube that fed into his vein. Two minutes later Dee was out cold, dreaming about the possibilities of bacon.

Chapter 18

Rio de Janeiro

"Damn, I have not had anything this potent in a long time." Gary said to Daryl as he took another shot, "Shit so strong it'll make a crazy person sane." Daryl just looked over at him with glassy eyes and smiled. They were sitting in back of a dance club, drinking for three hours.

"Christ, I'm so fucked up right now, my kidneys just put up a no vacancy sign." Daryl said.

"Tell me again why we never came down here for Carnival until now. This shit is slapping, half naked women everywhere, everywhere Daryl."

"Yeah they everywhere alright, let's not forget Rio is only the sex change capital of the world shall we."

"True, but believe me, I can tell the difference right away and so far, what I'm seeing is all women."

"Please Gary; all you're seeing right now is blurs, blurs shaking their tits and ass. You wouldn't be able to tell the difference between a transgender and a real woman right now even if you were his doctor."

But before Gary could respond a tall light skinned, big breasted woman approached the table, "Hello boys, what a surprise." she said.

Daryl had to take a second look before he responded, "Well I'll be dammed, Sergeant Mendez, what a surprise it is." Daryl stood up, "Please join us and have a drink."

"I think I will, and since we're not working, you can call me Katrina." she said as she flashed Daryl a big smile showing off her perfect white teeth.

Gary who was feeling the vibe said, "Excuse me for a second, I do believe I hear a urinal calling my name. And since I'm up what would you be drinking tonight Miss Katrina?" She looked around the table, "I'll have whatever you boys been busy with all night, please." With that said Gary disappeared in the crowd and Katrina turned to focus on Daryl.

"So is he always that friendly?"

"Oh no, he'll usually be much friendlier with a little bit more alcohol in his system."

"Is that right? She said with seduction, "How?"

Daryl straightened up in his seat, he was thinking about the possibilities he could have with this fine specimen of a woman in front of him; so much he started to get an erection.

"Oh you know how it is, never do nothing that I might regret later."

"Believe me handsome, there will definitely be no regrets, I promise." Katrina said.

"Are you always this open or have you started your drinking before you joined this party?"

"Of course, only when I see something I want. And no, I have not had a drink all night." she said as she put her hand on Daryl's leg and moved it up to his crotch and squeezed.

"And apparently I'm not the only one who knows what they want."

Daryl just sat there as she rubbed him for about five seconds before he took her hand politely said, "Would it matter if I told you that I am in love with a beautiful woman who is carrying my baby back home?"

A brief look of disappointment came on Katrina's face, and then she smiled, "Nope, I don't want to marry you; I just want to fuck your brains out for one night. Then you can go back home to your beautiful woman and that white picket fence."

"Sorry Katrina, believe me I really want to, more than you can possibly know. If this was a different situation where I was not involved with someone else, I would make it my mission to fuck you so hard, you'll hate your pussy afterwards. But you caught me in a transitional period where I am truly in love with another woman."

Katrina smiled, "No hard feelings, can't blame a woman for trying. At least I know someone still wants to fuck me hard." she said nudging Daryl in the side. They both started laughing and exchanged a mutual look of respect towards each other. Just then Gary returned to the table carrying three glasses, a full bottle of Absinthe, some sugar cubes, a strainer, and a bottled water. Katrina asked, "All on the company account huh, how does one justify the tab?"

Gary and Daryl looked at each other. Daryl spoke first, "Technically since you're here it will be billed as a business meeting, discussing some evaluation of the week's exercises." Then Gary added, "And since it's your government that's footing the bill, why the hell not?" With that said, drinks were readied then poured, followed by a small toast to thank God for wormwood. This went on in order until the bottle of Absinthe was gone. Everyone at the table was drunk, some more than others. Daryl looked at Gary who was looking at him, while pointing at Katrina, "So how long have you been on the police force?"

"Oh, I would say about four years now." she slurred.

"How long have you been on the special operations team?" Asked Daryl.

"Going on about two years now. How about you, how long have you been doing this type of work?"

"I'd say about two or three years now. It's fun, I get to travel, explore the world, get into mischief, and meet people like you." Katrina blushed and then put her hand on Daryl's bicep.

Gary saw the movement, looked at Daryl and silently mouthed the words, "If you don't fuck her, you're gay." Katrina turned to Gary right when he was finished speaking silently. Gary who had the look of a guilty man caught in the act excused himself from the table.

"So Katrina," Daryl said, "Where's your place at?"

Katrina with excitement in her eyes quickly said, "About a fifteen-minute drive from here. Why are you taking me home for a night cap?" she purred.

"Not tonight beautiful, I am taking you back to my hotel, which is about two blocks from here. And get that look out of your eyes; you're too drunk to drive home, so you might as well stay until the morning."

"Sure handsome, whatever you want to call it."

As they were getting up from the table to leave, Gary came back smiling, "I was just about to tell you that I had to go, I got one of those cage dancers coming over to the hotel in twenty minutes for a little strip show, and since watching strippers ain't cheating, I'm good."

"Be careful Gary, as much as I don't like your wife, please don't do anything stupid, ok?"

"Oh yes, advice coming from a man who has a drunk lady in his arms, getting ready to leave."

"You know it's not even like that, she's crashing there because she's too drunk to drive."

Katrina slurred, "Yeah, I'm too drunk to drive, so I am going to sleep in his bed tonight."

Gary looked at Daryl, "Just make sure you record it, will ya?"

Daryl shook his head and escorted Katrina out the club.

Twenty-five minutes later there was a knock on Gary's hotel door. Gary hurriedly answered the door, saw Daryl and was disappointed, "Damn that was quick, was it sloppy? What, did she just lay there like a dead fish or something? Where her tits real, where they soft? They were soft as a pillow, huh? Where's the tape, you did record it right? Quit playing with me, let me see it man."

"Man if you don't get your horn dog ass away from me," Daryl said as he pushed Gary out the doorway to let himself in, "Where's this stripper you supposed to have come over?"

"Not here yet, where's Katrina?"

"Back in my room passed out, snoring and fully clothed might I add."

"What's wrong with you man, once again a fine ass woman throws herself at you and you do nothing. I could understand if you were married with a ball and chain on your ankle like me but you're not. If I was you I would be fucking every piece of pussy I can, then settle down with Keri."

"Been there, done that already Gary, how many times are we going to have this conversation?"

"As many times as it takes for you to do the right thing and go back upstairs to your room, strip that cop naked, and beat her with your baton."

There was a knock at the door before Daryl could rebuttal Gary's tangent. Gary moved with lighting fast movement and opened the door. Standing in the doorway was a tall, about 6'2, long dark hair, big, size 36DD tits, and a phat ass Brazilian woman clad in tight pants and a bikini top. "I thought it was only going to be you tonight." she said.

"I was just on my way out." Daryl said.

"Yeah he was just on his way out." Gary repeated.

The woman smiled and said, "You don't have to leave just yet, I have not danced for you guys yet."

Gary looked at Daryl, shaking his head yes.

"Alright, you got me." Daryl said as he sat in the empty chair in the corner, with Gary sitting on the edge of the bed. The woman walked across the room, turned on the radio to a salsa music station, then walked back over to Gary and began dancing seductively for him. About three minutes into it the woman took off her top and gave Gary a big surprise with her size 36DD tits.

Daryl, who was in the corner of the room, was also impressed. Next came off the woman's tight leather pants, to reveal a pair of pink 'Hello Kitty' boy shorts. Gary grabbed her ass as she backed up and started shaking it in his face. He looked over at Daryl, "Still not cheating." He said smiling. After about two minutes of shaking her ass in Gary's face she bent over and took off her panties, her backside still exposed to Gary. Daryl, who was watching from his spot in the corner, immediately got an erection. All of that went away in a blink of an eye when the woman turned around and revealed she was not a woman at all. She was a him, with a very big, limp dick in his hands. It took Gary about three seconds to realize what was going on. He stood up and pushed the he/ she away from him yelling obscenities. The man yelled back at Gary telling him to keep his hands off of him. Gary went to go push the man again but was slow and was rewarded with a right cross to his chin, knocking him out cold on the bed.

The naked man looked at Daryl, "What, you have a problem too?"

"Hell no," Daryl said, "As a matter of fact that was a damn good performance." Daryl stood up and reached into his back pocket for his wallet, found two-hundred dollar bills, and handed it to the naked man, "You're very talented, but I think we're done here;

my man here has to sleep it off. We got a very long flight back to Canada in the morning."

The naked man started to put his clothes back on, when he was done he asked Daryl, "Are you sure I can't do anything else for you tonight handsome?"

"Um, quite sure." Daryl said as he opened the door to let the man out. Then he turned around to look at Gary, who was snoring on the bed. "Where they real Gary? Were they soft?" Daryl sarcastically whispered to Gary as he was passed out, and then he flopped down on the bed next to Gary and passed out.

****

As Daryl walked through the door he was bombarded with hugs from Melody and Devon. He fell to one knee and gave them both one big hug and kissed them on the forehead, then asked, "Where's your mother?"

Melody said, "She's downstairs in the shower. Did you bring us something back from Brazil?"

"As a matter of fact, I did, Daryl reached into a backpack he was carrying and pulled out two big logs of Carrillo chocolate, he handed each of them one, "Now don't go losing all of your teeth at once, pace yourselves, ok?"

They started jumping up and down thanking him and then ran upstairs to enjoy their newfound gift. Daryl walked downstairs to the master bedroom, dropped his bag, and then made his way to the bathroom. Keri heard the door open and peeked her head from behind the shower curtains, saw who it was and ducked back in the shower. She asked,

"How was your trip baby?"

"It was interesting." Daryl said as he started to undress.

"How so?" Keri asked.

Daryl who was already naked, pulled back the shower curtain and stepped into the shower with Keri. He gave her a long hard kiss and then rubbed and kissed her belly.

"Let's just say if I tell you, Gary will kill us both."

She smiled, and then whispered into Daryl's ear, "Did you bring me something back from Brazil?"

Daryl looked at Keri, "Oh yeah." he said as he turned Keri around, grabbed her ass and spread her cheeks as he entered her from behind. Keri gasped then moaned in pleasure.

Later that night as Daryl and Keri laid in bed next to each other, Daryl asked, "What do you think about us living together on a more permanent basis?"

Keri looked over at Daryl, "What are you suggesting?"

"Well I figure since I spend more time over here than at my own place, and the fact that you're about to have a baby. I might be useful around the house."

Keri was looking deeply into Daryl's eyes, "Only if you're serious about us."

"What are you mad, I've been serious about us since the first day I saw you Keri. I love you baby, more than anything in this world. You should know that by now."

"Alright, let's do it then, but we might run into space problems when the baby comes; it's going to be crowded here."

"Sure will, but I already thought of a solution to that problem. I was hoping this weekend you and the kids and I go house shopping. You know, browse the market and see what's available."

Keri smiled, "You've been planning this awhile, haven't you?"

"I've been planning it for the last two months to tell you the truth. I have a realtor meeting us at a few spots already."

"Are you sure this is what you want?" Keri asked.

"More than anything I've ever wanted in my whole life Keri."

Keri kissed Daryl lightly on the lips, "I love you Daryl."

Chapter 19

The Crapaudine- Karsten was stripped naked with his ankles tied together and his hands were bound behind his back. Then his ankles were lashed to his wrist, and he was thrown to the ground. After being punched and kicked the Sergeant –Chief decided it was time to put a gag in his mouth and pour honey all over him. When the black ants came, they came with force, biting Karsten on every part of his exposed body. Karsten was on the ground in this position getting eaten by the ants for around two hours before his screams through the gag become agonizing to listen to. At that point the Sergeant-Chief repeatedly kicked Karsten in the head until he was out cold; the ants didn't mind one bit. Coming up on the third hour like this, Karsten was doused with buckets of warm, soapy water to remove the ants. Then he was carried to the infirmary for a few shots, given some rash/bite cream and was told to report back to his unit in forty-eight hours. From that point on Karsten never laid a hand on a superior officer again, and he never slept with one's mistress either.

"A Moi La Legion." was heard screamed as a scuffle amassed leading outside of the bar. Every Legionnaire, whether he was in civilian clothing or proper dress attire, immediately stopped what they were doing, jumped up from their seats and headed outside toward the scream. The Wolfpack was no exception, Karsten, Rone, Nordeen, McLean, and Tiekert all took off to go outside. Once outside they punched and kicked their way through the crowd and came upon several Legionnaires who were outnumbered by four to one fighting in the road with several skinheads, who were yielding clubs, knives, and bats. The Wolves didn't hesitate; they charged head on into the fight.

Karsten grabbed one skinhead who was swinging a knife; he hit him on his chin, took the knife from him, and stabbed the man in his right hand. As Karsten was retrieving the knife out of the un-willing man's hand, he was rewarded with a club to the back of his head. He dropped the knife and stumbled forward trying to get a look at the assailant who hit him. As he glanced back, he saw Tiekert round-house the man on the side of his face. Momentarily stunned, the attacker turned his back on Karsten, who had then regained his wits. Karsten lunged at the man Tiekert had kicked, picked him up off the ground and slammed him into the asphalt road. Tiekert began kicking the man; Karsten rose up from the ground and joined him. They began stomping the man until he lost consciousness.

As Tiekert was going to administer the 'Coup de grace', Karsten stopped him by pushing him back and shook his head no. Tiekert nodded, turned around and disappeared in the mob. Karsten too turned around and saw a Legionnaire who was on the ground getting worked over with an aluminum bat. As the man with the bat went to go swing again, Karsten pinned his arm by the shoulder, threw his body weight with a sweeping kick and took the man to the ground. Karsten punched the man in the face; rapidly delivering seven quick blows. The Legionnaire who was previously getting beat with the bat, crawled on top of the man and began throwing loose, wild punches to the face, as the man on the ground tried blocking the blows. Karsten picked up the bat swinging it and hitting the left knee of the skinhead, shattering his knee. The skinhead was screaming and moaning in incredible pain as the other Legionnaire rose up from the ground and Karsten handed him the bat. He immediately swung the bat and smashed the other knee of the skinhead who was already on the ground screaming.

Satisfied with their work, Karsten and the other Legionnaire smiled at each other, shook hands and went their own separate ways, joining back into the fighting frenzy. The sight of flashing lights and the sounds of sirens brought everyman there to the reality that their freedom was at stake.

As people begin to scatter, helping their own up, Karsten ran into Rone and McLean who were jolly as ever laughing like crazed bandits. Karsten could not help but to smile himself. "Help the wounded and find Nordeen and Tiekert, we meet at the Café La Grand in twenty." They nodded and disappeared. Karsten began helping the other Legionnaires to their feet and away from the mayhem, before the police could slap handcuffs on anyone. He didn't want to be involved with the law anytime soon.

Forty minutes later Karsten walked into the Café La Grand and saw the other four Wolves sitting in the corner entertaining five beautiful women. Rone waved him over' Karsten walked over to the table and was immediately asked, "What you do, take the scenic route Sarge? We were worried that we might have to put our meager funds together and bond you out." Rone said.

"Oh yea, I see you were so concerned about my freedom that you were out looking for me this whole time."

"We were," said Mclean, "And we found these beautiful ladies, who looked a little thirsty. So we decided to replenish their thirst." he winked at Karsten. Not wanting to be left out of the conversation, the woman closes to Karsten spoke, "My name is Nadine." she said as she extended her hand to Karsten.

"Daniel." Karsten said as he took the woman's small hand into his and shook it.

"Will you be joining us?" she asked.

Karsten looked down at his watch, it was 1:48 am, "Sure, the night is still young and my mother isn't expecting me home until morning." he said as he took a chair from the neighboring table, he pulled it closer and sat down. As Karsten sat down, another woman at the table named Sissy asked, "Where you guys involved in that street brawl that happened downtown not too long ago?"

Karsten looked at the Wolves around the table, "Involved, why heavens no, we were just making sure no Legionnaires got into any trouble is all."

Around the table the Wolves started to howl, drawing the attention of the whole Café. When they were settled down Karsten asked Nadine, "And what are you ladies doing patrolling the streets by yourselves at this hour?"

Nadine looked at the other four women and smiled, "Oh you know, just looking for a little mischief to get into." as she put her hand on Karsten's knee. Karsten flagged the waitress down, "A round of Kronenbourg for the gentlemen," he looked at the table see what the women were drinking, "And a bottle of Pierre du Rogue for the ladies please."

Two and a half hours, three bottles of red wine, and thirty-five bottles of Kronenbourg later, Karsten was standing in the doorway of Nadine's flat.

"So are you going to come inside and take me to my bed?" she tried saying it seductively but slurred half the words.

Karsten opened the door and said, "Nope, I am going to take you inside your flat, fuck your brains out until you pass out, then slip out of here like a thief in the night, go grab me a bacon baguette from the deli down the street, hoping all the while I'll never see you again."

"Oh, you are bad, ain't ya?" Nadine said as she grabbed Karsten by his belt and pulled him all the way into her flat.

****

Two hours later, Karsten was enjoying his bacon baguette with frits on the outside patio at a small café three blocks from Nadine's flat when his cell phone rang.

"Karsten." he answered.

"Oui Mon Captain, Oui Mon Captain, right away Mon Captain." then Karsten heard the dial tone.

Shit Karsten thought to himself, always something with his men. He quickly finished off his sandwich, downed a cup of espresso, hailed a cab and begun his short trip back to base. At the gate he was greeted by two PM's (Police Military) who whisked him into a jeep and drove directly to the base H.Q. building. Once there he was escorted two levels down and into the Captain's office. Once inside he saw the rest of the Wolfpack standing at attention in the back of the room, not saying a word.

Karsten made his way to the front of the Captain's desk, saluted, and waited to be spoken to. The Captain, who was still sitting behind his desk was on the phone, "Oui Mon Major, I have the man responsible in my office right now, merci Mon Major." The captain hung up the phone, looked at Karsten and smiled, "Well, well, well, did we have a good time in town last night Sergeant? I've warned you countless times Sergeant about your unit's reckless behavior. I've told you that it would catch up with you one day. And you know what, that day is today Karsten. Today, my wish of seeing you and your men being disbanded will finally come true. Let me tell you a quick story before the Major comes down here and hands you your ass. Last night in town a riot or brawl you might call it, irrupted between some locals and some Legionnaires.

Apparently, some real serious injuries occurred and even just this morning a man died in the hospital. Witnessed put you especially, along with the rest of your unit on the front line of this whole debacle, yielding weapons and attacking innocent bystanders. And when I say witnesses, I mean the police commander's son in law, who by the way is also a policeman. You do remember the police commander, don't you? He sure remembers you. But wait this story gets better, in a report filed last night, the commander's son in law stated that as he was pulling up to the scene he personally saw you and another un-identified Legionnaire hitting a man who was on the ground with a baseball bat, crazy huh?"

The Captain waited for a few seconds to see if Karsten would respond, when he didn't, the Captain finished speaking, "As you can see this is a huge problem for you Karsten. I would love to help you but my hands are tied. I got orders to turn you over to the local authorities. I do wish I can be there when they slap that cold ass iron on your wrist. Whatever tricks you know to try to wiggle your way out of this one won't work. Not even God's son himself can get you out of this one." The Captain was smiling, "Sad really, I was just hoping you and I could put our differences aside and start working on a professional relationship, maybe even share a few laughs and a Kronenbourg." Just as the Captain was about to start another sentence his door flew open and a very upset Major came storming into the room. Karsten who was still standing at attention in front of the Captain's desk didn't move an inch.

"Is this the man responsible Captain?" the Major asked.

"Oui Mon Major, this is Sergeant Karsten, he runs the infamous trouble making unit known as the Wolfpack."

The Major began walking around the Captain's desk, stopping when he was directly in behind the Captain looking directly at Karsten. Karsten looked the Major in his eyes and immediately remembered who he was; he was the Legionnaire who was being beaten with a bat. The Major stared at Karsten, not showing the slightest hint of who he was, then he spoke to the Captain, "Is this a joke Captain, do you like wasting mine and the Legion's time?"

The Captain was confused, "But Mon Major, what are you talking about? These are the men who are responsible for last night's mayhem, there were witnesses…" The Major cut him off, "I don't give a rat's ass about your so called witnesses Captain, and these men are not the one's responsible."

"But Mon Major…"

"Shut up Captain, these men were in the regiment recreation center all night playing pool and drinking Captain. I should know, because that one right there," he pointed to Rone, "Hustled me for two-hundred Euros."

The Captain's face quickly became sad and scared, "But Mon Major…"

"But nothing Captain, are you telling me that my word means nothing Captain?"

"No Mon Major, it's just…"

"It's nothing Captain, this matter and conversation is over. You can call the police commander and inform him that there was a mistake in the identification of his suspects, am I clear Captain?"

"Oui Mon Major."

"And Captain, pour on the ass kissing hard would you, we wouldn't want him to think that we aren't going to find the men who are truly responsible, investigations take time."

"Oui Mon Major."

The Major looked at Karsten, and then passed him toward his men, "Dismissed gentlemen."

Karsten saluted the Major and was rewarded with a small wink from the Major. As the Wolves walked out of the building together and were making their way back to their unit's building, Rone asked, "Do I even want to know what the hell that was all about Sarge?"

Karsten looked at Rone, "You heard the man Rone, we were on base shooting pool all night, and we leave it at that."

Rone looked at the others and then back at Karsten and smiled. Almost simultaneously the Wolves began to howl as they started a slow in sync jog.

Chapter 20

"So how does it feel to be out of the S.H.U. after so long?" asked Daisy.

"What do you mean, how do I feel; I spent a fucking year in a Goddamn box the size of a broom closet, fighting for my life in this so called justice system protecting for myself, stressing over whether I am going to spend the rest of my life in prison because I had to kill a man who came at me with a blade when I was taking a shit minding my own fucking business. Let's not forget to mention the whole thing was caught on camera facing the damn restroom, and yet I was deemed the aggressor because I came out on top. With my military training, I could have easily walked away before it got too serious the prosecutor said. Clearly that bitch did not review the tape. The slow ass police couldn't get in, how the hell was I supposed to get out? I got stabbed, stomped on, thrown around like a rag doll, spent a fucking year in a freezing cell with the A.C. on full blast, with nothing to wear but a paper thin T-shirt and a pair of boxers. No socks, no blankets, no sheets, no pillow, no books to read, no TV to watch, lucky to get a shower once a week if the C. O's were feeling gracious, no mandatory 'hour' out, and to throw the cherry on top, one roll of toilet paper so thin it disintegrated when I went to go wipe my ass, that was given to me once a month. So you ask me, how do I feel? How the fuck do you think I feel Doc, peachy? How I feel huh? I feel like I got the fat round mushroom head of a dick stuck up my ass, followed by the long twelve-inch shaft it was connected to. What am I supposed to feel, grateful that I am out of S.H.U? Am I supposed to feel great that I beat some bullshit murder charges? I'm still in prison Doc, with no pussy, no freedom, and no gun. I have a big ass target on my back for those who might want revenge for killing Ham, and a punk ass L.T. who wants nothing more in his life than to see me hang from a nice fat oak tree."

"So you feel resentment then?"

"Resentment, are you serious right now? Have you heard nothing I've said? You know what, better yet, how the hell would you feel Doc if you were in my shoes?"

She thought about it for a moment, "I guess I would probably be mad at the world."

"Exactly Doc, I wake up every morning with two middle fingers to the sky screaming fuck the world."

"It can't be that bad, according to your file you have less than a year before your mandatory release date."

"That's true, but I have to make it that long first Doc. Ain't a day in here guaranteed, I have to earn that right every day. Especially now, everybody is going to want to beat up the man who killed Ham, so they can get props. And then what, I just beat one case, do you really think they are going to let me beat another assault/murder case, even though I'll be in the right? Hell no, I'll rot in a prison cell at C.S.P. (Colorado State Penitentiary) in solitary confinement."

"Ok, how do you feel about killing Ham?"

Dee took thirty seconds before he answered, "I don't feel a single bit of remorse Doc. That man had it out for me since I came into this prison. I really did not set out to kill him, and now that he is dead you want to know how I feel about it. He should've never picked a fight with a Marine, he'd still be alive if he didn't, that's how I feel Doc."

"You seemed to have a lot of built up rage, is this the attitude you're going to have when you get out?"

Bitch if you weren't so Goddamn hot, I would've been told you to go fuck yourself, Dee thought. "Whenever those nice white people let me go, that day will be the happiest day of my life. I will kiss the ground, jump for joy, and pull my pants down for the Warden and tell him he can suck my dick."

She made a comment in her notebook she was holding, "I see, so when all of this is done, what is your end game, your final goal in life?"

"Well Doc, since my dreams of being the next Russian Czar is out the window, I'll settle for a life where I can just die happy, having my fair share of pussy from around the world. My drive is simple Doc, I strive to be the best no matter what I am doing, well that and the love for a good piece of ass. Without pussy I don't think I would have a purpose to live, truth be told, I am God's gift to women. Who am I to deny them this righteous gift?"

"I see you're still as narcissistic as the first day we met. Do you ever see yourself settling down, having kids, the whole white picket fence thing?"

"Nope, I can't fathom just fucking one pussy for the rest of my life. Hell, I'll blow out her asshole the first year of marriage, she'll most likely want to file for a divorce and take half of my nothing." Dee smiled.

"A gentlemen you're not." said the Doc.

"I thought you knew that already Doc." Dee said.

****

A knock brought Dee out of his sleep. He looked over to the small window on his cell door, it was Tony. He got up off his rack, walked toward the door and opened it, "What's up Tony?"

"Damn cuz, I ain't seen you in over a year and here I find you hold up in this cell. Which by the way, I heard you won't be getting a celly since you don't play well with others." Tony smiled.

Dee ushered Tony in the cell and shut the door. He then walked over to his bed and turned on the radio, he looked at Tony, "Just trying to stay low key and suck a fee pimp. I see you've been hitting the pile since I been gone, what you weigh now?"

"Around a buck ninety-five," Tony lifted up his shirt to reveal his six pack, "And a washboard so cold I'm about to put those Arab laundry mats out of business when I touch down in three months. Would you believe it, these faggots actually paroled me cuz?"

"I heard, who did you have to blow to make that happen?"

"Let's see, I started with the Major, then I got passed on to the Assistant Warden. Did such a good job that he told his boss, next thing you know I was blowing the Warden himself. Who by the way had me choking on his big white dick; the fucker even made sure I had it all in my mouth before he busted his salty load down my throat. If I had known all these years that's what I had to do to be free, I would've been out years ago." Dee started laughing, shaking his head, "So are you going back to the Springs?" "Yeah, while you were in the hole trying to check-in, I posted myself on one of those prison pen pals web-sites and ended up pulling some dumb ass fat white bitch who wants me to move in with her. You'll like her too, she works at the Law Office of Hagen and Daz, just kiddin, nah she works at a bank."

"How big?" Dee asked.

Tony looked down at the ground, "Three and a half chins, working on four. But fuck it; if she's going to help a nigga get on his feet, I'll dick her down until I get my shit together." "Man I ain't even mad at you, do what you have to pimp. Just don't get that bitch pregnant, cause then you'll really be stuck."

"Shit, she can't get pregnant if all I do is nut in her ass and mouth."

Dee grinned, "A man after my own heart, you're learning son."

"What about you Dee, don't you M.R.D. later this year? Are you heading back to the Springs?"

"Man, I don't even know, I'm stuck with this five-year tail that I really don't want to do, but ain't trying to be on paper my whole life, so I'll just have to chalk it up. That fat bitch gotta friend or a sister who wants a bad boy?"

"Good question, I'll ask her when she comes up to see me this weekend. I would think so though, herds of buffalo normally roam the plains together, don't they?"

They both started laughing for a while, then Dee spoke, "Seriously though, I have no idea where I'm going. I only know where I've been, and where I've been I don't want to go back to."

"What are you a philosopher now, you've been rapping with Socrates' when you were in the hole? Because what you just said makes absolutely no damn sense." Tony stated. "Well then listen to what the fuck I am saying Tony. I don't have shit out there waiting for me; I am going to walk out of here with a damn hundred-dollar debit card and some dress outs. Not a pot to piss in, no fat bitch; I'm solo, a lone wolf, a predator on the hunt and I'll be damned if I starve, all the while I'm being hunted for my fur. When that time comes to make a decision, I have to be ready to run with it full throttle, no matter what it is."

Tony stared at Dee, "You know what you need?" he asked.

"Yeah, some pussy and a gun."

"Technically yes, but you need to relax. Calm your nerves a little. That's why I brought you this." Tony pulled out a fat ass joint.

"That's what's up playa." Dee said as Tony handed him the joint. Dee looked over and smiled, "I see you rolled it in my favorite paper, 1st Peter 4:12-14, a fine choice my good man.

Tony grinned, "Enjoy it cuz, and take your time, you know Peter burns slower than John."

****

"So I bet no you think you're the toughest guy on the yard, don't you?" Dee was sitting in a hard chair facing the L.T. across from his desk.

"Nah, just still harder than you, you gave it your best L.T., I'll give you that. But you should know better than to send a boy to do a man's job. But hey since you think you're a man, why don't you give it a try."

"Is that a threat I'm hearing?"

"Why of course not sir, I was just merely suggesting fear and common sense would tell you not to corner a wild beast, especially if all you brought to fight was a nice sharp pointy stick."

"A wild beast huh? Is that how you see yourself boy? What I see is a cocky coon who needs to know his place on this good white earth."

"Oh but I do know my place masta, it's between the legs of the pure, white, innocent Christian woman. Somebody has to satisfy them; you didn't really think your little pink willy was making them happy did you? Oh you did? How sweet." "I am going to wipe that shit eating grin off your face sooner or later, for that I give you my word. And when that day comes, you will know that it's my little pink willy going in your ass doing the fucking."

"If you could've you would've and besides how many times do I have to tell you that you're not my type? But I tell you what, when I get out, I'm going to come back up here to this shit town of Sterling just for you ok. We'll go out, shoot some pool, have a few drinks, and I'll pretend I am so drunk, that I don't know it's you who's sucking my dick. And when you're done sucking me dry, I'll kiss you on the forehead and promise to keep our little secret. Then on my way home, I'm going to upload it on Clearclips.com to show the world that I was telling them the truth when I said that you were a mean cocksucker."

The L.T. glared at Dee, and was making his hand into a fist.

Dee saw his hand, "all you have to do is swing L.T."

"All I have to do is write a report and your black ass won't be going anywhere."

"Well, if it was that easy you would've done it already."

"Just remember, you're not out yet, there's plenty of time for you to have a misfortunate accident."

"Really, I thought this facility ranked pretty high on O.S.H.A standards L.T."

"Get the fuck out of my office!"

"Nice talking to you sir." Dee said as he rose up from the chair and walked out of the L.T.'s office.

Chapter 21

Moscow, Russia – "Serious Gary, how in the hell did we end up with this shit assignment? Counter-Terrorism is what we specialize in, not stinking V.I.P. protection. I'm clearly no body guard, nor do I want to be one. There is not enough money in the world where I will willingly step in front of a bullet for some rich, fat as CEO or politician; so they can continue on living while I'm rotting in a pine box. More than likely the fucker deserves the bullet to begin with, probably stole someone's life savings or somebody's idea. So would you please kindly remind me why I am standing in the freezing cold, snow falling on my nice shaved head, in front of a five-star hotel waiting to be picked up by a bunch of fellows who wear cheaply made suits and carry guns, who's willing to die for a complete stranger?"

"Um, let me see, how about the fact that you were personally asked for, I told you that reputation of yours will get you in trouble one day. Also don't forget that this is a personal favor from your boss, my boss, the damn president of our company. And oh, let's not forget the fact that you actually know how to speak Russian, a fact I still scratch my head over, seriously how does a black man learn Russian, mind boggling really. And if all that did not answer your question, this surely will, it's your damn job." Gary said. Daryl looked at Gary with a blank stare, "I don't like it Gary, not one bit. The fact that I don't like it should be noted somewhere."

"Will you shut up, here comes our ride. Now smile, be polite, drink some vodka, and do what you're paid to do, ok cupcake."

Daryl started to smile as the limo pulled up in front of them and spoke through gritted teeth to Gary," Kiss my ass."

A twenty-minute ride later Gary and Daryl pulled into a razor wire fenced off compound with no visual markings of what it was. They were escorted into a small building where they immediately saw a group of around sixteen men, all wearing jungle print B.D.U.'s, standing on flat blue mats being instructed on unarmed fighting techniques. As they approached one of the instructors walked over to Daryl and Gary and greeted them in rapid fire Russian. Daryl immediately responded with proper Russian dialect that had the man look twice in amazement before he switched to English.

"Your Russian is outstanding Mr. Keener, where did you learn it if I may ask."

Gary jumped in, "Yeah Daryl, where did you learn it from?"

Daryl looked at Gary sideways before he focused his attention back on their host, "Night school at a Russian massage parlor."

The instructor whose name was Gorki started to laugh, "It must've been rough to pass that course eh?"

"Let's just say I had to put in a lot of extra hours to stay on top."

Gorki smiled and then stuck out his hand, "Pleased for you to come to Mother Russia."

Daryl took his hand and gave it a nice hard squeeze, "No sir, the pleasure is all mine. I've wanted to come to Russia for a long time now. You think I could take a picture tour of the old K.G.B. headquarters?"

Gorki looked a little suspicious and then smiled, "Of course you can, and after that the F.S.B. will give you the grand tour of our city in the trunk of one of their finest." Daryl got the joke but Gary didn't, "Gorki, this is my friend and co-worker Gary." Gorki shook Gary's hand and then pointed to Daryl, "Is he always this full of shit?"

"Oh no, just wait until the vodka starts flowing, you'll swear you were standing in a sewer."

All three started laughing and then Gorki walked over to the men who were wearing the jungle B.D.U.'s and pointed to them, "All of the men you see here are all former Spetsnaz soldiers. When they heard that outsiders were coming to Russia to teach them how to fight and shoot they thought it was a joke. And no offense, now that you are here, a Black and Hispanic, I don't think they're too happy and I am willing to bet they won't be friendly."

Daryl looked the men over, the smallest man was around 6'2 and 235 lbs., "Ah fuck it, I'm use to that by now, may I?" Daryl asked.

Gorki gave him a nod and Daryl stepped onto the blue mats and started speaking Russian to the soldiers. He asked that the mats be cleared except for their top three fighters amongst them.

As the men were doing this Gary whispered to Gorki, "Three bottles of Red Army say he floors them all in fewer than eleven seconds." Gorki looked as if he just got slapped.

"You did hear me when I said they are all former Spetsnaz, right?"

Gary shook his head yes. "Alright then, care to add night's drinking rampage for my boys here on your company expense account?"

"You're on." They shook hands.

Meanwhile Daryl had just finished explaining to his soon to be attackers that this would be full contact, no holding back assault on a would be threat to the person they are protecting. The soldiers looked at each other and grinned to themselves. Daryl was standing in the middle of the mats with one man to his left, one to his right, and one directly in front of him; all were standing around six to seven feet away from him. Without waiting for a signal from Daryl they attacked. The man standing in front of Daryl was the fastest and came at him with lighting speed. Daryl was ready for him, he gave the man a front kick to the gut, knocking him back slightly and leaving him semi hunched over. He immediately followed through with a knee to the face, knocking the man out cold. In his peripheral vision he saw movement to his left and right and judged the eminent threat was to his left. He ducked down just as a huge fist barely missed him by centimeters.

As he ducked he slightly pivoted to his left and gave an uppercut to the groin of the man who tried to knock his head off. Stunned, the man gave Daryl the time he needed to reposition himself to deliver and elbow to the man's chin, sending him down on his ass. As he did that, the last attacker grabbed Daryl and pinned his hands to his side as he held him from the back. Instantly Daryl put his right leg behind the attacker's right leg and it went limp, giving no resistance at all against his attacker as he started to fall to the ground. His attacker, who expected a struggle seemed perplexed for about a second or two as he started to hunch over to get a better grip on Daryl. Daryl, who got the time he needed, used his upward momentum to rise up and hit the man who was holding him on his chin with the top of his head. Blinded him temporary by the blow, the man's grip on Daryl loosened just enough for Daryl to get an arm loose and elbowed the man right in his mouth. That blow caused the man to fully release Daryl. Daryl then rolled to his right, and behind his attacker, putting him in a very nasty but effective choke hold. Daryl has his grip around the man's neck like a python. Three seconds later the man was out, snoring in Daryl's arms. Daryl released the man and he hit the mats like a suitcase of bricks. He then looked around the room and began to address the soldiers in Russian.

When this was going on, Gorki looked at Gary in amazement, "How the fuck did he do that?"

"You know Gorki, I don't ask the devil how he does his tricks," Gary said, "But I do know my Panerai said he did it in ten seconds flat. Which means when we are done for the day, I hope you have enough rubles in your pocket to satisfy our thirst. And F.Y.I. Daryl over there, like the expensive shit." Gary smiled at Gorki who was watching Daryl take on another three of his men.

****

"Damn woman, you're as big as a house." Daryl said to Keri as he stood behind her and started to rub on her stomach.

Keri put her hands on is, "It's your fault you know, if you had any self-control, I wouldn't look like this."

"Ha, self-control, try telling yourself that. I thought you were picky about the guys you rape. But ha, ha, the jokes on you. Now you're stuck with my ass for a very long time."

Keri turned around to look Daryl in the eyes, "I think I can live with that." She said as she kissed him.

Just then the realtor walked into the kitchen near where they were standing and asked, "So what do you think? It's close to two schools; one's a Junior High School and the other is a High School. A city bus route runs around three blocks from here, and the community center with a pool is located just a ten-minute walk from this house."

Daryl, Keri, and the kids had been looking at houses all weekend long, this was the second time at this particular house. It was a five bedroom, four baths, and three car garage home that was approximately 5,281 square feet, sitting on a half-acre lot. What attracted them to the home, was the large ten person Jacuzzi and sauna it came with. Daryl spoke to the realtor, "What's the asking price again on all of this?" The realtor clasped her hands together, "The asking price is $381,000.00."

"Ok now, be truthful with me, how many offers have you had on this house in the last nine months?"

The realtor looked at the ground quickly before she answered, "Honestly, not one Mr. Keener."

"Alright, I'll tell you what; we'll make you a cash offer right now, how does $371, 200.00 sound?"

The realtor eyes went wide, "Cash you say?"

"Cash, or E.F.T. in an account of your choice if you prefer."

"I have to call my boss and see if it's ok to drop the price that low, can you excuse me for a few minutes while I make the call?"

"Sure, but let your boss know that my price is firm, either take it or leave it." Daryl said.

The realtor walked out of the kitchen to make her call.

Keri looked at Daryl, "Are you sure about this, I mean all of this? Me, the kids, and the house?"

"I had better be, that woman is about to come back in here from her imaginary phone call with a whole bunch of papers for me to sign, so she can take a boatload of money from me." He smiled. "Seriously Keri, will you stop worrying, I've told you a thousand times already, you're my girl and will always hold my heart. I'm not going anywhere and I'll be damned if I let you go either. Even though you gained all of this weight on me, what are you doing, eating gallons of ice cream when I'm gone?" Keri smacked Daryl on his left cheek and then kissed him.

The realtor, back from her fake phone call came back into the kitchen and reached into a thick file folder she was carrying and took out a large packet of papers and handed them to Daryl. "If you would like to read this tonight when you have time, we can close on this property as early as tomorrow if you'd like."

Daryl smiled, "I'll have my lawyer call you first thing in the morning." he said as he extended his hand to shake hers.

She grabbed his hand eagerly and said, "You two are going to love this house. By the way, do you know what you're having?" she pointed to Keri's stomach. "A baby." Daryl said jokingly.

"Don't mind him," Keri said hitting Daryl in his side, "To tell you the truth, we are waiting until the baby is born to find out."

The realtor shook Keri's hand, "Well technically since the house is yours, I'll leave the keys so you can explore some more if you like. I'll be looking forward to your call tomorrow; you two have a lovely day ok." she said as she strolled happily out of the kitchen and then out of the house itself.

"Melody, Devin, get your bad narrow asses in here!" Keri shouted.

The kids came running from different directions, each giggling and laughing.

"So what do you kids think about this house?" Daryl asked.

Melody spoke first, "Oh my God, it's really, really big and it has a hot tub downstairs."

"Yeah, and there's a basketball hoop in the driveway." said Devin.

"Well, I'm glad you two approve," Daryl said, "Your mom likes it too. And that's why this is going to be our new home from now on."

Melody and Devin started screaming in excitement.

Chapter 22

Kourou, French Guiana -3° R.E.I.

"Was that fast? That was fast right? It had to be fast. "Damn well felt fast. Do you think that was fast Sarge?" asked Rone. Karsten, who was breathing hard replied, "Shit, I believe my lungs thinks so. Tiekert what do you think?"

"I think those, slow, lazy ass Seals from America are still trying to find out which way is up." Tiekert said.

"Damn, I thought Navy Seals were supposed to be the best America had. Those pussies won't be at the finish line for at least another two hours or so the way they're going." Rone mumbled.

"Watch it Rone, those Seals are the Legion guest for the next three days," Karsten said, "Try to be a little friendlier uh? They came to learn from the best, and when I say the best, I mean the Wolfpack. It's their first time on the obstacle course."

"Uh, excuse me Sarge, but wasn't that our first time on the course as well?" asked McLean.

"Indeed grasshopper, but Wolves are bred to run in the wild, seals on the other hand are bred to be eaten by sharks." The Wolves all shared a brief laugh before Karsten continued, "Look on the bright side boys, we are getting paid to show some Americans how to make fire, it's a fucking vacation if I ever saw one."

"I agree Sarge, but I think I speak for the rest of us when I say we ain't in the teaching business, we are in the looting and shooting business." Nordeen said.

Nordeen was right, Karsten thought, "Ok look, I don't like it any better than you. I'd rather be sipping a Kronenbourg and finger fucking my Famas. But these Seals are our brothers in arms. When push comes to shove, they get the job done. So if it means that we have to babysit them for three days so they can learn the things that will get them all home safely after an operation, then that's what we are going to do. And quite frankly, since we've landed here three hours ago, all I've heard is a bunch of ladies fussing over whose period's the reddest. This ain't a democracy Wolves; you will do the job asked of you, period."

Just as Karsten was finished speaking a Sergeant- Chief and a Corporal pulled up in a beat up jeep, the Chief looked around and then asked, "Are you Karsten?"

"Oui Mon Sergeant-Chief." was the reply.

"Get in." The Chief sounded an order. Karsten obeyed.

"What do you make of that?" asked Rone.

"I don't know, maybe they found out about that kangaroo we smuggled on the plane." answered Tiekert.

A ten-minute drive later Karsten was escorted into a dull, red, two story building that had no marking on it. He was ushered into a large conference room where two Captains were already waiting for him with documents and pictures spread before them on a large wooden table.

One of the Captains spoke, "Karsten I presume?"

"Oui Mon Captain." Karsten answered.

"Take a seat Sergeant." the second Captain said; Karsten sat.

The first Captain resumed speaking, "I've been told that you and your Wolves are ghosts. I've been told that you men are the Legion's best. I've also been told to lend you every available resource I have that you may need. And for the record Sergeant, I don't like being told what to do on my base. So let me make myself clear Sergeant, I don't like you or your Wolves. I didn't ask for you to come down here and sure as hell can't wait for you to leave. And if I find out that you or your men have anything to do with that damn kangaroo running around here with a dress on, I will personally take it upon myself to fuck you in the ass with my boot, are we clear Sergeant?"

"Oui Mon Captain."

The second Captain handed Karsten a thick file folder with a picture clipped on top and then spoke, "This is Julio Carrico, and he's wanted in a dozen countries across the world, mostly for human trafficking and weapons smuggling. He is one of the major players in moving women and guns into Europe and the Middle East via various well developed pipelines. Nobody has seen him for years; he's evaded capture many times like Houdini.

Only through blind luck and inter-agency cooperation with the N.S.A. and M.I.6. have we been able to pick up transmissions of a possible location of a supposed meeting he is supposed to be at in two days. A meeting with the Baraga drug cartel in Columbia. This operation will be an S.A.D. (search and destroy) mission. The file in front of you will have everything you need to plan your op. You will be given four hours to brief your men, plan your insert and extract, and report back to me with the particulars. Your ride will be leaving in exactly five hours, I suggest you use the time wisely Sergeant, you're dismissed."

"Merci Mon Captain." Karsten said as he picked up the folder, stood up, saluted and exited the room.

Trunja, Columbia- "Firing a rifle is like being with a woman." McLean was speaking to Tiekert. They were both lying in the prone position on the jungle floor looking through hi-powered scopes attached to their modified Steyr AUG 20 assault rifles, which was loaded with A.P.I. rounds (Armored Piercing Incendiary). They were looking for any activity on a makeshift airfield.

"First you inspect it and make sure it's clean. Then you grab it by the butt, take your magazine and jam it in; and if it doesn't fit, you make it fit. And then you squeeze that trigger until you unloaded everything you got."

Tiekert looked at McLean, "Seriously, I think you chose the wrong profession. You could have best served the world as the guy who goes around stealing old lady's pensions. You don't make any sense; none of the shit you say makes any sense. And we all know old ladies don't make any sense either. It's perfect for you, you're like the anchovy that nobody wants to touch."

The sound of rustling leaves behind them brought them both to attention. They both turned around with their weapons hot and ready. It was Karsten, Rone, and Nordeen; they were all crawling on all fours to reach them. When they reached McLean and Tiekert, Karsten spoke, "We've been up and down on both sides of the airstrip, no sign of any recent activity of any kind. Kind of makes me wonder if we're out here on a wild goose chase."

"Why don't the powers to be just drop a bomb on this fucker?" asked Rone.

"Oh I can think of a couple reasons Rone, for starters it wouldn't be covert if they did, secondly, there will be too many people in on the loop to send in an aircraft in an unwilling host country. It's a lot easier to send in a bunch of expendables, if who get caught will surely be tortured before they're killed. And lastly, close quarters killing is a sport we're good at. A bomb is only good if you're that Unabomber guy in America, or Bill Clinton, all depends on your choice of how to be blown."

"Just had to throw that in there huh Sarge?" Rone asked.

"Hey that man is a legend."

"Not really," Rone said, "Every leader in the world is doing what he's done every day."

"True, but how many of them bang their intern with a cigar afterwards and then smoke it. And then go on live TV addressing the nation and lie about the whole thing, while his wife is holding his hand and smiling?"

Nordeen cut in, "Yeah, as much as I would love to hear more about your hero Sarge, wouldn't our time be best well spent if we say; I don't know, focus on the task at hand maybe? Because if our intel is right, our guest of honor should be arriving in about eight hours or so, which gives us less than two hours to plan our nasty surprise." Every Wolf's face went serious, "Alright then," Karsten said as he pulled out a map of the area they were in, "Two hours is not a lot of time people, so we have to move quick. That airstrip is about one-hundred and thirty meters or so long. We will have to be able to maintain and control our firing positions that whole distance. On the east side of the airstrip is a small clearing through the jungle that can accommodate vehicles and personnel to move through. Rone, you and Nordeen will take around twelve claymores and conceal them along that clearing and all along that side of the airstrip where the jungle meets the runway. Set them up for remote detonations, I don't want any creepy crawlies notifying anyone where here too early. Tiekert, I need you to go on that runway and bury ten one pound blocks of C-4 in a staggering pattern throughout the whole thing. McLean, you set up a firing position here," Karsten pointed to a dark spot on the map, "On the southern end of that runway with that M-35 MGl grenade launcher. I want you to first use H.E. (High Explosive) rounds for the first of your two barrages, and then switch to thermite rounds. After you finish with that come around and meet up with us on the west side here," he pointed again to the map, "As for myself, I'm going to seek out some alternative routes for our quick departure just in case the op goes F.U.B.A.R." Karsten looked around the group at his men as he continued speaking, "We all meet back here, except you McLean, in ninety-five minutes. No go be merry and fruitful my sons; the light is leaving quickly." The Wolves started to move out, each with their own task on their mind.

Nine hours later Karsten looked down at his spec op watch, it was 03:19. Karsten, Nordeen, Tiekert, and Rone were lying about six feet from each other in a straight line on the jungle floor nested in some bushes around fifty meters from the west side of the airstrip. Nobody had moved for hours.

"Tell me again how long we plan on staying here Sarge?" Rone whispered softly.

Karsten, whose face was completely painted black, looked over at Rone and spoke through gritted teeth, "As long as it takes, now shut the fuck up, please." Karsten touched his throat mic, "Ares to Tin Man, what's your sit-rep?"

"Tin Man here, quieter than a mouse pissing on cotton Sarge."

Karsten thought to himself as he put a cherry jolly rancher underneath his tongue, *either a wild goose chase or the location was compromised and changed at the last minute.* Either way his orders were to stay on location for the next forty-eight hours if necessary. Karsten looked at Rone who was closest to him on his right. "Rone, I'll be right back, I want to check something out." Rone acknowledge Karsten by nodding his head once. Karsten crawled backwards and disappeared in the morning darkness. Fourteen minutes after Karsten had left the sound of vehicles approaching in the distance became apparent, and the sounds were getting louder and closer.

Through the small jungle clearing came seven military grade hummers, two of which had what appeared to be 50. caliber machine guns' turrets' on top. The wolves watched in silence as about twenty men exited the vehicles, all wearing body armor and tactical vests, carrying various models of automatic weapons. By the way the men moved, every Wolf was thinking the same thing, these were not amateurs, they were professional soldiers/mercenaries and they were armed to the tee. They watched as the men quickly set up a perimeter around their convoy and a small area on the north side of the airstrip. Rone touched his throat mic, "Dragon fly to Ares, over."

"Ares, go ahead."

"We have movement all over the east side of the airstrip, what's your twenty? Over."

"Ten meters from the clearing on the north end of the runway. Hold your position; can you verify the target is here?"

"That's a negative, over."

"Ten-four, sit tight and wait for my signal, over."

Rone looked at Nordeen and Tiekert and mouthed the words, 'wait for my signal.'

Tiekert and Nordeen just shrugged their shoulders. Ten minutes after Rone and Karsten's conversation, the sound of a small plane came from the distance. Four mercenaries lit flares and were placing them along the runway to guide the plane in. The plane made a smooth landing on the rough runway, taxied to the north end of the airstrip before turning around and sat idling. Karsten was just meters away from the plane as six men surrounded the plane in a very professional protective manner. He watched for two minutes before he was satisfied. Inside the plane sat Julio Carrico. Karsten who was cradling an AA 12 automatic shotgun, loaded with his special rounds he called 'good mornings' basically a two-inch slug and buckshot together in the same shell, touched his throat mic, "Ares to Oxford."

"Oxford here, go ahead."

"Get ready to blow the runway charges on my mark, over."

"Roger that."

Karsten, who was smiling from ear to ear, edged himself closer to the runway clearing. When he saw Julio Carrico getting ready to exit the plane, he made his move. The Wolves all watched as Karsten came out of the darkness like a black ghost. Still undetected, Karsten clicked his throat mic three times, Oxford flipped the switch. The runway began exploding in an awesome show of pyrotechnics. Karsten used this distraction to his advantage by unleashing fury with his auto shotgun. Killing the first four mercenaries' closet to him before the others realized what was happening. As the other two started to turn their guns on Karsten. They were brought down by Tiekert's hot A.P.I rounds to the chest and face, melting through their vests like butter. Karsten, who was now focused on the pilot and Julio made a mental note to buy the Wolf who just saved his ass a case of Kronenbourg.

McLean who was down on the south end of the runway was now unleashing a barrage of 40 mm H.E. rounds at the hummers. The rest of the Wolves were also in the process of sending hot lead down range from various positions located on the west side of the runway, pushing the mercenaries back into the jungle were earlier Rone and Nordeen had concealed they claymores. Karsten, who was on the left side of the plane blew the pilots head off and sent another round into his torso for good measure. Julio, who saw Karsten coming, began firing at the plane's door hoping to hit his attacker. Karsten, who was now on the opposite side of the plane, began unleashing ten quick rounds of his 'good mornings' inside the plane to silence those pistol shots. He then boarded the plane to see a bloodied but still alive Mr. Carrico.

Carrico looked at Karsten, "Whatever they are paying you I will triple it my friend."

Karsten smiled at him and lowered his weapon, "Relax, I'm not going to kill you."

"So how much do I owe my new friend for his services?"

"Nothing, it's the shotgun who you should be talking to, he's going to kill you." With that said, Karsten pumped five rounds into the body of the late Julio Carrico, leaving nothing but a half of a torso. Karsten exited the plane to see chaos all around him. He tossed a thermite grenade into the plane and ran for cover. As he was running for cover he told Rone to blow the claymores and McLean to send the thermite rounds in. The plane exploded in a bright, white ball exposing Karsten to the mercenaries.

Karsten was hit by what felt like a hammer in the middle of his back. He fell on his face into the ground about three meters from the jungle's thicket. He immediately got back up without looking back he continued running into the jungle. When he was fifteen meters in, he stopped, couched down, and turned toward the airstrip. The sky was bright yellow-white as McLean's thermite rounds were burning everything in sight. He held his shotgun at the low ready just in case he was being followed, he wasn't. Karsten touched his mic, "Party's over ladies, meet at location Zulu." Karsten didn't need a response from his men; he knew they heard the transmission. As Karsten began the three-mile hike to location Zulu, he stopped halfway and took off his tact vest and stripped off his Dragon skin body armor. As he examined it closely from where he felt had been hit, he found what he was looking for. Not one, but two rounds about an inch from each other, was still lodged in the armor. *Shit,* he thought, *the boys ain't never going to let this one down.* He pocketed the bullets, put back on his gear, and finished heading toward the meet location.

Chapter 23

"Seriously, what gives; is there really that many crazy birds out there in this world? It blows my mind just to think how some of these guys are still alive, let alone how any of them were getting pussy on the streets. I mean I have to sit down and rack my brain and try to visualize what woman in their right mind would let this man stick his dick in her; she has to be as crazy as him for even considering such an act. It's rare that a man doing time will come across a 'celly' that is actually decent, someone who's not a complete 'daffy'. It never gets old, how someone can come to prison and become anybody they want to be. I mean come on, I had a celly who swore up and down he was moving more keys of coke than Pablo. Bragging to me about how many cars, how many houses, and how many hoes he had, but yet he's trying to survive on the State of Colorado sixty cents a day state pay he makes from working in the kitchen. And then when I asked him about all of his luxuries he simply says, "The Feds took it all." Cut it out, if the Feds really got all of your stuff, how come you're not serving federal time? How come you don't even have a federal charge against you? And on top of that, how come you're only serving a three-year sentence for burglary? Couldn't have been doing that much out there if you're breaking into houses stealing Pokémon cards and costume jewelry, all I ask is my celly keep it real. If you were base head, then that's what you were. If you were shooting so much meth in your arm that you forgot what planet you were on, so be it. But don't give me a damn Ian Fleming James Bond story; hey you're in prison, how slick were you? And I'm not one to judge, I'm in prison my damn self for doing stupid shit. The thing is I acknowledge how stupid I was. I gave up a career, a family, all for loyalty to a friend. But to move on with this story, a liar is a lot better a celly to have than just a complete nut. A nut is un-predictable; you never know if you're going to have to kick his ass or not. One day the man is perfectly sane, the next day he's fishing in the toilet. Literally, the man made a hook from a paperclip and attached it to some dental floss, trying to catch the turd he dropped in there an hour ago. I mean who does that? It's crazy to think what type of life this man was living on the bricks. Only to find out he was an accountant or a real estate agent who's in here for fraud. Damn, what the hell happened to him from his transition from the court house to prison? A nut for a celly will turn you crazy too if you're not careful. Hell, for two months my old nut ass celly had me thinking and truly believing I can proclaim myself as a sovereign country and that D.O.C. could not hold me any longer because I was my own citizen. Now either he was spiking my coffee for two months with his psych meds or he was one hell of a salesman. If that nut was going door to door selling vacuums, he would've made a million dollars off of me, because his smooth talking ass would've had me believing that vacuum was going to end world hunger. I finally woke up one morning and told his crazy ass he had to move out. He agreed and I was blessed with a bible thumper in his place. I don't knock anyone's religion; we believe what we believe. Somebody's wrong, but we'll find that out when we become worm food. I don't need a celly telling me every five minutes I need Jesus. What, he thinks I don't know already? I believed for two months I was a country for heaven's sake, I probably do need spiritual guidance, but not every five minutes. These dudes will read the bible and try to preach to you about changing your life around. They walk around the unit going cell to cell trying to read the word to everyone.

They put on this façade like they're so innocent. News flash Moses, you're in here because you can't keep your hands off yourself around little children. And yet you're telling me how I need to change my ways. What scripture are they reading to think that what they did was alright? Now according to them they have a disease, they can't control it, that's why they turned to a higher power. Men like that, I won't even waste my breath on; you have to move out, next celly please. Sure enough, my next celly is a man who thinks he's a woman. Now remind you, I don't judge a man by his sexual preference, and I don't really care if he likes men or women. The thing is I don't want to know in detail what he wants to do to our neighbor. It's crazy is what it is. I had a celly that was 6'3, 230 lbs., muscular, cut, and was gay as all day. So after all this time he was my celly, I figured out he was the one who was getting served. I made the mistake of coming home from work early one day to only walk into the cell and see my celly asshole naked and on his knees asking for forgiveness to a man who was about 100 lbs. soak and wet. I thought I woke up in the twilight zone; like everything was opposite of what it was supposed to be. Come to find out later that day, he starts telling me how he's a woman trapped in a man's body and when he gets out he's going to Trinidad to have his wiggle removed. I can't believe what I'm hearing. The man is bench pressing 450lbs and talking crazy to me about how badly he wants a vagina and size 36DD tits, my mind is blown now. Then he starts telling me how sexy I am and since I'm not getting out anytime soon, how I should turn to the dark side. He's really trying his hardest to convince me on why I should let him give me a blow job. His exact words were, 'Only a man knows what a man wants.' I told him, 'hey I thought you were a woman. He responds by telling me, 'I'm an incomplete woman right now but you can just pretend if you want'. What I want is to kick his ass, but shit I'm not dumb. At any given time that man can knock me out and take what he wants, I can't have that. Really didn't tell him he had to move because we probably would've ending up scraping and had I lost, I would've lost. Nope, couldn't take that chance. He actually ended up becoming an alright celly. I just didn't like the 'come hither' eyes he would always give me. That and the constant asking if I needed a nice deep tissue massage." "Damn Dee, I think you have to lay off the weed for a while." Tony said as he took the joint back from Dee.

****

"So are you ready playa?"

"Man what type of question is that? That's like asking me if pussy is pink; you know damn well I'm ready, been ready for year's cuz. And I'm having my fat bitch pick me up at the gates. As soon as we drive off the prison's property I'm going to tell her to pull over on the side of the road and I'm going to stick my dick in her mouth and tell her don't stop until my nuts are the size of raisins. I ain't jacked off in weeks; she has a big surprise coming for her, literally."

Dee was slightly laughing, "You know I need you to get a bomb ass job so you can squeeze me in when I join you in a few months."

"My nigga, don't even trip, I'm gonna have it all set up for you. Might even have you a buffalo waiting for you to tackle on your first day out." Better warn that mammoth to make an appointment for the next day in advance to the proctologist, because they are going to have to sew her ass back together. You know my motto, 'Leave em gapping'."

Tony and Dee shared a brief laugh and then Tony said, "Real shit though, I have to get my shit straight so I can be a father to my kid's man, their almost teenagers now. It's never too late to try right, I want them to understand why it's so important to keep their life on the right track and not fuck up like me. I don't want my kids ending up in prison like me; just a statistic in a politician's bill."

"Then get out and do what you have to Tony, it ain't hard staying out of the mix. The only question you have to ask yourself; is how bad do you want to stay out? That should be a no brainer; you being free means pussy, you being locked up means no pussy." "I feel ya, I just hope I don't end up with a piece of shit parole officer who wants to ride my ass instead of leaving me be and let me get on my feet. Those faggots got nothing better to do than to wait outside your pad and watch you show up two minutes later past your curfew; just so they can throw you back in prison for six months."

"Just don't show up late Tony. Don't give those pussies any reason to send you back. Bite your tongue and jump through whatever hoops they want you to."

"Yeah, you're right, but right now my kids are my motivation. Just watch, when you see me in a few months. You won't know who I am anymore. I'll be Sponge Bob Square Pants ass wearing brotha who's working nine to five."

"Oh, I can picture that. A man with a tattoo on half his face working a white collar job," Dee said jokingly, "I wish you the best Tony, but really I don't have to. I know you'll do alright."

"Thanks pimp; I'll see you on the other side cuz."

Dee and Tony embraced each other with a half hug and hand shake, and then Tony left Dee's cell to go back to his unit to pack, he was getting out in twelve hours.

****

The lights in Dee's cell went on full bright and his door was being un-locked and pushed open. Dee looked at his clock; it was 3:21 AM. He looked toward the door and saw the L.T., a Sergeant, and a rookie C/O slowly walk in about three feet in his cell and demanded he get up off his bed slowly, get on his knees and put his hands behind his head. Dee looked at the intruders in his cell; two of them had their Tasers pointed at him, their red dots pointing at his chest and face. He complied with their demands. Once on the floor, he was handcuffed, and the L.T. smiled and then punched him in the mouth. "Wake up boy, we're sorry for the inconvenience, but we have reason to believe you have weapons and drugs in this cell. Do you wish to tell us where they are now, or are you going to deny the allegations?" the L.T. asked.

"Suck my di..," but Dee couldn't finish his last statement. The Sergeant had shot him with his Taser and Dee was on the ground shaking uncontrollably. All three men were laughing as the Sergeant kept his finger on the trigger, shocking Dee for a period of thirty seconds. When the Sergeant finally let up, Dee had pissed himself.

The L.T for good measure gave Dee a kick to the ribs to remind him he was there, "What were you saying coon? The Sergeant here doesn't like it when a nigger gets lippy. If I

was you I'll be watching what I say from here on out."

Dee lay on the floor silently, in pain as he watched the rookie and L.T. throw his TV on the floor smashing it. They then went on to break every appliance he had in his cell, even his wristwatch. When they were done trashing his cell, the L.T. refocused his attention back to Dee, "Well, sir, we apologize for the inconvenience we caused you, we'll leave you a shakedown slip indicating nothing was found, taken, or broken." as the L.T. was filling out the slip the Sergeant reached down to Dee and without hesitation yanked the two Taser prongs out of his back; ripping skin and flesh. The L.T. then again gave him another kick to the ribs before he had the rookie un-cuff him. The L.T. looked him in the eyes, "I told you, you're not gone yet, you have a long road ahead of you Toby; you have a good morning now." The three officers left the cell and slammed the door shut behind them, leaving Dee still on the ground holding his side.

Chapter 24

Daryl was sitting at his desk playing online poker on his laptop when Gary strolled through his open office doors, "What's up brother?"

"Shit, just sitting here watching the raping of myself as these two clowns work together stealing my money; what you up to?"

"Just stopping by to see if you want to grab a bite at this new mom and pop joint three blocks away. They're supposed to have this supreme mouthwatering buffalo burger. I'm going to need one; maybe two with bacon piled a mile high, you interested?"

"Let's see," Daryl said, "Buffalo, bacon, bacon, buffalo, hell yeah I'm game. Go ahead and have a seat though and give me a few minutes, there's something I want to show you."

Gary sat down in one of the two soft comfortable chairs in front of Daryl's desk. Daryl reached into a lower side drawer of his desk and pulled out a small black box and threw it at Gary. Gary caught it and before he opened it, he asked, "What the fuck is this?"

"You know what it is Gary."

"Ok, I know what it is, what the fuck do you have it for? Are you holding it for somebody?"

"Yes, actually I'm holding it for Keri."

"Why?" asked Gary.

"Man, are you going to open the damn thing and look at it or interrogate me all afternoon?"

Gary rubbed his chin, "Interrogation sounds good."

"Open the damn thing will you?"

Gary reluctantly opened the small black box. Before his eyes was a huge diamond ring, with small chocolate diamonds surrounding a bright clear diamond in the middle, "Damn man, did you rob Tiffany's for their precious?"

"More like they robbed my ass, let's just say that whole three months' salary for a ring went out the window on this one."

"Get the fuck out of here, you're telling me this ring cost more than forty thousand dollars?"

Daryl put down his head and spoke softly, "Yeah, something like that."

"Damn, I gave Casey a ring I got from a fifty cent gumball machine."

"Don't even try to front, if Casey ever goes swimming with her ring on she'll sink straight to the bottom."

"Are you sure about this? You're my man and all so I am going to give it to you straight. Don't do it, please don't do it. Have you learned nothing from my misery, my pain? You don't see the limp I walk around with? That ball and chain is heavy my friend, really heavy."

"Enough with your theatrics, you love your wife and kids, you ain't fooling no one."

"Love my kids yes, love my wife yes, hate my wife, hell yes. And before you start asking me why I don't get a divorce; the answer is, I'm scared. Casey ain't going to let me walk out that door. She has that if I can't have you, nobody can have you attitude." Daryl was just sitting behind his desk smiling at Gary's bullshit.

"What's so funny, you think I'm joking don't you?" Gary asked.

"Give me my ring back."

Gary closed the box and tossed it back to Daryl who caught it and put it back in his desk drawer. He then stood up and looked at Gary, "I'm so hungry I could eat a buffalo, let's go." Gary stood up and they both started for the office door.

****

"So what are your plans when you get out?" asked Daisy.

"Let's see," Dee said, "Go get a piece of ass with that hundred-dollar gate money, followed by a large Butterfinger blizzard from Dairy Queen, and if I have any money left, I am going to go find that same hooker again and have her suck me dry. Then and only then will I decide to go down to the parole office to check in with my new master, uh, I mean parole officer, and listen to him/her give me a long ass speech about how if I fuck up, they're going to send me back to prison where I belong. To which I would tell him/her they have nothing to worry about because I learned my lesson in prison and I do not wish to return. And then we'll play the cat and mouse game for my duration of parole; me plotting on the mouse trap about snatch the cheese, them putting the cheese on the mouse trap."

Daisy shook her head, "Seriously."

"Shit, I was being serious Doc. I ain't jack off in like a month. In ten days I'm going to blow that hookers head off."

"Can't you do better than a hooker; I thought you were Casanova, the man with a Diamond dick?"

Dee smiled, "I am who I am. I don't exactly have a lot of time to find daddy's little girl. Because when I find her where am I going to go, back to the homeless shelter where I'll be staying? Or perhaps maybe back to her place, and then have her drop me off at the shelter before my curfew? You see where I'm going here doc, the keyword is homeless shelter. Life is so much better when I exchange cash for services rendered, don't you think?"

"And you're not worried about catching anything, huh?"

"Please, of course I'm worried. But I do have one hell of a track record. I made it through years of fucking five-dollar hookers in Cambodia and Thailand without catching anything. And besides it's a fifty – fifty chance anyway with any chick. Who's to say that nice young church going girl I met at the library just didn't have four dicks in her ass that morning before we go out? Exactly, you don't, women are more scandalous than us men. You put on a show like you're so sweet and innocent, but you're not, you're only fooling yourselves. The thing is I acknowledge I'm a whore and I'm comfortable with it. I let it be known off top that I like having sex and if they ain't with it, that's cool. I'll go find one that is."

"So have you heard back from your friend Tony?"

Dee shook his head, "That dumb mothafucker only made it three months out there. I really thought he had his shit together. That was until I was watching the news and saw his mug on TV. Fool was arrested for shooting at Johnny Law. His girl called the cops because he hit her. Next thing you know, he's getting in a shootout. It's unbelievable that the police didn't kill his ass; he ended up getting away for a long three hours before they found him. Dumb ass was having a drink at South Side Johnny's like nothing happened; which by the way that place is a cop bar, idiot. Those cops did beat the shit out of him before they hauled him off. Now he's looking at twenty plus years back in this bitch, more if they file the bitch on him."

"How does that make you feel?"

"What, how does it make me feel? I don't feel a Goddamn thing, his life, not mine. I got nothing but love for him, but he's on his own right now. Later down the road if I can send him some bread to help him, I will."

Daisy looked at her watch, "It's almost count time, if I don't see you again before you leave, I wish you luck." she said as she stood up and extended her hand. Dee stood up and shook her hand, "Don't kid yourself, you know damn well I am going to find a way back to this shanty town so I can show you what the Diamond dick is all about."

Before Daisy could respond, Dee was already out of her office.

****

"A toast please, Wolves, to our very own Rone, who through all these years of ass kissing is finally being promoted to Sergeant. And let's not forget he will also be leading the pack in four months when I, your humble leader will no longer be with you on your marauding escapades. And to the rest of you cubs, I love you all." Karsten looked around the group at every man there, "You're my brothers, the only family I have left. Wish I could say that I'll miss you, but I won't. I'm going to be shit faced, face down in some broad's crotch, on an island where they serve drinks in coconuts with little umbrellas. I won't even know my own name for at least a couple of months."

There were some small laughs around the group, and then Karsten finished, "Seriously though, I couldn't have served with a better group of men in my life. I came into the Legion a lone wolf, and now I am leaving the pack to start a new adventure. So raise that Kronenbourg high, this here is for the Wolfpack." Everyone howled loud for about ten seconds and then began chugging their beer. Every man finished his beer and grabbed another.

Rone put his arm around Karsten, "So tell us Sarge, tell us the answer to the question that's been on everybody's mind for the last ten years, how you really ended up in the Legion?"

The room went quiet; every wolf was looking at Karsten. Karsten looked around the circle, "There once was a boy who knew no love, who became a man who will never love again." Nobody said a word, just a lot of blank stares at Karsten. "Look, if you really want to know, come find me when each of you leaves the Legion. Then we'll discuss it over some steaks on the grill and a cold Heineken in our hands. Until then it ain't none of your damn business, and I'd appreciate it if you assholes stop asking me." Karsten said with a smile.

"I sure wish you'd be here for the four new recruits hazing uh, I mean official testing." McLean said with a mischievous smile.

"Yeah." Said Tiekert, with an even bigger smile on his face, "We're trying something new with some potato sacks and a few sheep, it should be interesting."

"I can only imagine." Karsten said.

"So what's the first thing you're going to do as a civilian?" Nordeen asked.

"That's a good question sir, I was thinking about either heading up to Holland to show them girls and boys how to truly hit a Graffix or head South, down to the PiPi islands and eat lobster every day for a month."

"You know you're going to miss it Sarge." Rone said, "The action, the excitement, the full Legion sketch. You were made for this Sarge, that's why they picked you to get this unit off the ground. Let's face the fact Sarge, you are a killer, and a killer has to kill. You're not going to know what to do out there as a civilian. Might as well go become a Merc and put those skills to work."

"You know you're probably right Rone, who's to say what the future holds. But I do know one thing, that I am going to take from the Legion," Karsten looked around the group, "That the highest courage is to dare to be yourself in the face of adversity. Choosing right over wrong, ethics over convenience, and truth over popularity. These are choices that measure your life. Travel the path of integrity without looking back, for there is never a wrong time to do the right thing."

****

"This is Daryl," Daryl said as he picked up his cell phone that was laying on his desk, "Slow down Melody, take a breath and calm down. Now tell me what's going on?" "Mommy is at the hospital, we're all at the hospital, she's about to have the baby and you're not here, you're not here!"

"Melody, calm down alright. Now, has she had the baby yet?"

"No, but she's about to."

"Ok, how did she get to the hospital and what hospital are you at?"

"We're at Quebec Memorial, and the ambulance brought us here."

"Ok, did your mom bring the bag we always keep by the front door in case of emergency?"

"No, I don't think so."

"Fine, look I am on my way ok. I need you to go tell your mom that I am on my way. Tell her that I am going to swing by the house first since it's on the way, grab the baby bag, and be there in less than thirty minutes. Tell your mom not to have the baby without me, ok sweetie?"

"Ok, just hurry please daddy."

"I'm on my way right now baby, I love you, bye." Daryl pressed the end button on his phone and then pressed a button on his intercom to talk to Stacie.

"Yes Daryl?" Stacie said.

"Cancel all of my appointments, my girl is about to go in labor and I am out of here, wish me luck."

"Good luck Daryl." Stacie said.

But Daryl didn't hear her; he was already out of the office, running down the stairs because the elevator was taking too long. When he reached the parking garage his cell phone rang again, he looked down at the screen, it was Gary. "Can't talk Gary, Keri's going into labor!" Daryl said as he started his car.

"What hospital brother?"

"Quebec Memorial."

"Ok, I'll see you there with a couple of Cubans my friend, and congratulations you fag."

"Yeah bye." Daryl said as he hung up the phone.

****

The prison bus had dropped Dee off on the side of interstate 25 in Colorado Springs, right by the Nevada street exit. As the bus sped away he looked around. There was a check cashing place with an ATM about half a mile away, he started for it. When he reached it, he activated his D.O.C. debit card and withdrew the little hundred that was on it, and called a cab. Twenty minutes later the cab arrived and he got in the backseat.

"Where to mister?" the cabbie said.

"Actually I have two quick stops if you don't mind. The first is the Ace Hardware Store which is about two minutes' drive away from here in the Southgate Shopping Center. And the second will be the Evergreen Cemetery, off of Hancock and Fountain."

"No problem, the cabbie said.

Dee sat back and relaxed, then looked at his cheap prison watch, it was only ten am on a nice warm Thursday morning. The cab stopped in front of the Ace Hardware Store, "Could you give me about four minutes please?"

The cabbie nodded. Dee was back in three minutes, fifteen minutes later the cab pulled up in front of the Evergreen Cemetery. Dee paid the cabbie, gave him a twenty-dollar tip, exited the cab and started to walk toward the cemetery. He hopped a small wall and continued walking for about another three minutes. When he was satisfied he was at the right spot, he reached into his small bag he bought at the Ace and took out his retractable shovel and began digging. After five minutes of digging he finally came to a medium sized metal box. He pulled it out of the ground and brushed it off. He then opened it, inside was a vacuumed sealed plastic bag with his passport, his driver's license, a copy of his birth certificate, his social security card, thirty thousand dollars' cash in hundred dollar bills, and a Detonics Combat Master sub-compact 45. Cal handgun with a small of the back holster. He ripped the plastic open, grabbed the gun, found the magazine, locked the magazine in place and then loaded a round in the chamber. He then put the gun in the holster and clipped it behind his back. He took around two-thousand dollars and put it in his pocket. The rest of the stuff he left in the plastic and put it in the leather tool bag he had brought earlier at Ace. He looked at his watch; it was now a little past eleven am. He walked out of the cemetery and down the road about four miles until he came to a 7-11. Dee called a different cab company and waited on the cab. While he waited, he went inside the store to use the restroom and to pick up a few snacks and a bottle of iced tea. When he stepped back outside, the cab was pulling in the store's parking lot, he got in.

"Good morning sir, where are you heading to?" the cab driver asked.

Dee handed the driver two-hundred dollars, "Three quick stops please, the first is the El Paso County jail, the second will be the Law offices of Saul and Pearson on Tejon and Dale street, and the last will be the Citadel Mall."

The cab driver started to drive, when the cab pulled up in front of the county jail, Dee got out and told the cab driver, "five minutes max." He entered the building and walked directly to the cashier window.

"Can I help you?" the cashier asked.

"Yes, I would like to put one-thousand dollars on Anthony Arnell's books please." Dee said as he handed the woman the money through a slot in the bullet proof glass window.

In two minutes she handed him a receipt and he was on his way out the door. Ten minutes later the cab pulled up in front of the law offices of Saul and Pearson, "Ten minutes max." Dee said as he exited the cab. Inside the building he meets with an attorney, Harim Saul. Dee gave him fifteen thousand dollars' cash and asked him to get Tony the best deal possible. Hands were shook and Dee was on his way to his third stop. When he arrived at the mall, he told the cabbie to drive around to the east side of Dillard's entrance. In front of Dillard's Dee gave the cab driver a fifty-dollar tip and exited the vehicle. Inside Dillard's, Dee bought himself four suits, a Geneva watch, some cologne, five pair of boxers and socks, three pair of dress shoes, one pair of tennis shoes, a small luggage set, two pair of shades, and a nice looking silver chain. At the cashier stand he asked the cashier to please call him a cab; she did.

He waited ten minutes before the cab came; when it did, he got in the back seat.

"Where you going?" asked the cabbie.

"Two quick stops." Dee handed the driver a hundred-dollar bill. "The first is that Sporting Goods Store around the corner and the second is the Springs Airport please." The cab driver pulled up in front of the sporting goods store, "I'll just be about six minutes at the longest." Dee walked into the store and came back five minutes later. The driver made his way to the airport. When he arrived at the airport Dee tipped the driver a fifty, collected his bags from the driver and went inside. He made his way to the Delta Airline ticket counter, where he was greeted by a big breasted, smiley, red head named Sally, according to her name tag. "Welcome to Delta Airlines, how may I help you today?" she asked.

"Yes, I need a first class open ticket on your next available flight to Oslo, Norway please."

"May I please see your passport sir?"

"No problem." Dee said as he handed her his passport. While she was putting the required information in the computer for his flight, he reached into his pocket and pulled out a bag of apple jolly ranchers he had purchased earlier. He opened the bag, took one piece out and unwrapped it and put it underneath his tongue. Right then Sally asked him, "How many pieces of luggage will you be bringing with you sir?" "A small carry on, and these three pieces." He pointed to his new luggage, "And this baseball bat is all."

"Ok Mr. Keener, you're total is $4,678.98."

"Please call me Daryl." He said as he paid the lady. She handed him his ticket, "Your flight doesn't leave for another six hours Daryl. If you decide to wait at the airport, we offer a first- class lounge on the west end of the terminal."

"Thank you Sally, by the way, has anybody ever told you how beautiful your smile is?" Sally blushed, "Not lately."

"Well, Sally, your smile is very beautiful and addictive. If you get off before my flight leaves, I would love to buy you a drink."

She looked Daryl up and down and then said, "I'm off in five hours, and you can keep your drink, I was thinking more of having some chocolate for an early desert." She said in a seductive tone.

Daryl smiled, "Touché, I'll be in the lounge all day dreaming about the possibilities." Daryl said as he winked at Sally as he walked away.

Aubagne, France

The place where a Legionnaire starts and ends his career, Karsten had just got done signing his discharge papers in H.Q. and was out the door when he heard a familiar voice, "Karsten!" He froze in his tracks, turned around to see Captain Sprazzo walking towards him, "My jeep is outside, I'll give you a ride to the gates. And that was not a request Karsten."

Karsten followed the Captain to his jeep that was outside and got in. The Captain started to drive at a snail's pace towards the main gates. He looked over at Karsten and spoke, "So Mon infant has grown up and decided to leave the nest eh?" Karsten didn't respond, so the Captain continued on, "Let me ask you something Karsten, why do you think you were chosen to start a brand new elite unit?"

Karsten looked at the Captain, "Because you wanted to see me fail Mon Captain."

The Captain squinted his eyes at Karsten, "You don't believe that lie Karsten. You know why you were chosen. When are you going to wake up, you didn't need to join the Legion. I personally think you joined because you wanted to punish yourself, which the Legion will be more than happy to accommodate. Perhaps right a wrong from your past life, maybe even running from something."

The captain studied Karsten's face for any sign of recognition from the last statement, but was only rewarded with a blank stare; so he continued, "Even with your new French citizenship, you already know you can never go back to America without being arrested, don't you? Not unless you sneak across the borders of Mexico or Canada."

Karsten looked at the Captain with guessing, surprised eyes, "What?"

The Captain said, "You think I didn't know that you are a wanted man? Or perhaps that maybe you were a scout/sniper in the Marine Corps? No, why do you think I've rode your ass since day one? I was grooming you from the start Karsten. and the only way I knew you could succeed was to make you have so much hate for me and the Legion that you'd do anything just to prove your worth." The jeep stopped at the main gates, "Karsten, never forget who you are, a leader; always have been and always will be." Karsten got out of the jeep and grabbed his gear from the backseat; a duffle bag with ten years of his life in it. The Captain got out and walked around the jeep and stood right in front of Karsten, "The Legion thanks you for your sacrifice. And I personally thank you for showing me that time can change the essence of a man." The Captain extended his hand; Karsten took it and gave him a firm handshake. Afterwards the Captain saluted

Karsten, and Karsten returned the salute. As Karsten was five feet away from the main gates the Captain ran up to him and handed him a business card. "I have a close friend who would love to have a talk with you Karsten."

Karsten looked down at the card; it read Tom Basher, Recruitment Director, Global Security Inc. "I'm done being a soldier Mon captain." Karsten said.

"But you're not done leading Karsten." Karsten took the card and put it in his breast pocket, and then walked out of the gates.

"Karsten!" the Captain yelled, "Who should I tell him will be calling since Karsten is no longer your name?"

Karsten smiled, showing his white teeth, "Tell him Daryl Mon Captain, Daryl Lamont Keener."

****

Daryl was speeding on the freeway and side streets trying to get home in time to pick up the baby bag and make it to the hospital before Keri delivered the baby. All he was thinking about was how he was going to be a father. How he was going to cherish this baby with all of his love. How he was going to show his newborn how a person can succeed if they apply themselves.

Daryl was already thinking and smiling to himself, how if he had a daughter, how he was going to threaten her boyfriend's when she started dating. And if he had a son, how he was going to take him to a full service massage parlor when he turned sixteen. So much was on Daryl's mind when he pulled into his driveway, that he didn't notice the out of place dull grey truck parked across the street from his house. He was in such a hurry to get inside the house that he left the car door wide open and the car still running. Not paying attention to the man who got out of the dull truck and who was making his way across the street to his house.

Daryl opened the front door, looked down and saw the baby bag and picked it up. As he shut the door and turned around, he was greeted by a smiling familiar face, it was Mark. Mark was about ten feet in front of him pointing a loaded 44 Magnum to his head,

"Not so tough now huh?"

But before Daryl could even react, Mark shot him twice, once in the head and once in the chest, killing Daryl instantly before his body hit the ground.

"Freedom from jail, the sound of clips being inserted, at the same time a baby is born and a man is murdered, and it's the beginning and an end."

Made in the USA
Coppell, TX
15 March 2021